D0095446

TIME TOGETHER

By Marian Seldes

The Bright Lights: A Theatre Life
Time Together

TIME TOGETHER

A NOVEL BY

Marian Seldes

BOSTON

Houghton Mifflin Company

1981

Library of Congress Cataloging in Publication Data

Seldes, Marian.
Time together.

I. Title.
PS3569.E553T5 813'.54 81-7661
ISBN 0-395-31264-7 AACR2

The author is grateful for permission to reprint from the following source: from "Burnt Norton" in *Four Quartets* by T. S. Eliot, copyright 1943 by T. S. Eliot; renewed 1971 by Esme Valerie Eliot. Reprinted by permission of Harcourt Brace Jovanovich, Inc.

Printed in the United States of America

V 10 9 8 7 6 5 4 3 2 1

for Katharine

Time past and time future
What might have been and what has been
Point to one end, which is always present.

T. S. ELIOT,
"Burnt Norton"

TIME TOGETHER

Part One

On October 30, 1960, the day before her seventy-fifth birthday, Ermina Ives Dennison summoned her children in the usual way. She had her butler, Evans, dial their numbers. When he heard a voice he handed the telephone to his mistress who issued the command into the receiver. "Seventy-fifth, my dears! Here at the apartment. Come at five and I'll throw you all out at seven. Informal. Just the family." And to her youngest daughter's invitation she added: "How's Nell?"

"Fine, Nana. Oh, may I bring — ?" Leonora was still speaking when she heard the dial tone. She smiled. It meant Evans was dialing her sister, Martha, or their brother, Dwight. She pressed down the receiver and called the liquor store and ordered a magnum of champagne. Then she called the florist for a bouquet of pink carnations.

Across the room at a card table her daughter, Nell, was playing double solitaire, slowly and pleasurably, with Arnold LeVine.

"Arnold, would you like to come with us to Nana's tomorrow?" She made it sound like a casual invitation.

"No, I don't think so," he said without looking up.

"We can't put it off forever. She knows you exist!"

"I doubt it." He had seen her once, at Leonora's wedding, where he was her husband's best man. The mother of the bride ignored him then and he knew that fifteen years later she had no curiosity about him or anyone connected with that part of Stephen Tannenbaum's life. "You and Nell go. Tell me about it. Your reports always make me laugh."

"Please come, dear," said Leonora.

Nell kept studying the cards, smiling, playing with care.

Martha Ives drove up to the building where she had spent the winters of her childhood. It looked like a dungeon in the afternoon light. The iron bars on the lower windows bulged outward in curves, the awning was black with city grime, the marble floors ingrained with dirt that had been covered with polish until it appeared shellacked. The elevator was a metal cage. It was a relief to walk into the elegant rooms she had decorated for her mother and to see attractive, familiar things in their correct places.

"Have a drink, my dear," offered Nana, "and bring me one."

"And me one?" Dwight asked playfully. He was sitting on the floor and for a moment Martha remembered him as her brother, adorably funny and dear, not the haunting drunkard in a tweed suit who greeted her at each ritual celebration at 67 Riverside Drive. Dwight had married four times. One wife had died; the others had stayed with him for a time, but eventually quiet divorces had followed legal separations and another member of the family was not heard from again. He hardly seemed to care. He rarely mentioned any of his wives or the children they took with them except in jest. Dwight joked his way out of marriages, friendships, and jobs, his beloved bourbon allowing him to ignore how stale his wisecracks were. His face was coarse, choleric, and his long-fingered, idle hands shook.

Martha had placed the drink in his unsteady grasp and was sitting, gossiping with her mother when the doorbell rang.

"They're late," announced Nana, rising to intercept Evans as he moved toward the hall.

The latecomers were helping each other with their coats, Arnold taking particular care with Nell as she switched the bouquet from one hand to the other.

The alcove where they struggled to make themselves presentable was lit by a chandelier hanging high above an oval mirror. As always, Leonora wished she had taken more time with her make-up and hair. Martha would notice the gray streaks. But Arnold looked at her approvingly as he inhaled the soft perfume from the potpourri hidden in the Adam console. "What is it?" he asked Nell.

"Roses and lavender leaves, coriander and cloves, and oil of cinnamon." She had looked in the drawer once and read the label on the jar. "I know it by heart."

Nana appeared on the threshold. "Oh, Mother, you remember Arnold — "

If she did, she pretended not to. She avoided his open hand.

"I said *just* the family!"

Leonora looked at Arnold helplessly, knowing her mother saw a thin, dark, plainly dressed nobody on her threshold.

"Would you like Arnold to stay out here with the coats? He doesn't have to come in." Nell's outstretched flowers were ignored. Nana's fat, pump-covered feet were marching her back to the living room.

"What shall I do with the carnations?" asked Nell. She spoke cautiously, as if the problem might need an elaborate answer.

Annoyed by the way her mother had treated Arnold, Leonora said, "Give them to me, dear. I'll put them in a vase. Could you take Arnold in and introduce him?" Her question, too, was carefully articulated.

"Yes. I'd like to."

It solved a problem. Leonora knew Dwight would think Arnold was her lover. This way they could avoid the look of appraisal he was sure to receive. When Leonora came back from the kitchen, with Evans carrying the vase of pink flowers, she heard her mother's reedy voice questioning Arnold. "What do you *do*? What are you interested in, Mr. —— ?"

"LeVine. I'm a writer, Mrs. Dennison."

"Ives. I do not use Dennison."

"Ives. LeVine."

"What's that?"

"My name is Arnold LeVine."

Dwight and Nana exchanged a look with Martha. Leonora's ex-husband, Stephen Tannenbaum, had not been accepted as a member of the family. If he had behaved more diplomatically, he might have been forgiven for being Jewish, but he had no wish to be a part of Ermina Ives's circle. His sole interest was in the daughter who was his wife — and in whether she was to have money. But it never came to a climax. Leonora and Stephen had been divorced in 1954 and he was now on the trail of an heiress. This had been the subject of their gossip before Leonora's arrival. Dwight thought it perfect of Stephen, entirely true to type. Nana found it appallingly common, but loved talking about it, for the lives of other men and women were her recreation, that and radio serials.

"Do you ever write radio plays, Mr. Lev*ee*n?"

"No, nothing like that." If she had been kinder, he might have reminded her of their first meeting, instead he offered the information he presumed she wanted to hear. How he made his living: "I'm a newspaper writer. But lately I've been working in the newsroom at WNYC. I write the news."

"Do you?"

"I mean I rewrite it. I take the stuff off the Associated Press ticker and turn it into sayable material."

"Sayable material?"

He knew he had misspoken. He had been anxious about seeing this woman he had heard so much about through the years, and his tongue felt heavy in his mouth. While he was talking he was trying to look at all the faces at once. The Iveses: the imperious mother, the sad brother, the confident, attractive sister, the scruffy animals, and now Evans, impeccable in his uniform, rearranging the flowers, which bloomed brightly, freed from their grass-green wrapping paper.

Nana's attention left Arnold and shifted to her beloved Pekinese, who jumped up on her lap, and to the large calico cat sprawled in the exact center of the Aubusson carpet. It was stretching, curling, and uncurling, and now lay flat on its back, four paws pushing in and out in the air, eyes closed. "Wantonly amorous," said Dwight.

They all watched it now, pushing its claws into the carpet, stretching again, and turning over on its back in a pose of supreme sexual invitation.

"What sex is this animal, Ma?" Dwight asked.

"My dear, I haven't a clue. Evans brought it home one day and it's been here ever since." She regarded the cat for a moment. "Probably female." Knowing Dwight was about to make a remark she did not want Nell to hear, Leonora offered to get him a drink.

"Another?" he asked, smiling. They had been taught never to say *another* drink. It was not done. Perhaps if it had been done, thought Leonora as she refilled his glass, he would not be grasping for this one as if it were his first drink of the day.

She glanced at Arnold. He was sitting on the couch with Nana and Peke, a bundle of silky brown and black fur with no shape except where a rhinestone collar glittered in the vicinity of its neck. Arnold was asking the questions now. All the right ones. Nana's mood had changed. As she finished her second drink, she became mellow and loquacious.

"I wish it was serials you wrote. I listen to them all afternoon."

"I don't write fiction, Mrs. Ives."

"Ermina."

"Thank you. Ermina. I'm really *just* a reporter."

"And what would you report about this gathering?"

"I'm so fond of your daughter my opinions would be slanted."

Dwight looked at his mother, then at his sister, and Leonora received the look she had missed at the door.

"How gallant!" said Nana, pronouncing it the French way.

Arnold felt flustered again, tongue-tied. He attempted to get her off the track of his life and on to hers. In a few minutes she was his once more, all attention, her fingers occasionally touching his sleeve, her glossy hazel eyes seldom leaving his face. The fascinator at work.

"I am ready to meet my maker," she announced, sucking in her cheeks.

Nell saw her aunt Martha shudder. No one else seemed to notice.

"Oh, God, don't talk about death," said Martha. "Please."

"It comes to us all," said Nell, and everyone burst out laughing. It would be the youngest, most innocent, the farthest from that desired or dreaded goal who would comfort Martha.

"I mean I have had a good life!" Nana went on, "All right, I'll talk about life, my darling, not dying. I am proud of you all, my children *and* my grandchild. My family. I'll tell the world!" She used her mother's phrase. "Two marvelous daughters, two sons — no, don't say it, anyway he is *not* dead to me." *You* said it, thought Martha and wished it was time to leave. "I think each of you has done the best possible thing with your lives. You have given other people happiness and that's what we should all aim at. Be loving and giving. I've said it a thousand times."

"A million," said Martha aloud, rising from her chair.

"What? Did you want to say something, Mart?" In a moment she would call Leonora Leo and Martha's irritation would double. She stood by the window and watched the lights come on across the river.

Nell began to hum softly. Leonora was trying to think of something to say to please her mother when she heard her name.

"Leonora! Tell your daughter to help herself to some tomato juice, and then if she wouldn't mind" — an order was coming in the guise of a request — "could she get me the photo album from the study? I want to show Mr. Leveen something. And, Dwight, my boy, I need a square of ice in this."

Dwight got up, hitting the table with his knee, and the bowl of caviar and ice slid to the floor. The tiny shiny black beads and melting cubes fell around the legs of the table and chair and glistened on the nap of the rug. No one moved. Usually when there was an accident of any kind Nana called for Evans, but since she did nothing, Nell took a spoon from the cocktail tray and began to pick up the roe one by one, like a miniature Easter egg hunt in which she had no competitors.

Nell knew exactly what she was doing, filling the time with a chore no one else wanted to do. It was part of the way she spent her days. She was beginning to enjoy herself when Nana mentioned the photograph album again.

Nell rose and, carrying her precious fund of caviar, walked slowly to the sideboard, decided on a glass of ginger ale and disappeared into the study for longer than it should have taken to find the album. Leonora did not want to be caught helping her. It was a sore point with Nana.

"Leo, I've sent Nell away because I want to talk to you all about her. I think it is time we did something about her problem. She's in her teens now, and it seems a shame when they are finding cures for everything that something can't be done for Nell."

"What are you talking about?" asked Leonora, furious that her daughter's situation was to be discussed as if it were one of the financial problems Nana occasionally broached at family gatherings. It did not trouble her mother to see Leonora's face darken with embarrassment.

"No one wants the responsibility of taking care of her after I'm gone, I know that. It's not just the money" — she had a way of smiling when she said the word that made it sound like *minny* — "it's the time and the care."

"Really, Nana." Leonora could bear it no longer. "*I* can take care of her. I always have."

"Well you *can't* now. You don't have a husband and you don't have a job." Leonora looked at Arnold in supplication. He glanced from her strained face to Ermina's serene one and found it impossible to see where the resemblance he had been told of existed. Not in the eyes. Leonora's were almost too big for her narrow face. Not in the shape of the cheek or jaw. Ermina's bones were covered with a generosity of flesh that made her appear kind even when she was dictating her desires to her children, her servants, her slaves.

At that moment Nell appeared in the doorway. "Is this it?" she asked, holding a bright red leather album of Polaroid pictures from the seventieth birthday.

"No, that is not it. That is a *modern* album. I want the *old* one."

"Then why didn't you say so?" snapped Leonora.

"Be quiet, Leo, you'll only confuse her. Now listen, Nell. Take that one back and put it where you found it, and on the shelf below in the right-hand corner you will find the *old* one. It is dark brown and twice as large as the one you are holding in your hand at this moment. Is that clear?"

Now Leonora and Martha did exchange a look. Uncountable repetitions of that phrase had not blunted its sting. Lateness, supposed theft, questionable cleanliness, bad table manners — all the sermons of childhood failings that had echoed with that question which no one dared answer.

"Yes, Nana. Clear," said Nell and disappeared. Nana went on, "It's not only the money, which I will continue to provide for her after I meet my maker — "

"— it's the time and the care," prompted Martha.

"Exactly! But now there are drugs, you know, my dears, and we have waited *too* long."

Leonora watched Arnold's reaction as her mother's face went through its disturbing change, the mouth moving and widening. In a moment the tongue would appear and make its swift licking motion, dart in and out as she prepared her final word on the subject. Leonora turned her gaze to Nana, thinking: Like the serpent in Eden! I can't imagine that garden, but what I *can* see so clearly in my mind's eye is the serpent. I see the tongue darting out, in and out. I see the evil of the world beginning even though I doubt the garden and doubt the apple. Years ago when Nana was angry she whisked her tongue around the outside of her mouth in a way that taught me everything I know about terror and sin. It was a warning that too often I did not heed. Occasionally she would keep her tongue *inside* her mouth and make the circle there, her upper lip distended, her nose and the rest of her face pulled into a grimace. And if I wasn't watching, if I missed the signal, hostilities would begin without warning.

"Nell must be treated now for her illness."

Martha moved from the window and sat down near her sister.

"She is not ill, Mother. She is *slow*," said Leonora softly.

"All right, slow. That's what *you* call it. But if there were a way for her to catch up with the rest of the world I see no reason why she shouldn't take her place in society, get married, have children."

Just as Leonora was about to suggest a private meeting with her mother, Nell came in again. "I can't find it, Nana."

The flesh on her cheeks tightened as Ermina forced a smile. "Well then, *I'll* get it. It's really not that important."

Arnold got to his feet and said, "May I go with Nell and bring it back for you?" He was near the door. Before there was time for a reply he was asking Nell where the study was and in a few moments they were back with the album. "It had fallen behind some of the other books," said Arnold, without the slightest tone of reprimand, yet Leonora wanted to cheer. His tiny heroic deed saved the afternoon for her. She grasped his arm in thanks as Nana pulled the album out of Nell's hands. The leather was crumbling, the reddish-brown powder smudged her palms. "No matter, no matter. Come and sit down by me," came the order, and Nell obeyed, smiling, untroubled. Nana indicated the cushion on the other side of her and Arnold resumed his seat, trying to avoid the ever-present Peke, on whose silky coat Nana gingerly wiped her hands.

The afternoon faded, the room grew dark and the Hudson River looked misty from the windows. Evans came in, pulled the curtains, and switched on three lights. A standing one near Dwight, a small lamp with a pink shade on a table between the chairs where Leonora and Martha were sitting, and finally as he neared the door, the sconces with the small candle-flame bulbs. The room glowed.

Martha looked at the furniture, remembered pieces from her childhood, some of it recovered in materials she had chosen for her mother: the rug, richly patterned and showing only a few small tears after all the passing back and forth of friends, family, and servants; the portrait of her grandmother above the couch; the photographs of celebrated acquaintances on the piano; the cut-glass decanters for liquor; the silver jiggers; the ice bucket that had been a tennis trophy of her father's.

She caught herself dreaming and decided that if the piano were removed to the far corner and the bar put against the wall in its place, the room would look much airier. She must remember to tell Nana before leaving.

"Look, Nell," said Arnold, pointing to a page of snapshots taken at the island on Oseta Lake where the Iveses spent their summers, "these pictures of the costume party were taken on your birthday!" There was the date in Nana's bold hand, February 6.

"No, they were not taken on her birthday, that was February sixth, nineteen *twenty-six,* twenty years before Nell was born." Arnold kept looking at the faces, Martha beautiful in a Scandinavian peasant hat made of stiff lace, Leonora made up to look Japanese, wrapped in a delicate silk kimono. Lemuel Ives in blackface! He turned the page, a picture of Nana and Lem, both blackened, with glimpses of white skin visible near their eyes and hairlines. He wanted Leonora's opinion but could not get her attention. She was staring at her mother.

Nana's tongue came out of her mouth in a sharp pink cone. "Birthdays! Who cares! I don't. I've had too many of 'em. Enough to last a lifetime." Polite laughter. "Nell has them all ahead of her, but it's all an accident anyway, isn't it? Birth. I'm sure mine was, and I know Leo's was." Even Dwight looked up from his drink to catch what she was about to divulge.

Martha went back to her place at the window. Nell wanted to follow her.

"What do you mean, Mrs. Ives?" asked Arnold.

"If someone hadn't removed the Lysol bottle from my medicine chest, Leo wouldn't be here now."

Leonora begged, *"Please."*

"Someone took it out of the medicine chest! Oh, we all used it in those days, and when it was too strong it *burned!*" She shuddered at the memory of her own vaginal pain. "Children were expensive, and Lem and I weren't sure we wanted any more."

Nell watched her mother, saw the strength drain away with the color of her cheeks, leaving a blankness of hurt. What was Lysol? She had seen it advertised in magazines. Something to clean, to disinfect, to kill germs. She would have to ask Arnold.

A new page in the album: the wedding picture of Ermina and Lem. He looked handsome and ill at ease. She looked less appealing than in the other pictures, her jaw too strong for beauty and her dark hair piled carelessly around her half-veiled face.

"The day after we arrived at the Camp, Vernon Hammel came — "

"— with Dale?" said Martha.

"Yes, actually, she *was* there with him that time. Later they arranged a truly open marriage. It was understood that each could do whatever he or she liked with anyone. But there was one stipulation: not with anyone either of them knew. But of course, Vernon broke the rule. Twice. I was the second."

Dwight grinned at the looks of distress on his sisters' faces. He knew they had grown up believing that while their father lived Nana had been utterly faithful to him. Dwight knew better, and the presence of Natalie Hammel at the Camp each summer made sense to him. It was not simply as a playmate for the girls, but if Nana was busy with Vernon it was best to have his daughter around to play with her children. All so civilized.

Conversation dwindled. The animals again became the topic and Leonora heard herself asking Peke questions. Not since Natalie Hammel had asked her to speak to her myna bird over the telephone had she felt so foolish.

"It's time to go, Nell," she said, looking at Martha in the hope that she would make the leave-taking simpler. She did. In a rush of friendliness Martha arranged for them to borrow Evans and the car, for the piano to be moved, and to have dinner with Nana the following evening. Martha felt the failure of the occasion was largely her fault and wanted to make up for it. She suggested the guests take the glasses back to the kitchen. A small parade began, led by Nell.

"Oh, no!" cried Nana. "Don't do that. There'll be nothing left for Evans to do!" But she could not stop the collection of used Waterford from multiplying on the kitchen table. She called after them, "In the pantry then, for God's sake, the *pantry!*"

Martha had not heard her and told them all to bring the glasses back to the living room. Nell thought it was a delightful game, a completely new way to end an afternoon at her grandmother's. Confusion was restored to the tops of the tables in the room, which was now almost dark because Dwight had hit the light switch on his way out. They stood separately, inventing good-byes. Nell wondered what Nana would do after they left, and decided she wanted to pick up the glasses herself. It was *her* game.

Evans, wearing a chauffeur's cap, was polishing the chrome on the rearview mirror of the old black Packard. Dwight missed the door handle and Martha steadied him. Leonora slipped in ahead of them to the far corner of the back seat. Nell, as always, headed for the front seat and Arnold followed her. Evans opened the glove compartment and gave her a Hershey bar.

"We are going to drop Mister Dwight first," said Martha.

Evans nodded and started the motor. At that moment Nell began her favorite round, "White Coral Bells," and Arnold joined in. Dwight's head dropped to his chest. Leonora leaned forward and slid the dividing window closed. The song continued. Leonora stared out the window.

"What's the matter, Leo?"

"Don't call me Leo, Mart. Why did you let Nana tell that story. *Why?*"

"I couldn't stop her."

"You didn't even try. Will you at least call her tomorrow and tell her never to tell it again? Not to anyone."

Martha knew how it hurt Leonora for Arnold to have witnessed their family at its worst. "Nana won't remember telling it. She didn't even remember Arnold, did she?"

"Why should she remember my best man? She's forgotten the groom." Not quite, thought Martha, who had seen the look her mother had exchanged with Dwight. Leonora shook Martha's arm. "Call her and tell her I think it was the cruelest thing she's ever done and that I despise her for telling it in front of Nell. You have to realize," Leonora said, trying to control her anger, "that Nell is not an object you can play with. You can't say anything in front of her and expect her not to react just as importantly as anyone else. You can't try to change her without discussing it and finding out how she feels. You can't make plans for her as if she were a baby."

"*I* know that," said Martha.

"You know it but you don't abide by it. You and Nana are always trying to take over her life. Her clothes, her education, her time."

"She sees me once a week."

"She stops by after school before she comes home."

"Sometimes."

"Often. And you certainly know her mind and heart well enough to realize how ghastly it was for her to hear that story. I'll never know how it affected her because she won't talk to me about it, and I don't have the courage to ask her."

"Why not?"

"Oh, Martha, every child in the world has fears about not being wanted, why should Nell be any different? Then Nana tells that story to amuse Arnold, I guess, to show that she's 'modern' and up-to-date, and what can Nell think?"

"She won't relate it to *herself*. I think she just felt dreadful for you."

"I think Nana wanted to spoil something for me and Arnold. Something that really doesn't exist. She was jealous of me and Stephen in the beginning because she thought I had everything. Husband, child, perfect marriage. It infuriated her, and the fact that Stephen was Jewish *and* that I didn't provide her with a grandson. And, and, and —"

"Leonora, you're absolutely neurotic about Nana today! What's the matter?"

"The matter is that her telling that story in front of Nell was a kind of betrayal I cannot forgive. I can understand all the rest."

"Why are we quarreling? Let's talk tomorrow."

"I don't want to quarrel with you. I want to tell you that your loving Nell is one thing. Your being generous and kind to her. But you hurt her, too. We know what it is, the slowness with Nell. It's a condition she's lived with since birth and will continue to live with, I guess, until the end of her life. She will learn — assimilate — and she will get on in the world as long as someone is around to help her over the rough places. The wonderful thing is that she seems happy. I don't know anyone who is really happy. Were you ever? Are you now? I look at my daughter's face and it's peaceful. And at night — unlike the rest of us — she sleeps. I think that's what I envy most. Her capacity to rest without dreaming."

"No one sleeps anymore," said Martha lightly.

"Be serious, this isn't a cocktail party."

"How do I hurt her? Tell me."

"You dress her up and try to make her into someone else. You pull her into your way of life by showing her your happiness and making mine look bleak."

"Bleak happiness?"

"My life. I don't have rooms full of flowers and champagne and fires in the grate and music playing. I don't have a maid who cleans up after me. I don't have a job."

"What are we talking about now, Leo? You or Nell?"

Leonora was weeping. "Please, please don't take her away from me. She's all I have and you have so much. Don't make her want what she can't have."

"Leonora. I love you and I love Nell. I am truly sorry for what you think I have done. I never meant to hurt you. I love Nell as if —"

"Finish it!"

"— she were my own daughter."

The sincerity of Martha's words and the look in her eyes made Leonora ashamed of her rage.

"Let's go back —"

"— and face Nana. She's the one you want to kill, not me!"

Leonora laughed as suddenly as she had cried, because of course, Martha was right.

In the front seat, Nell begged Arnold to sing the round again.

Part Two

AT THE TURN of the century Ermina Pringle and her sister, Clara, were brought east by their parents. The money from their timberlands in northern California had multiplied, and their father had wanderlust. After the long train journey, they spent a month in New York City looking for a winter home and in the spring drove to the Adirondacks, planning to stay one summer. In New York State there was plenty of timber and the Pringles knew how to harvest it at good prices. They bought the island and 25,000 acres of wooded land.

It wasn't until 1919 when Nana's oldest son decided to hitchhike his way across America that one of the family went west again. Harrison, who had spent endless hours canoeing on the lake in storms without capsizing, was pulled under by the current of a mountain stream and drowned. A young woman he had met in Colorado wrote Mr. and Mrs. Ives: "Harry was happy when he died." The death of her sixteen-year-old boy meant the end of Nana's easy pleasure in life. It was as if she had undergone an operation and lived without the part of her brain that directed emotional responses. She tried to feel grief and could not cry.

Because his father had been a lawyer, Lemuel Ives was expected to study law. In high school in Plattsburg he joined the debating society and acted in a class play each year, trying to control his nervousness when addressing a group of people. When he was accepted at Williams College, he felt he was on his way to fulfilling his father's hopes, but after he received his B.A., he did not find work and had to teach history in a boys' school in Blackington, Massachusetts, for a year. Back to Plattsburg to apprentice with Van Gelder and Sons real estate and law office, from there to Columbia Law School. But it wasn't happening fast enough. Lem and Charles Van Gelder, Jr., were admitted to the Bar in 1893 but there were many months at the beginning of his practice when he feared he would never succeed.

He had no plans for marriage until he met Ermina Pringle. The loving approval of this striking girl, sixteen years younger than he, gave him confidence. Her wanting him to be a success seemed at last to insure it. Before the children were born he was an alderman of his district — "the twenty-first assembly," Ermina would throw into any conversation she could, her voice rising with pride.

Charles Van Gelder's father thought Lem had a good business mind and he knew he was fair and honest. He appointed him tax commissioner for two terms.

It seemed obvious to everyone but himself that he should go into politics. Alderman, mayor — and after that, who could tell? National office? He was not a dreamer and did not trouble himself about the future. A day at a time, just enough hours to solve that day's problems. No more, no less. He fell into bed tired and content.

Charley spent his summer vacation at the Camp with Ermina and Lem. Together they studied and tested each other on real and imaginary cases. Ermina was the jury. Charley was a damn good actor and that was important for a lawyer. He could make Lem believe anything. Lem felt he lacked the very energy and style that would make him a successful trial lawyer and, when Charley went to Washington to work for the government, Lem stayed on in tax law. Charley begged him to come, too, but the risk was too great. Three children now, and Ermina needed servants and nice things. He procrastinated, and one day said good-bye to Charley in Albany and did not see him again except in newspaper photographs when he was appointed Associate Justice of the United States Supreme Court.

Ermina wondered what Lem was thinking, looking at Charley's distinguished face in the paper, reading the favorable criticism of his career.

"My dear, do you think you have learned from your work — does it make you better able to handle the problems that come up in your own life?"

"I don't think so. If I had learned — all along — how to live my life by profiting from the vagaries of my clients, I wouldn't still be an ordinary attorney in an ordinary firm. I'd be secretary of state."

And if I had learned more, she thought, listened more carefully, remembered more accurately — I wonder, could I have helped make it possible? But the subject was closed. He folded the newspaper and relit his pipe.

"I used to daydream that your father would be the vice president of the United States," Ermina told her daughters after he died.

"Why *vice* president?" asked Martha.

"Oh, because I knew — in the dream — that Charles Van Gelder was going to be president." She moved her thumb rhythmically in a small circle around the inner flesh of her index finger and at the same time her tongue circled her lips. Leonora looked away. The daydream had left resentments.

The island was lush with greenery. The two-story stone house was crowded by tall pines, squat cedars, underbrush, ferns. Paths had to be hacked through it and every year in the spring the machete and scythe were put to use again to make the way to the water wide enough for two or three to walk together or for a child to run down without getting scratched by branches.

When Lem worked in his study, Ermina did her chores. Bathing, cleaning the rooms, rearranging the contents of a desk or bureau could become a task that took her time and thought and in turn gave her pleasure. But she was always waiting for the call of her name to summon her to his room, or the raising of his eyes from his work — her silent cue for life, real life, to begin again.

After the children came, she had less time to fill, and it took more care to find the time to share with him. No more making small tasks into large ones. There was always enough to do and she found that waiting for the cry of a hungry child started the juices of her body flowing, just as Lem's beckoning look had always done and would do later, at night. At his signal, they would prepare themselves at exactly the same time, and arrive washed and perfumed and newly dressed in clothes they would soon remove at the bed, where they discovered pleasure in each other, and, to her way of thinking, each other.

There they were one and the same. There they were separately beautiful to themselves and to each other. The ritual he had taught her had infinite variations and included everything from trepidation to exhaustion, from delight to an ecstasy that often caused them both to call out like drowning, dying creatures who had no vocabulary but sounds and cries.

When Martha's tasks were done — Nana made her responsible for Leonora's part of the bedroom as well as her own and for all their ironing — she swung in the hammock, half-awake, planning her life, or went down to the lake and climbed out on the fallen tree and sat with her legs in the water. If their neighbor Abe was free, she would ask him if he could take her out to the raft in the rowboat. He'd leave her there to read in the late afternoon before the sun set.

It was from the raft that she saw Abe bring the carcass of a deer to the front of his cabin, throw it to the ground, spend nearly an hour hoisting it up on a frame he'd constructed, and with the precision of a surgeon, slit the fur from the body, strip it off still attached to the magnificent antlered head, and spread it out on the ground to dry. If he knew she was watching, he did not let her know. His concentration was perfect. She watched, sick and fascinated, wondering why he didn't call the boys to watch. He took the hose and watered down the stones until the blood washed away, then he rinsed his hands and the knife and went inside his cabin to rest. He had killed it out of season. She had watched him committing the end of his crime.

Lem described Abe Langhorn as "the best man I know." The children grew up learning from Abe the ways of the fields and the lake and how to take care of animals and what herbs and mushrooms to pick. He did seem good and wise. Not fatherly, yet gentler than their father. A man with more time than other men, he sat in his little house near the fire, talking, never looking at the clock. Walks with Abe did not have to have a destination. His muscular body looked packed into his immaculate clothes. Olive green jacket over light brown trousers tucked neatly into polished dark brown boots. There was never mud caked on them, nor did he seem to sweat like other people who came to work at the Camp.

The boys feared they loved him more than their father. The idea of the Camp without him was unthinkable. The girls felt his careful indifference to them. Neither was particularly drawn to hunting or boating, but Martha was quick to find and identify the edible plants. "You get an A for that, my girl," was the first compliment she had ever heard from him.

Martha went back to the house and knocked on Lem's study door.

"Poppa, can I come in?"

"At once, my dear." He settled her down on the floor by his chair and finished reading a court transcript. She waited, inhaling the smell of his tweed trousers and pipe tobacco and bay rum. She felt calm when it was time to ask him about Abe. She thought if she knew what he was like she could understand what he had done. She did not betray Abe by telling her father what she had seen. She was learning the way to keep secrets as her father confided in her the story of the best man he knew.

Grown up, Martha was godless; in childhood she invented a god and built an altar to him in a cove of the lake where not even the boys would go because Abe had invented some story about eels and snakes and quicksand. They went elsewhere to sail their boats. Martha had no intention of going in the water. She found a sandy curve, as long as her body stretched out on the ground, and to it she brought treasures from her walks. Stones of shapes and colors that glistened in the water. A pile of stones, no higher than the lake grass, which she added to and changed whenever she came to it. Squatting rather than kneeling, building and rebuilding her pyre — to whom? — she did not pray but willed her thoughts into questions and waited for answers. It was there that she found out what she wanted most in the world, and without an answer of how to find it, knowing the question was as comforting as the cool water running through her hands and the warm earth beneath her. Was it all in one summer or were there two that she went there to the cove? No one ever knew, no one asked her where she was. On the days she did not go there she felt it waiting for her.

She would use her life to find a person who needed her. Someone who would be her god: Him. No name, no face. No one like him yet in her living or reading or dreaming. It did not matter how long it took. She would fill the days with some kind of work and through that work perhaps find him. It was clear to her that she would have to improve herself. There were things she did that made her furious. Repeating the same mistakes, knowing she was going to make the wrong choice and making it, turned her open nature into a closed and angry one.

On those days she barely spoke to anyone, and Nana called it one of her moods. Working on the bad part of her character was to take up many hours of the summers and too much of the winters. Her teachers would call her name and reprimand her. "Where *are* you today, Martha?" Miss Dunn would ask. The answer was, at the cove hunched over her stone altar longing for the future.

She did not hear Abe come down the bank. He must have watched her for quite some time and walked on. As he did, she heard the branches moving and turned to look. He saw her and said, "Martha." She could think of nothing to say even in greeting. She hated being discovered in her sanctuary and wanted to erase the memory of his placid face when it suddenly reddened and darkened. She could not look away. He dropped his bag of tools on the ground and carefully unbuttoned and lowered his trousers. She tried not to shift her gaze, but his eyes willed her to. She looked at him and when he decided she had seen what he wanted to show her he just as slowly dressed himself, picked up his tool bag, and walked away.

It did not happen again. She pushed over the stone pile and went back to the house and that was the last time she consorted with a spirit without a shape or form and the first time she was aware of a shape and form that would haunt and fascinate her in her growing up, waiting there in her memory and changing the plan of her life.

She would not look for a partner. She did not want one anymore. She wanted a life without *that*. It would be harder to achieve than the discovery of the person without a name, the him. No one knew of her earlier quest, no one would know of this decision, which was to give her a strength she did not know she possessed.

"Martha, are you asleep?"

"Yes."

Leonora laughed. "I've got to tell you something. I've come

to a decision." Martha waited. Leo loved to talk at night. Martha wanted to sleep. In the day they were not so much sisters as gentle adversaries jousting for the attention and respect of their parents. "Martha, I'm not going to wear hair ribbons anymore."

"Nana will scold you. She can't stand the sight of hair in your face." Martha's imitation made Leonora giggle.

"No, it's more than that. When I get back to school I'm never going to wear black or navy blue again except for the uniform. I'm going to take the feather out of my winter hat. And if I ever have a child she won't wear black velvet for good and middies with red ties for — "

"— bad! Oh, I know what you mean. And no more high shoes with buttons and laces."

"I lie awake dreaming about a pair of low-cut patent leather pumps."

"And you know what else would be wonderful? To throw away our hairpins!"

"Cut our hair!"

"It's too late for talking, girls. You have all day for talking. Go to sleep now." Nana's firm voice sounded uncannily like her daughter's mockery.

Martha lay awake thinking about Abe and what she had seen. Odd to be talking to her sister about hair and clothes now. Leonora was still a girl. Martha felt like a woman.

Martha did not see Abe for years after the last summer they were all together at the Camp. In 1943 when it seemed sensible to sell off part of the land, they all met in the main house on a bleak autumn day and, while they were sitting around the fire discussing the terms of sale with the surveyor and a relative of Abe's who was not introduced but looked like his son, Abe walked into the room with an outsize pot of coffee and a fistful of mugs and silently served them. When he came to her, she stopped him with her eyes as surely as if she had tugged his sleeve. His expression did not change as he murmured, "I still look for you." He was a widower then, and had not married again, became a selectman, respected by all who knew him. Fair and levelheaded. She could hear her father's voice: The best man I know.

In summer when the branches were heavy with the heat from the damp air and Nana's sister Clara came for her annual visit, the porch was a haven. The slanting roof and the pale blue ceiling underneath gave the semblance of a cooler shade than the verdant trees.

The chairs were old, the rocker creaked and the wicker settee caught threads from clothing and women's stockings and pinched the children's upper thighs when they wore bathing suits or shorts.

Clara sat at the far end of the porch — she called it the piazza — with a neat pile of clothing that needed repair. Nana made a collection and for eleven months not a thing was darned or hemmed, not a button tightened or a collar reversed. When Clara came she was handed the laundry case that held her "work." She insisted that she loved to mend and would feel cheated if everything were not saved for her. It seemed to the children that the amount of sewing took exactly as long as her visits. When the things lay folded on the sideboard in the hall and the case was hanging on the line freshly washed, it meant Clara would pack her suitcases.

Leonora wondered how Aunt Clara could sew and rock in the wicker chair at the same time. When she saw her threading a needle and rocking, she laughed. "How do you do that?"

"The thread knows where to go, you goose!"

Why was it easy to be silly and have a good time with her aunt and not with her mother? Leonora felt embarrassed and guilty as she heard herself whisper, "Aunt Clara, I love you more than Momma."

"No you don't, sweetheart. You love me differently."

Leonora did not understand her and knew she would want to

ask Martha about it at night, but did not dare. She should not have said what she did, but it was as if she had no power to stop the words. Any endearment made Nana's eyes shine, she was always thinking of Harrison. Even Dwight could not hug her or touch her without sensing her pitiless despair, the shadow of the drowned boy coming between each demonstration of love.

Clara made all of them feel comfortable because she was so organized. Calm surrounded the circle in which she sat. They needed to be near that center, that sanity. It was the gift she shared with them and did not know she had. The cologne and powder and pretty handkerchiefs she left as thank-yous were reminders of the sweetness Clara brought to their childhood summers.

The winter after Harrison's drowning, Aunt Clara invited the Iveses to Christmas lunch. Nana was relieved. She did not want to prepare a feast for her diminished family. She had enough to do and no servant for the weekend. The children were no help — Dwight's room was in such a state of confusion she decided to give up on it, and the girls were sporadically neat, then suddenly piggish. "I can't cope with it," she said, and was delighted to accept her sister's summons.

The day began like most holidays: the children waiting for the adults to wake, attempts at quiet conversations developing into laughter, and footsteps too loud to allow sleepers to rest. There were no scoldings on holiday mornings. Eventually the sound of carols would be heard. Lem would find a station on the radio and turn the sound up as loud as it would play. That was the signal. It was not necessary to be dressed; they assembled in bathrobes and dressing gowns. Lem tucked his pajama top into his house trousers and threw a sweater over that. Coffee for the adults. Breakfast was a forgotten meal on the day of presents, casual worshiping, and family visiting.

In order to preserve some sense of decorum they opened their presents in turn. Harrison had always been first. Now it was Leonora. This particular Christmas, Clara chose to give the girls a doll house and Dwight a bicycle as their big presents. The size made wrapping difficult. Nana bought red and green tissue paper and taped tents of it over them in an attempt to hide the recognizable shapes.

The doll house was five feet long and two stories high. It was described in F. A. O. Schwarz's catalogue as an English cottage. It was carefully painted, each room a different shade, and vines and flowers were attached to the outside walls. Details of stairs, windowsills, and wall and ceiling moldings were exact. The windows looked leaded and the light fixtures, although not practical, were delicate copies of chandeliers and sconces. Rugs were painted on the floors and the bathrooms were complete, too, a wooden tub, basin, and toilet in each.

The furniture came in excelsior-packed boxes, some pieces with painted designs, some carved. The sofa was upholstered as were the armchairs and a hassock. The drawers in the bureaus were paper lined, the kitchen cabinets were metal, and a box full of miniature groceries was provided.

The back wall of the house had been removed so that to squat beside it was to have all the rooms available. If it was turned around and a light put behind it, the leaded windows glistened.

The only things that did not seem perfect in detail and size were the figures of a family of four in a separate box. They were stiff, clothed in felt and printed cotton and ill-fitting wigs. Martha wanted to throw them away. They did not go with the furniture. They were intruders.

Leonora insisted they be allowed to live in the house. "They belong there."

"They don't."

"A house has to have inhabitants," she replied.

Martha scoffed. "Inhabitants! Where'd you get that word?"

"Oh, you just want to play with the furniture all the time. It's no fun for me. You can't make up stories about furniture!"

"I can. Leave me alone with it for the afternoon. You can play with it tomorrow. I want to fix it up the way it should be now. Then you can move the 'inhabitants' in."

"Look! There's another box of them!" Leonora pulled another "people" box out of the wrappings and discovered a maid and a butler ready to go to work in their serving costumes. Both girls laughed and hugged each other. "Well," said Martha in Clara's voice, "the servant problem is solved!"

Leonora hid the little boy doll — something in his smiling round pink face reminded her of Harry. She did not want Nana to see it.

It was the first year Martha received jewelry from Nana. It was the second or third time that Dwight wanted and got adventure books and a subscription to *Boys' Life* as his small presents. But his favorite thing was still the long green. Why not admit it? There was nothing he liked better than the little decorated envelopes from relatives too busy or bored to shop. Inside, the neat checks with his name carefully written on the first line or, better yet, brand-new bills: ones, fives, and occasionally a ten. That was the best. "What will you spend it on?" he would be asked. He did not know. "I'm going to save it," he said. And so he did, but years later he could never place that money in his memory. Did he save it or spend it? The pleasure was simply to receive it.

The day went on, lazily. They had to go to church, of course, where Clara was the choir mother and her boys were the pride of her life. Their unruly hair glued down with some preparation (one of them swore it was liquid shampoo), their cassocks washed and pressed. They looked innocent and sang exquisitely. The rest of the service did not share that purity. The pastor was an unctuous man, his interest, like Dwight's on Christmas morning, was the long green. The sermon, including many Biblical and topical references, was like a carnival pitch. It was aimed at the pocketbooks of the congregation and the finale and the coda were always accompanied by the sounds of the organ pealing and ushers with velvet-lined silver platters getting into line at the last pew. Snap, snap, purses and wallets were opened. The children were nudged and took their coins out of their pockets and dropped them in, looking at the nearly filled plates with awe. Would the bills stay in place? More silver would hold them down, perhaps, but as the collection plates swept through each line of givers the paper money fluttered nervously like birds on top of a nest.

It would be wrong to catch the grownups' eyes when Dr. Deerfield likened society to "a bowl of jelly" or as he pronounced "God-uh, and Christ-uh, and the Lord-uh." They must not laugh. The girls were impatient to get back to arrange and explore the doll house. Dwight sulked because he was not allowed to bring his bike. After church they walked, no matter how snowy the streets were, arriving at one o'clock precisely for lunch at Aunt Clara's.

For Leonora, the marshmallows on the sweet potatoes and the hard sauce with the mince pie were the highlights of the meal. For Dwight the dark meat — "Can I have the *whole* leg, please?" — and the boiled onions were most important. Nana ate little; Lem drank several glasses of wine.

It was just family. A hired maid served and because no one knew what to call her, they smiled pleasantly and said thank you every time she came around with another tray of food. After lunch Aunt Clara praised her profusely, paid her, and sent her on her way to her own celebration provided by her half-day's work for the quiet, apparently wealthy family.

At home, the evening came with nothing planned. There was a pick-up supper, quiet talk, big cups of coffee, the radio still playing Christmas joys and laments. Nana grieved for her lost son. Suddenly without warning she half-stood from her place at the head of the table. "I didn't get anything I wanted," she moaned.

The children could not believe that an adult, any adult, had such feelings. Lem was appalled because he knew at once that he had failed her, yet didn't know how. She was so exhausted and embarrassed she could barely push her chair back and, holding first the table and then the sideboard for support, find her way out of the room. All her grace and quiet control gone in an instant of disappointment: of being too old for anyone to care about her Christmas dreams; of hating herself for envying Clara's decorated tree nearly buried in boxes from the most expensive shops, some still unopened; of life going by and no one seeming to watch it go. Strange sounds came from her tightened throat as she rushed down the hall, went into her bedroom, and closed the door.

Dwight put his head on the table and closed his eyes. His sisters rose at the same moment and began to clear the dishes. In the kitchen Martha said, "I saw tears in Father's eyes."

"It's her own fault. She just doesn't love anybody."

"I said, *Father's*."

"I heard you. It's Nana's fault."

Dwight watched them. "Well, well, well."

"Is that all you have to say?" said Martha.

"No. I am sure there is a great deal more to say, but this is neither the time nor the place." He was imitating his father and the girls were about to giggle in gratitude to him for letting the day end with a lessening of the tension Nana's pain had brought to all of them. At that moment Lem appeared at the door with his finger to his lips. Dwight shrugged his shoulders.

"Don't do that, Dwight. Your mother doesn't like it." Lem looked at each child in turn and said, "Merry Christmas" so softly that only Leonora heard it. She had run to his side as he appeared in the room. She trembled but did not know why.

"I felt scared, Mart. Not of father, just scared."

Every day Lem went to his law office in New York, arriving on time, leaving on time, accomplishing the amount of work necessary to fulfill his obligations. It did not occur to him to do more or less. But one day after more than twenty years of service to his clients and to various charitable and civic organizations, he did not go to his office and did not make any excuse by message or personal call. Everyone who knew him assumed that he was ill. For several days nothing was done by his secretary, Pearl, or by Nana. She thought he was at the office; Pearl thought he was at home. Three days without anyone telling him what to do or where to go. Days of floating, coasting, flying. When they were over, the diagnosis was that he was overtired. He was not able to figure out what to do to give his life meaning, he only knew he had to stop what he had been doing and wait until he could manage to replace his chores at the office and his conjugal duties with something else.

He decided to move his family to Oseta Lake as soon as he could arrange to give up the apartment. When he was settled, he would send for them. Nana and the children were panicked by his decision. The time before he came to it — the quiet time — was difficult for them to understand, but this new plan was untenable. Each had a reason why he or she did not want to leave.

The girls had each other and their secrets from each other. They did not seem to be lonely. Dwight chose to be by himself. His days were arranged so that he could wander through the woods in the summer and the streets in the winter and, as long as he did his chores, neither Nana nor Lem chided him.

Harrison had been Nana's audience. From his earliest years he trained his eyes on her and as she made a salad or threaded a needle for her petit point or poured the talcum on the buffer to shine her nails she felt her boy's gaze. He was her darling Harry and she hated to have him out of the room. Even at night she thought of him and, as Lem grew less ardent, thoughts of her son obsessed her. She had not wanted him to take the trip that led to his death; she had not wanted him to spend the night at a friend's when he was small. She needed his eyes.

It was her selfish little obsession: her desire to know what impression she made on others. Wherever she went, whatever task took her attention, it was split with the need to know how she was doing, whatever she was doing, and when, as she twisted and turned in her sad husband's bed, it occurred to her to wonder how he really felt about her and how she was responding to him at that moment, her body froze and he held her stiff shoulders so that he could look straight at her and wordlessly question what was going on in her foolish female head.

Nana wondered if she could live the rest of her life in the same manner. Finding no talent to explore she made a kind of dry peace with herself and accepted what each day brought. If it were not for reading the novels the girls sneaked into the house and left hidden in their rooms — where she found them and later returned them — she would not have been prepared for her only important infidelity.

How did Nana and Lem start playing it, the name game? The children played it carelessly, but with adults there was something devilish about it. Lem and Nana sat in the parlor after dinner and, without a cue or a warning, he would begin. The game had no rules, it was too simple to need them. He would simply say the name of a friend or acquaintance and choose a subject — money, sex, potential, looks — and off they'd go on a roller coaster of criticism and cruel laughter. Carefully dissecting the chosen name until there was virtually nothing left unsaid by either of them.

After a few glasses of wine or an after-dinner brandy, it was easy to start, but tonight Nana was feeling depressed and unsure of herself. It was unbearably difficult. Impossible to concentrate as one tore a reputation to shreds.

It was Lem's turn. A new name but the same subject, not fair to change that until the next time they played. Andrew Dennison's name was his first choice. The subject: potential. "You first," he suggested.

"I don't know him well enough," she lied.

"Don't cheat. Say what you think without thinking!"

"I imagine . . . I think . . . he could succeed in any position he was interested in . . . I mean, he could rise to the top . . ."

"In what way?"

"He's serious. Not frivolous. He doesn't seem to have many outside interests. He's hard to talk about because he's so guarded."

"I don't find him that way at all. He's dull certainly. Abstracted sometimes. Doesn't contribute much to the conversation . . ."

"You just play cards with him, don't you? No one talks much at your club."

"You don't have to defend him, my dear. He's perfectly affable."

"Affable? What does that mean?"

"He has nice manners. Polite."

" 'Politeness is fictitious benevolence' said Boswell."

"Johnson?"

"Johnson. Of course."

Why did the quietly witty Andrew Dennison give such an impression of himself to other people? Nana wondered. Was it possible that no one else saw the *other* person contained in him, the one who when aroused became passionate and overwhelming? And if her name were to come up in someone else's game what would be said? Was *she* affable? Courteous? Dull?

Andrew Dennison was a fine card player, good at billiards, drank conservatively, and dressed that way, too. He had what his law partner called "a nice little sense of humor" and a soundless laugh. When amused he would rock back and forth with his mouth in an open smile, but no syllable of mirth passed his lips. This sense of humor lurked in his eyes. Nana saw it, he knew she saw it, and they were friends at their first meeting.

Nana had been married to Lem for twenty-five years and had borne him four children. She knew Andrew before Lem died, and he flirted with her and touched her and she did not stop his words or put his hand away from her neck, her cheek, her breasts. He did not touch her often, an occasional caress as she arrived at or left his table or his car or, later on, his rooms. She excused herself by thinking that Lem no longer touched or spoke to her with the same soft strange sounds that had made her melt when she was younger. There was no place for that now in his life, and if he no longer felt the need to reach out to her, what was surprising to her was that she no longer desired it.

When Lem was ill at the Camp, when he was dying, it did not occur to her that she would be free to marry again. When Andrew asked her, she was overcome by a prolonged spasm of painful crying she could not control. He held her and calmed her. "You don't have to say anything. You can forget I asked you."

"I won't forget," she sobbed, and hoped he would not forget.

He did not mention it again until after Lem's death and by that time it no longer sounded like a proposal, but a friendly arrangement between loving friends. There seemed to be a rightness to it and when the time came for them truly to join their lives it was impossible for her to remember anything else that had ever been as right. He, the more experienced, older of the pair, refused to compare any emotional experience to one that had preceded it. This gave his life, his encounters with both men and women, intellectually and casually, a kind of newness and, in the case of Nana, a freshness that was unique.

It was arranged. There would be a small wedding ceremony with just her children and Natalie Hammel, a party at Delmonico's and a drive out to Long Island for a few days by themselves.

Halfway through my life, she thought, and I am so happy. Why do I feel threatened? By whom?

She sensed it would be Leonora and it was. From the time they announced the wedding plans her attitude was condescending and quiet. It was as if by taking another husband — which meant a new lover — Nana had abandoned the role of mother. Leonora, at eighteen, could not accept such a situation. By choosing to be happy with Andrew, Nana lost her daughter's affection.

After Lem's death, Nana realized that almost nothing Leonora said was directed to her, and what she did say was often remarked upon by Martha to fill the silences. If Andrew was in the room, Leonora found an excuse to leave. At meals she rarely spoke. It made Nana furious but she did not dare express her rage. She knew her daughter's withdrawal would win the day. She did not want to discuss it with Andy because it meant admitting to him that she had failed with one of her children. But one night he said something that made her think he had sensed her uneasiness.

"Mothers and daughters, fathers and sons: strange, isn't it? No way of knowing how it will all turn out." She looked up at him from her place by the fire. He was reading the *Law Review* and went back to it, commenting later on a quarrel between a brother and sister over their parents' estate. He discussed the legalities involved.

"But what would you do if you were handling the case?"

"I try not to touch problems like that, my dear. Families are too complicated for me. Business is a cinch compared to mothers and daughters —"

"— and fathers and sons."

"What is ideal," he said, "is to live fully every minute and to die with no debts and nothing left behind. Nothing for the monsters to fight over."

"Do you think children are monsters, Andy?"

"No. I was one once, remember! No, I think the situation brings out the worst in all of us. Fighting over something that really never should have been ours in the first place. By the way, do you have a will, my darling?"

He grinned at her. She did. "I'm going to change it. Give you everything. I don't want the children fighting over my possessions."

"They'll fight worse if you leave them to me. What've you got?"

Lem had all the real estate and whatever monies he had earned in his name at the bank. But in his will he had left everything to her. She then divided it evenly among herself and the three children and put the results of that simple mathematical problem on a piece of paper that became her will. It was a considerable amount.

"Let me look at it sometime, will you?"

"Whenever. It's all yours now. What there is of it. The timber on the shore property and the island. I don't think the outbuildings are in good condition. Whoever bought the place would have to remodel."

"Do you want to sell it?"

"No, dear. I don't know why I said that. We'll go there in the summers, won't we?"

"We'll see. We'll see," said Andrew. A chill of excitement made him straighten his neck and shoulders. He decided at that moment to spend the rest of his life working the Ives estate into a fortune.

It was Leonora who had found Lem sitting in his Morris chair, the pipe he favored above all others still in his hand, the *Albany Times* lying in unnatural folds on the floor. She had come into his room quietly as always, knowing that he would find time to talk with her if she waited. "Hello, Father," she said softly. The stillness did not alert her to what had happened. She straightened some papers on his desk, checked his calendar, and added the last few appointments he had told her about before she realized he was not awake, not alive.

"It seems to me," said Dwight, "that as long as there are trees, we'll be rich. That land in California and the Adirondack forests will take care of us for the rest of our lives."

"It all belongs to Nana," said Martha.

"And *Mister* Nana," said Leonora.

"Who else is she going to give it to?" asked Dwight. "It's ours. I mean, we're the family."

"Innocent! She can do whatever she pleases with it," said Leonora. The conversation made her uneasy. She rocked in Aunt Clara's chair and hated the sound of the creaking boards beneath her. The waves on the lake lapped against the stones. Martha wanted to leave her brother and sister and walk down to the cove but something held them there together. Leonora thought she knew what it was. They were all afraid to leave the Camp now because it meant deciding what to do with their lives. Martha wanted to be a decorator but there was nothing definite in her plans beyond looking up a friend of Clara's in New York. Dwight talked of hitchhiking to California. He wanted to take the trip Harrison had never finished. He lit a cigarette and started wheezing like an old man. His sisters looked at him, recognizing for the first time his uncanny likeness to their father in the last months of his life. They had never acknowledged the resemblance before.

"I think the money is going to ruin us as a family," said Martha.

Leonora looked up. "Just what I was thinking."

"Don't be dumb," said Dwight, clearing the phlegm from his throat. "What would we do without it?"

"What other people do," said Leonora. "Work."

"I'm going to travel. I'll find some kind of work. What're you going to do, Sis?"

"I don't know. I wish I did."

Dwight disappeared into the house to have his afternoon nip of Old Forrester. He would sleep until dinnertime. The sisters left their chairs and sat together on the top step listening to the water.

"I wish I'd talked to father about what to do, Mart. I don't want to be a disappointment to him."

"You won't be."

"I *will,* if I don't do something with my life."

"Here's what we can do. Go to the city with Nana. Stay at Riverside Drive until I get settled in some kind of work and then we'll find a place together. Meanwhile you can look for something to do. If you could choose anything in the world, what would it be?"

"That's what I'm scared of. I just don't know. I'd like to —" Leonora put her hand to her mouth and bit her finger.

"Say it." Martha waited.

"Make someone happy."

"I'm sure you will. And until then, while we're here, you

know what we can do? We can go into father's room and arrange all his papers and notebooks."

"No, we can't. He told Abe to burn them. They're all gone."

"Does Nana know?"

"Nana doesn't care."

Part Three

THEY WERE THE only two people left on the top of the double-decker Fifth Avenue bus by the time it turned up Riverside Drive. The man studied the woman, while the woman worked on the *Times* crossword puzzle. Presently she felt his gaze, stronger than the sun on the page before her. She looked up. He did not smile at her, he simply waited for her expression to change. His look was one of immense interest without being personal. She might have been a painting or a photograph. She knew it was time for her to look down at the column of numbered words again, but she kept looking at him until he spoke.

"Do you like word games?"

"I'm not very good at them."

"It all depends on whom you play with, doesn't it?" Now he was grinning and his face charmed her. He looked bright and clean and intensely masculine. She blushed. He introduced himself and sat beside her until she reached the bus stop outside of the forbidding stone mansion where she seemed to have an appointment. He saw the doorman greet her. He got off at the next stop, walked back, and questioned the doorman about the woman who had just gone in. He made up a name. "No, that was Miss Ives, sir." He thanked the man who had just played a tiny but important part in the play of his life. He never saw him again because he was not to be welcome at 67 Riverside Drive.

He looked in the telephone book. There was an "M. Ives" in the East Sixties. He dialed, and a maid answered and told him that Miss *Leonora* Ives lived with her mother and gave him the correct number. He dialed again and asked for Leonora.

"This is her mother," said a brisk voice.

"May I leave a number for Miss Ives to call? This is Stephen Tannenbaum." He gave his number and hung up when she started to ask what he was calling about. He knew that the whispery voice of her daughter would be his next call. An hour later he was talking to her and wooing her and three days later they met at the Palm Court for tea. A year later they were married at the Plaza Hotel. She had fallen in love with him on the open-air bus.

The Second World War affected Leonora and Dwight in oblique, tangential ways, but Martha was more involved because after many months of requests and rejections she finally received permission to go to Europe with the Red Cross. She was put in charge of decorating the interiors of the clubs and mess halls in the vicinity of London, and later in Ireland and eventually in France. This made it possible for her to be with her lover, Laurence Parrish, an American banker who was with the Office of Strategic Services in Paris.

Dwight successfully avoided active service because of his age and the fact that he was still married to his second wife, Grace. He enlisted in the ROTC and was sent to Camp Crowder in Kansas. He did office work and was the morale officer for a month. He was back east before Grace had a chance to get rid of their apartment. She had left him without a word and he returned to the rooms he had shared with her to find the furniture covered with white sheets.

He invited Leonora to come and see him. The room she entered was still shrouded. He thought it would make her laugh. Leonora tried to make the place into a bachelor apartment for him. "And you can rent two of the rooms. Space is at a premium in the city now."

"I'd like to rent the whole thing and go up to the Camp."

"Then why don't you? You look thin. You could get some rest." He shrugged. She touched his shoulder tenderly. "Was it dreadful? You never wrote."

"Old Nana won't like what I have to tell her. I was a lousy soldier. I hated basic training. I was too old for all that. And then I got too sick for it."

Leonora wondered if he meant hung over.

"One fine day I just couldn't breathe, that's all. They took me to the hospital and x-rayed my chest and the next thing I knew they were talking to my C.O. about a medical discharge. They found out I had T.B."

"No!"

"Yeah. I made some feeble joke about sending me to Saranac. Didn't Abe's family have something to do with one of the sanatoriums there? I thought it would be so convenient —"

"Dwight, be serious."

"Well, you goose," he said, smiling, "it wasn't anything like that. The x rays weren't mine, some sort of foul up. A couple of shots of that new stuff, penicillin, and I was feeling fine. But I was mustered out of the service and here I am fit as a fiddle and unemployed."

His sisters felt that his serious drinking began at that time. The war meant getting black market whiskey and sitting in Third Avenue bars to Dwight. He did not stay at the Camp with his mother. He lived at the City Athletic Club and she paid the rent for him. Nana had lost her second son.

Leonora shared her butter and sugar and shoe ration stamps with her mother. She wrote long letters to Martha once a week and waited impatiently for her replies. She lived through the bombings weeks afterward when Martha's reports arrived. She followed her sister's progress with the service clubs by the postmarks: Manchester, Buckden, Lichfield, Duxford, Tidworth, Sudbury, Ipswich, Taunton, Tavistock. She envied Martha the work and the excitement, but even more the possibility of romance. The letters referred to Laurence Parrish by his initials, and Leonora had a copy of the code Martha and Larry used to explain where he was. Each European city had its American counterpart. Some of them made Leonora giggle: Munich was Coney Island, Nancy was Cleveland, Ulm was Jones Beach, Frankfurt was Newark.

Months of working and living compared to Leonora's months of filling time and waiting: volunteer work at the Junior League, at the USO, at the British War Relief office. Nothing she was proud of. On D-day she was listening to the radio. Martha was in London: "I dined alone and went to bed early and was awakened by LP's voice telling me about the landing."

She wrote of trips to Ireland. She sent snapshots of herself in her Red Cross coat and cap, black Army-Navy store shoes and thick gloves. Even Nana thought they were the best photographs even taken of Martha. Then nearly a year of letters came from France where she set up clubs in Dijon, Nancy, Reims, and Cannes. The initial *L* appeared more often, the codes were less cryptic, the war was coming to an end. But Martha did not want to come back to America. Her connections in Europe had become her friends. She waited for her sister to send word of *her* friends, but Leonora's letters were rarely autobiographical. "I seem to live vicariously," she wrote in answer to Martha's questions, "so please remember everything and tell me, *tell me*."

The Ives family remembered its dead in words and pictures and memories. For Stephen Tannenbaum each mention of Lemuel or Clara or Harrison or any of the aunts and uncles of the Pringle family was infuriating. All he had to remind him of his mother, who had died when he was eight, was a wood-framed sepia photograph that bore no resemblance to the person he remembered. Occasionally the aroma of bread baking, herbs simmering in soup, or the warm smell of ironed shirts would overcome him and make him believe she had lived, had loved, and had taken care of him. His father rarely mentioned her name and he knew no one else called Ida, so even those syllables were strange on his lips. He had so little to tell Leonora about her.

"I would have loved her, Stephen."

"That's sentimental."

"I would have loved her! She was your mother, your hands and wrists and the shape of the back of your head and your beautiful feet — they are all part of her. All the things that delight me."

"Stop it," he said, but he looked pleased.

He blamed his father for his mother's death and yet he could not forgive her for dying. He wanted her back, the sweet warmth of her breast to comfort him, her soft words, her kind eyes. She left him alone in a world he ached to escape from. He did not tell his father what he planned to do. Sidney Tannenbaum tried to be there when his son came home from school. He prepared the same food his wife had made, but the boy ate little. He had no appetite for food or school and no talent for friendship.

From the time of his mother's death until he was graduated from high school, he lived in rented rooms in a brownstone house. It was while he was sitting on the stoop reading from his collection of Big Little Books that he first saw Arnold LeVine. Stephen was nearly fourteen, Arnold just five years old. He was a serious, quiet boy and it did not bother Stephen to have him sit or stand beside him. Without anything being planned, he would appear at Stephen's house every afternoon and soon became his friend. Mr. Tannenbaum no longer hurried home from work: the boys were busy doing something together. Sometimes he would find a note on the table from Stephen saying he was taking Arnold for a walk. They always came home in time for dinner and with three of them at the table conversation was easier.

"That kid was the first person I ever knew who made me

feel I was somebody," Stephen told Leonora, and when she met Arnold she understood why. He gave her, too, the feeling that what she thought and said was interesting, even important. He had given Stephen a sense of identity and was the single acquaintance from his past whom she came to know.

"When I was a kid," Stephen told her, "I figured I wouldn't be spending my life in school. What mattered came later. I did my best and that was it. I got by. I was looking for a way to live my life until I could really live it. You know what I mean?"

"Yes. In a way. But I wanted to be the best at every subject, sport, test, friendship. I used to leave school exhausted in the afternoon and have to rest before I could do my homework."

"I never did mine," he boasted. "I figured whatever they assigned I'd do in my free time at school but I wasn't going to give them my home free time."

"What did you do with that time?"

"Played ball. Sneaked into movies. Imagined I was on the prowl for girls."

"Imagined?"

"Oh, listen, I wasn't any good at it. No one is at thirteen or fourteen, that's when you pretend you're a lady killer and a stud!"

"Girls don't feel they're really any good at attracting boys either, but we try. We buy make-up and worry about our clothes and, most of all, our complexions . . ."

"Girls don't change."

"You're right."

"Boys do. You know you're a man when you don't have to think about it anymore. When you just *know* how to approach a girl or a woman."

"A woman?"

"Oh Jesus, yes. It's the real thing then. You hit the sack with an older woman and—" He stopped himself. "Am I offending you?"

"No."

"You looked shocked."

"Surprised. I'd love to know what it's like for a man. No one has ever told me anything like this before. How are women supposed to understand men if they never exchange confidences? What your girlfriends tell you is either silly or what you already know, and men are so — well — reticent."

"We're that way so you won't trap us. You tell most women something and they twist it out of shape. The next time you see them they start in on you."

"I won't do that."

"Sure you will. Some day you'll say something about my being so knowledgeable about women and connect it to the way I talked to my secretary on the telephone and the next thing you know we'll be having a real go-round."

"I won't do that, Stephen."

"You would've if I hadn't warned you."

"You think all women are alike?"

"There you go!"

"No, I meant that seriously. Do you? Because I think all men — I mean the men I've known — are absolutely different. I think that's the reason I'm so curious — and so grateful to you for talking to me — because I can't seem to figure them out."

"Don't try so hard, Leonora. Let yourself alone a little. Relax a little. The thing I figured out at school works in life, too, you know. You don't have to finish the assignment on time if you don't want to. Make your own schedule, your own timetable for work and play. That's the trick about being grown up."

"I waste my time. I'm dependent on the letter that comes in the morning mail or a telephone call that starts my day or an engagement written on the calendar for what I do with my time."

"And if nothing was there? If there was an empty day?"

"I'd do crossword puzzles or wash my hair or clean the apartment or — " To stop her trembling he took her in his arms and held her. "I don't know what's the matter with me. I'm sorry."

"There's nothing the matter. Life is small sometimes, you just want a bigger life."

She took a deep breath, pleased by his thought. "Yes, I do, but

I wonder if I could handle it if I got it. Maybe I'm safer the way I am."

"Safe. What's safe? Nothing."

"Safe is happy. I wish I could be happy."

He kissed her forehead, pushed her gently from him, picked up the telephone and made a reservation for dinner at Charles's. She went into the bathroom and washed her face with cold water and sprayed cologne inside her dress. When she came out he was lying on the couch waiting for her. They were an hour late for dinner.

Leonora knew there were certain topics to be avoided with Stephen. She learned it by being told "N.I." This code, which he picked up from his stepmother, meant "not interested." On the list were the weather, meals, weight, health, and personal attributes. Even a compliment was shrugged off with impatience. Plots of novels, plays, or films were on the list, too. "Don't spoil it for me," he'd say even if he had no intention of reading or seeing them. Careful reading of reviews gave him the gist of everything current and a great deal that he had missed in school. He appeared to be as well informed as most of the critics.

What did interest him was money. How it was made and spent and saved. And the people who had it.

He wanted to be asked to parties and events. He wanted to make a killing. It did not seem unusual to him that a man should crave the look and touch of money as much as close contact with another person. He did not think of getting up in the morning without making a call to his broker. His plans were based on his income, and if he caught himself craving something beyond his means he would force himself to work out the cost to the most minute detail. His ambition was to make enough money to support his habit of greedy dreams. In the process of making money he intended to make himself and whoever cared for him happy. He would educate, entertain, and endow anyone who would stay on his side. Why he appeared ungenerous he did not know, but he was certainly aware that he had that reputation. Perhaps it was because he did not talk like a generous man. He found himself remarking on the cost of everything and knew he had spoiled many restaurant meals by commenting on the price of the food and wine. It angered him that foolish, feckless men who talked about art and life and "the humanities" were considered more valuable members of society than he. When he met Leonora he realized she could be his guide through the doors that had been closed for so long. As her husband he would at last be comfortable in the living rooms of the quasi-intellectuals, and in the dining rooms of the cultured. He took her hand and promised her a fur coat, a string of pearls, and a trip to Europe.

"I don't want a coat. I'd love to have a Siamese cat!"

"I'll get you one tomorrow," he said, wondering why she didn't mention the jewelry or the journey. He gave their dinner order to Charles.

"I'm an awful liar," he boasted as they enjoyed the pasta. "I can lie my way into anything."

"Into, not out of?"

"Both really," he continued, grinning. "Once I told a millionaire's daughter I was a millionaire, and she believed me."

"I don't."

"It's true. I was on my way to Europe. I saw her name on the passenger list and I went to the purser and asked to be moved to her table."

"You were in first class?"

"Does that surprise you? Yes, when I travel alone I treat myself like a king. The best of everything, in every way, and this heiress — she was the best on the ship."

"How the best? The prettiest?"

"The richest."

"Was she single?"

"Married. I didn't know it at first. I knew very little about her, just recognized the name. Oh, I checked the list for her husband, but there was no other name like hers there. I didn't sit next to her, I was put opposite her at a circular table, but after two meals I simply changed my seat and no one seemed to mind."

"Was she easy to talk to?"

"Shy. Talked so softly I missed a lot of what she said, but I didn't care. I just wanted to —"

"Don't say it, please."

"No, not that. I wanted that, wanted to get that, but most of all I wanted to show her I was on a level with her economically."

"And socially?"

"It's the same thing to people like that. They can't be comfortable with anyone who isn't what she called 'well off.' She actually asked me if I was well off!"

"And you said?"

"That's what gave me the idea to show this little dame that I could top anything she had. I invented a father in the steel business and a mother whose family had made money in plumbing fixtures. I'd been to Woods Hole where the grandest house was owned by the Crane family, so I used them for my mother's family. She never asked me my father's name, she didn't even ask me mine. I think she was crazy about me the first time she saw me."

"Really?"

"Yeah. She just stared at me."

"Why was she traveling alone?"

"Family troubles. Some rich old aunt was dying and she was elected to go over and hang around until she croaked." Was he trying to make her laugh or was his vulgarity part of the story? "I don't think she gave a damn about the old girl. I don't know what she gave a damn about. Not me, certainly. I mean she had a hell of a time in my stateroom and I had an even better one in her suite, but she was bland, you know, white bread."

"And when the voyage was over?"

"That's the end of the story. And she never knew who I was. I told her I was traveling under an assumed name because of some business dealings in Germany. Didn't want my father's competition to know I was in Essen, stuff like that."

"And she believed you?"

"What the hell. It was better for her, too. She got a nice American going over and I had a terrific time. Living a lie."

"I think it's sickening."

"Then why did you ask me to tell you?"

"I didn't."

"Sure you did. You loved to hear it. Just because you don't have any nerve doesn't mean the rest of the world has to be milk and honey. Nobody got hurt. A good time was had by all."

While Stephen was ordering their dessert she tried to think of a subject to divert him, but he continued to tell her of his conquests.

He told Leonora about his discharge from the Army at Fort Ord when he went to San Francisco. He noticed an ad in the *Examiner* for a job as the caretaker of a large house in the Ojai Valley. He decided to call instead of write, made easy contact with the owner of the orange ranch, and was there the next day, ready to begin. He wore his Army uniform, which pleased the women working inside the ranch house and inspired the young men who worked in the orchards. It wasn't a difficult job, and it gave him time to look around for other work.

For a short time he had an affair with the ranch owner's wife, Helen. He simply waited in his shack for her to visit him as she did the first time. She appeared at the door and looked at him as he stood there, holding the doorknob in one hand and a cup of tea in the other. They said nothing and after a time he shut the door and put down the tea and they went carefully to the cot and she let him undress her. She stayed with him for less than half an hour each time. He could not remember the sound of her voice, she said so little, and she was silent when they made love. Not love. It was a sexual release without any complications and they were grateful to each other for it, for the depth of each other's need being answered. After one month, during which time she came to his room nearly every weekday at precisely three o'clock in the afternoon, she stopped coming. She went to

San Francisco to visit her mother. Without her visits he became restless, began to dislike the pungent smell of fruit ripening on the trees and the stillness of the warm nights. He decided to look for another job, but his luck did not hold. His telephone messages went unanswered and his letters received mimeographed replies. He wanted to get away from California and begin a career in New York at last. He told Ted, the ranch owner, that there was illness in his family.

"But what happened to Helen?" asked Leonora.

"She lost the baby. Ted said they'd have to try again."

Leonora gasped. She did not dare ask the question that had been in her mind since he said that Helen had gone to San Francisco. She did not want to know the answer.

Stephen's apartment on West 12th Street was a series of narrow, low-ceilinged rooms. The largest, painted and carpeted in light gray, was hung with water colors, several signed with his initials and the rest with a faint "M.B."

The largest and most vivid was a sailing scene hung over the marble mantel where Stephen stood, glass in hand, half-telling, half-inventing his life story for Leonora. He did not seem to have a plan. She wondered if he considered including her in his future.

"I don't like to plan. My life's going to turn out the same with or without my trying to direct it, right?"

"What?"

"Right or wrong?"

"I don't know. Isn't there something more than simple destiny?"

"Destiny! What a joke! I'm not living out my destiny, I'm living out my life. There'll be just so many days, and nights — thank God."

"God?" asked Leonora, trying not to mock him.

"Shut up. I mean I *prefer* the nights. And I will do whatever I can to fill them up with some sort of sensible living."

"But you're brilliant. There should be more to your life than that. Goals. Hopes. Dreams."

"That's what women have. I have enough trouble getting from one day to the next."

"What makes it worthwhile then?" she asked.

"You. Sometimes. And me sometimes. Some of the time I like what I'm doing. I seem to be getting somewhere."

"Tell me where?"

"Don't ask so many questions. You've made your own life all complicated with dreams you can't possibly fulfill."

"Why can't I?"

"Because, dear girl, you have an illness: You want perfection, and it's not to be had. If I could cut that desire out of you with a surgeon's knife and leave no scar, I think you'd have a better life."

"And now?"

"You're never satisfied. Don't protest. Even when you think you are, you aren't. I know it and so do you and I'm not just talking about —"

"I am satisfied, then. You know I am."

"Then let's say you are."

"You don't believe me, Stephen?"

"You haven't had all that much experience. You don't really know what you want. It isn't a knight in shining armor, is it?"

"It's you."

She was thinking: Whatever happens I do not want to hurt this man. In all his stories the man and the woman leave each other with nothing. I want to give him something. Myself. And more. What can I give him? How can I avoid giving him pain? I want to be perfect for him.

"Why are you smiling?" He always knew when she was thinking of something she could not say.

"I'm content," she answered, wishing she could express her sense of being a woman at last in a room with a man whom she loved. But it was like falling off a precipice and she could not catch her breath or order her thoughts into words.

"That's nice. But you'll get bored with me after a while. Wouldn't you like to have other people along sometimes?" She wondered if Dwight would like to meet him. "Your brother, perhaps?"

It was arranged that they would meet at a restaurant and later come to the flat and have a drink. But it rained the night of the engagement and Stephen did not want to go out. Instead he sent her to Charles's, where they wrapped a fresh-cooked Virginia ham and some sweet potatoes in waxed paper. There were vegetables and salad greens, French white and Italian red wine, and apple juice in his icebox.

The restaurant was no more than seven blocks away, but never having ordered food to take away, Leonora was apprehensive. The manager was surprisingly accommodating. He made her feel that the half-homemade dinner was a delightful idea.

On the way home she skidded on the slippery wet pavement and dropped the package in the gutter. Looking both ways and seeing no traffic she stooped to retrieve it and was shocked to find herself wondering whether to tell Stephen what had happened or to try to get away with the food as uncontaminated. "I'll never lie to him. That's what will make everything work with this man. I'll tell the truth, even about trivial things," she decided, and rushing up the stairs and into the flat she fought for breath between laughing and telling what had happened to their main course. He joined in her laughter and made her feel adventurous for coming back with anything edible at all.

Stephen came into the bathroom as Leonora was combing her hair.

"Do I look all right?"

"Well if you can tear yourself away from that mirror I'll give you my opinion."

Leonora turned slowly from her reflection to Stephen's gaze.

"Stand up straight," he commanded.

"I am."

"No, you're not. You think you are but you have a kind of funny slouch, my sweet, see — one foot out to the side that way."

"You're joking with me."

"I think you are a very handsome young woman, Leonora, but there are a few things you could do that would make you look beautiful: You could carry yourself with more pride and that would give you some height. You could wear brighter colors and you might visit a beauty parlor for some tips on how to wear your hair."

"Anything else?"

"You asked me, didn't you? Don't get glum."

"Stephen darling, I want to be so beautiful for you," she said as she went to him. "I only feel that way when we're in the dark."

"Well, *that's* nice."

"I didn't mean it to sound like that. But when I first met you I thought you liked the way I look and now—"

"I don't set too much importance on looks, Leelee."

"I think you do." She looked in the mirror again and was ashamed of herself for begging praise from him. Somewhere, she was sure, there was a girl who looked exactly the way he wanted her to.

She did not like her reflection. The dress she had chosen for Dwight to see her in as the fiancée of an attractive man looked dowdy. Why had she bought it in beige instead of rose? Her hair hung limply over her ears. She pushed it back with her fingers and secured it with bobby pins.

"Take those out of your hair. I hate them. Ugliest thing ever invented."

"But my hair—"

"Get it cut."

She envied him. His looks were a part of his being. His hair grew in tight curls around his finely proportioned face. His eyes were large and blue, his limbs straight, his torso strong. "Oh, Stephen, I'll go tomorrow. I'll get all fixed up."

"Don't bother."

"But—"

"I like what I see and smell and touch and I was really just teasing. If you were any prettier you'd get vain and if there's one thing I don't like it's a vain woman. Come here. I've got a present for you." He reached in his pocket and pulled out a jeweler's envelope. "Open it," he ordered, and she pulled off the flap. A string of perfect white jade beads poured into her hand. She kissed them. "Kiss *me,*" he ordered, and she did.

The doorbell rang. It was Dwight.

Over coffee and brandy Stephen quizzed Dwight about his childhood and avoided questions about his own. The talk turned to the Camp and brother and sister spoke almost as one, their interruptions dovetailing, their laughter mingling. Stephen listened until it sickened him.

"For Christ's sake! Didn't you ever do anything, feel anything? Did you just go from your city place to your country place and *talk?*" He said the word as if it were one of the forbidden words. "Talking, for Christ's sweet sake, *talking!*"

She could not defend her family to him. They had talked too long as it was. Afraid of boring Stephen, they left out much that would have made him more understanding: all the ugliness and cruelty. They had omitted the bad parts the way adults did when she was a child.

Leonora wished she had waited until they were alone to tell her story, which was really the story of other people's lives. "I have no life of my own," she said. "Everything that has happened to me and everything I am is the result of *others'* being, acting, and existing." She looked over at Dwight. His eyes were half-closed.

"Existence! That's all you have," cried Stephen. "Your indolent, feckless forefathers. It's all white bread. What have they done? What have they contributed?" He gave her no time to answer. "And what about him?" He nodded toward the dozing Dwight. Leonora waited for him to go on. He lit a cigarette and stood at the mantel. "I think of *my* ill-begotten father, hardly knowing his parents because they were always at work, getting up in the morning by himself in a two-room place in Brooklyn. Making himself something to eat if there was anything, and running to school so he wouldn't die of the cold. He couldn't get sick the way you did. There was no one to take care of him. I don't know what he did with his life when he wasn't at school or doing odd jobs. He never told me about a book he'd read or a concert he'd heard." He paused to sip his wine, saw Leonora's stricken face, and tried to control his irritation. "His father was always moving through the city, looking for a better deal on the rent, a steady job. It was the same for my dad. He married young and his wife died because he neglected her health. He was so afraid of doctors' bills he wouldn't take her to be checked up." Angry at himself for talking about his mother whom he could not forget or forgive, he raged on. "What did Dad end up with? He was a good accountant who never stole or missed a day of work and, when they retired him from his last job, which he held for twenty-nine years, I couldn't stand visiting him and my silly stepmother because all they talked about was the price of cheese and cigarettes and what was on the sports page of the *Daily News!*"

"But, in the end, there isn't that much difference in people's lives then, is there? They had few comforts, little pleasure but" — Did she dare ask? — "they weren't able to accomplish anything either, were they? They just, well, lived."

"They *struggled.*"

"I think my father did, too. I know he wanted to be more than he was. There was a time when he thought of politics. He knew an important man who was a judge. They became good friends and respected each other's opinions. If my father had followed him to Washington he might have become — your word — 'somebody.' "

"But the other guy would have fixed it for him."

"No, it wasn't like that. They'd have been partners. Men have to help each other. I don't think anybody does anything entirely alone."

"You don't know what it's like to be on your own. You and your brother had everything given to you by your 'Nana.' " He baby-talked the word. "You thought your parents were perfect." He imitated Dwight's slight drawl. "And you depended on them for everything. I bet your sister's just the same. The whole soft-skinned breed of you." He moved restlessly about the room, glancing at Dwight, avoiding Leonora's eyes.

"I can't go back and change it now," she said. "I did — once — love my mother more than anyone in the world. I thought she was perfect because I had never known anyone as kind. But when I started disapproving of her, the kindness turned into coolness, she made that piggish face and I felt angry. I didn't want to explain my position to her and yet I knew that if I didn't the next day her coolness would be there, and not her kindness." She saw Dwight's eyes close with sleep and moved away from him toward Stephen. "My father wanted me to *do* something with my life. I have a feeling that except for Martha we've been a disappointment . . . I wanted to graduate from school, not to get on with my life but to escape the sameness of each day. When Nana suggested I learn to type, I saw myself trapped in an office and refused to take the course. I'm sorry now. I suppose I would have found a job if I'd learned shorthand, or tried something else, but I could never think of the something else. And because Nana had never had a job, she felt self-conscious about urging me. And meanwhile our friends, the same ones Martha and I used to talk about and ridicule, were finding jobs or getting married or busying themselves with projects that seemed like work. Even Natalie Hammel found something to do."

"Which one was she?"

"Our closest friend when we were growing up. She started a travel service. She'd visit places, find everything — hotels, side trips, shops, restaurants — and book identical vacations for her friends. Of course, it caught on and it was written up in *The New Yorker,* and a year later she had a staff of five and her project became a career."

"And so you just — what — hung around?"

"I knew I'd have to leave home. It didn't occur to me that I might fall in love or get married any more than I imagined I might find the perfect job. I had lunch with Natalie and she suggested that I go to San Francisco — Nana's city, where all her dreams took place. I asked Natalie about the modern city. I knew it was silly to go there with the past so vividly in my mind. All my questions got the same answer: 'Destroyed in the fire.' "

"What about fellas?"

"I met the first of several men there. Men who were to teach me some of the things I couldn't find out at home or at school or in my few careful wanderings away from those places in my earlier years."

"Has Dwight ever heard this?"

She shook her head. She wondered if Stephen had been in Ojai, California, when she was there. She decided to go on with her story, hoping that his anger had subsided and that the evening could be redeemed.

"I got a job after three weeks of wandering around that magical city. An assistant in an art gallery. I lied a little, told the manager I had worked for a relative in New York who had a gallery in the Village. She didn't doubt me and I went to work for her. I catalogued her collection, filed her correspondence, and paid her bills. By the time my first paycheck was due she relied on me to pick up her son at nursery school and to order her lunch from the delicatessen at the end of the street. I had to remember *not* to get any Jewish food. Anything else was fine. Bacon and tomato sandwiches on *white* bread, egg salad on rye, tea with lemon, occasionally a slice of pound cake. 'Surprise me,' she'd say."

Stephen smiled. "Anti-Semitic was she?"

Leonora ignored the question. "Well — her tastes in food and art were limited. But she was a nice woman, open and friendly. And she taught me how to run that gallery. Sometimes I'd be in charge for several weeks at a time and I loved having the responsibility. I stayed with her for three years. I learned a little about California — the place the Pringles came from — and it made me proud."

"Proud of the Pringles?" he singsonged.

"No, I mean patriotic. It made me love America. When we were growing up I thought there were two worlds. New York City and the Adirondacks. It took me a long time to get a sense of the reality of other places. I learned to read maps in school, but I wasn't good at it."

"I'll teach you. So you stayed there and worked and what else?"

"Not much. I met some nice people."

"You mentioned several men?"

She blushed. "At the gallery I met a young man who wanted to sell his sculpture and woodcarvings. They were crude, bold works. Not the sort of thing my lady liked, but *I* did. He was the first person I'd ever met who claimed to have faith. He felt he was in communication with God."

"What church?"

"They just called themselves The Believers. There were lots of groups like that out there in the thirties."

"And you were his girl?"

"I stayed with him. But nothing ever happened."

"I don't believe you."

"It's true. I'd spend the night with him, lie beside him on his bed, wearing my clothes, and he'd talk and talk and I'd listen until I fell asleep."

"A family habit?" asked Stephen, looking at Dwight who was crouched in his chair like an uncomfortable dog, limbs like paws, hanging from his inert body.

"I thought, this odd boy —"

"What was his name?"

"Max Fenley — was joking at first. I thought the 'He' he kept mentioning was his father or his art teacher. He indulged me, he was sure he could win me over to his beliefs and he never stopped relating what I said to his passionate calling. He said it was a power greater than anything we knew or could know on earth."

"Then how could *he* know?"

"He didn't, Stephen. Of course he didn't. His faith failed. We went to Mexico for his work, but he painted nothing. He started drinking red wine and smoking marijuana. He said he was going to be a whole man again . . ."

"And what's the end of the story?" he asked impatiently.

"There is no end. I stayed in San Francisco and kept looking for some kind of life. When my aunt Clara died, I came home. It seems rather blurry now, you've blotted every other person out of my mind."

"I hope to Christ I have," he said angrily and walked over to her and hit her across the face. She cried out and Dwight woke, startled. He reached out to Leonora.

"Take your hands off her, you drunk," shouted Stephen. "And you take yours off him." Leonora swiftly pulled away from Dwight.

"I'm sorry," she said. "I'm sorry," but she didn't know why she was apologizing. She must have had more to drink than usual. Why had she told Stephen about Max?

Dwight straightened his collar and tie, asked for his coat, and muttered his good-byes. She tried to hug him in farewell, but Stephen held her away and pushed Dwight out of the room. "You can find your way out." He locked the door and looked at his wristwatch. Leonora hid the red patch on her cheek with her cool, empty wineglass.

"Dinner could have been better."

"I'll learn to cook something delicious and we'll ask him back."

"Right."

"We'll have a good time, you'll see."

"What is your definition of a good time, Leonora?"

"Being content with people I'm fond of."

"You'd settle for that?"

"Well, I don't expect to have a good time all the time."

"What do you mean?"

"Nothing."

"Can't you define pleasure?"

She wanted to answer: Being with you. Really with you, when we are alone and no other thought or desire enters my mind except you and your entering me in every way, in every place, and never leaving me. She looked at him for help.

"Don't you think by the time you have finished school and started out on your own that you have the right to expect something more from life than comfort?" he demanded.

It was the time to tell him her secret. The one fantasy that had haunted her in her first year of history class in high school: She wanted to be important to someone else. She wanted to be remembered. It seemed so long ago that she had forgotten it, but his steady gaze had brought it back to mind. That sweet ambition was with her again. Then it had seemed an outrageous possibility. Now?

"What are you thinking?"

"I was wondering if through you I might achieve a small immortality."

"I doubt that."

He did not understand. Time to put the childish dream away again.

"Your brother's sad. I feel sorry for him."

"But he's a saint."

"A *saint?*"

If only he would lead her to his darkened room the things she was saying would not sound ridiculous. Take me there, she pleaded with her eyes. But he was looking for something else. He wanted her honest answers to his questions, not the replies rehearsed through years of living with protective parents and teachers, and polite, careful acquaintances. There had to be more to her than that or why was he considering her as his companion?

"I mean he takes care of people in a way that expects nothing in return. I think that is one of his finest qualities. And he's uncomplaining. When you are with him you feel important, and, of course, he's dear-looking."

"Is that why you put your hand on his leg?"

"What? When?"

"All the time. You never stop touching him, that *saint,*" he sneered.

She was still talking when he hit her again. His palm slapped her cheek twice. "One for that simp Max Whatchamacallit and one for your stupid, lazy brother. You're mine now, Leonora, and if you're going to stick around with me, you're just going to have to shape up."

The color rose to her skin in an instant and the tears poured over her stinging cheeks. Immediately remorseful, he pulled her to him, furious at himself for his jealous outburst, unable to forgive her for provoking it or to assuage it in any other way than to give her what her eyes had been pleading for since Dwight stumbled out of the room.

When their long lovemaking was over he turned away from her and muttered, "Go into the other room. I can't sleep if you stay here." She obeyed. She gathered her clothes in the dawn light and looked around for any other evidences of her stay, smoothed the sheet where she had just lain, and felt her way between the furniture and the walls until she reached the front room. The bed was not made up so she put her coat on like a nightdress and curled up on the counterpane. Was it always to be like this if she stayed with him? Was she not to be his partner in sleep?

Treasuring the depth of pleasure within her, as if he were still there, she fell asleep remembering and awoke only when she needed to use the bathroom. Should she risk waking him? It was like being a child in the car wondering when one of the adults would want to stop for gas or to stretch, and longing to ask permission to jump out of the car and squat on the ground. But this was worse because it was unromantic, so far from her image of herself as the mistress of an overpowering man.

She looked for a book in the living room. There were plenty to choose from. Not in bookcases but stacked in neat piles on tables and on the floor next to the sedate Victorian loveseat near the fireplace. The sun brightened the room, each piece of furniture gleaming where the wood was polished. Her eyes ached, and the world blurred. She must have had less than an hour's sleep. Stephen discovered her dozing with a book in her hands.

Before too many nights had passed, he no longer asked her to leave. He fell asleep directly after his pleasure reached its highest moment and he made the strange choked sound that was his signal of delight. She lay still beside him until she was sure he was asleep, then she went into the bathroom and luxuriated in his large old-fashioned tub that stood above the tiled floor on ugly iron claws. Refreshed and clean she returned to his bed, and if he awoke, he pulled her to him for more of what he needed from her and what she wanted so much to give him: What she thought of as her self — what he called a name she had neither read nor pronounced — so protected was her life before he chose her as his partner.

He had taught her ways to satisfy him that she had not known existed. He guided her head and shoulders into position above him and her hands around his erection. And at the moment when his greatest tension was released in her mouth he swore or called her name. One night he cried out two names, neither of them hers. "Oh Christ, oh Peg, oh Christ."

"Am I big enough for you?" he asked.

"You're perfect."

He wanted a more explicit answer, but she was not able to give it to him. His question, coming in the center of the experience, nearly made her pull away from him, but so completely was she caught in the deliciousness of his moving within her that she intercepted her reaction and held him harder, clasping her arms around his back and her legs around his legs. The question would be repeated, rephrased, and she would have to have an answer. It could never be discussed when they were not in bed. Their entire life together as lovers was to be kept separate from daily living. She had said "Thank you," quietly and directly to him several times, but he had not replied. As a child they told her she had said "I'm welcome," when people thanked her. She thought of it in the pauses he might have filled.

What would happen, have to happen, was a series of comparisons and what was hardest for her to tell him or to admit to herself was that she did not remember enough about her previous experiences to describe them. It was as if she had dreamed them and her life with him was the beginning of important sex, living sex that would eventually lead to children and contentment and happiness.

He tired quickly; after he spent himself in her, he slept. The questioning was postponed.

In a taxi on the way to his apartment, Stephen asked Leonora, "Do you ever think about it?"

She stared at him. "What are you talking about?"

"I do. All the time."

"Tell me what you mean. I'm lost."

"Suicide."

Startled, she answered, "No." Then: "Yes." He was expecting more from her. She needed time. If it was true that it obsessed him, why had he never mentioned it before? Was he playing a game and would she be sorry if she took him seriously? "Let's stop somewhere and have something to drink." She had never been the one to make a plan, now he looked surprised. "It's late," he said.

"I don't care. Let's find a quiet place." He gave the driver instructions that were so precise she knew they were going to a bar where he had talked to other women, beguiled them, made them long for him. She forgot for a moment why she made the suggestion and floundered in her self-inflicted jealousy.

When they sat in the dark hotel taproom and he ordered Black Velvets, it did not seem possible to get back to his subject again. There were three other couples chatting easily and several men standing at the bar, each one silent, avoiding contact with the others who were dressed and shod as if they had gone shopping together for their correct dark suits, blue shirts, and patterned ties. What do they do, she wondered. Three unrelated men in the same place doing the same thing, but separately, perhaps one was a doctor with a wife and children and a large practice of adoring patients, the second, heavier, man . . .

"I hate to interrupt . . ." Flustered, she turned herself away from the room and toward his angry face. "I thought you wanted to stop somewhere and talk. Now it seems my competition is the financial backbone of the city."

"Do you think they're bankers? Or in the stock market?"

"I don't give a damn who they are. Drink your drink." They drank in silence. She did not dare ask what he meant by his question in the car.

When Leonora began to stay in Stephen's apartment she did not know where to put her things. His clothes took up the space in his large bedroom bureau and small closet. There was no provision for storage in the front room. Leonora realized that a locked door in the hall on the landing was a closet belonging to the apartment and Stephen gave her the key. She rearranged the cartons and cleaning materials and made room for her suitcase, which she used as a drawer. A smaller empty suitcase on the shelf near the light bulb could provide another one. She asked Stephen if she might use it and took it to the front room for her nightgown and robe.

It was not completely empty. A white prayer book, some underwear, and a flowered cosmetic case containing a pink rubber bag and nozzle and a diaphragm lay in the bottom of the satin-lined, much-traveled piece of luggage. She decided to put it back in the hall closet when Stephen called her.

"Come on in here, woman. I'm waiting for you."

Her panic made her a poor partner. She hesitated when he gave her what were now familiar signals. She knew she was spoiling it for him.

"What the hell's the matter?" he muttered.

"I'm afraid to tell you." But she told him about the suitcase. "What should I have done with it?"

"Nothing. I'll get rid of it. I forgot it was still there. Were there any letters in it?"

"I don't know."

"In the side pocket?"

"I didn't look."

"Look now." Like a sleepwalker she went to get them and brought them back to him. He had pulled the blankets around his naked body. She sat on the edge of the bed and shivered. He did not reach for her to come near, so she stayed at the point farthest from him. He threw her his robe and she put it on.

"Can I ask you something, darling?"

"You *may*," said Stephen.

"Will you tell me why you asked me about suicide? I can't stop thinking about it, now that you've mentioned it. It's something we never talked about at home. If it happened to someone Nana knew, she refused to discuss it. That's why I had no answer for you in the taxi. I don't know anything about it except from books."

"Then let's forget it."

"But it's something you think about, isn't it?"

"Sometimes."

"And it has something to do with me — in a way — hasn't it?"

He looked at her for a long time and then he said in a low, kind voice, "All right, little Leonora, get me a bottle of booze and a glass and put on some records and I'll try to explain something to you."

She rose and pulled the robe around her, tied it tightly, and slipped her feet into his bedroom slippers. She put *Madame Butterfly* on the record player. Then she brought him a tray with a bottle of bourbon, some soda and ice, and a bowl of mixed salted nuts and put it beside him on the bed.

"Don't you want anything?" he asked.

She shook her head. "I just want you to tell me things."

"It will take a little while. You may not like it, but you have to give me your word that when I'm finished telling you there will be no more questions. This is a once and for all telling."

"I promise."

"And don't interrupt me."

"I never do."

"You always do."

"I won't tonight," she promised and sat beside him resisting the need to hold his hand, to rest her body beside his, to cover herself with his blanket.

The light from the window changed from moon to sun as he talked. His voice became softer and harder to hear as the hours went by, but she did not move except to refill his glass.

"I have to exorcise a ghost or nothing will be right between us. I thought I could get away without doing it, but I can't. I can't stand the way you look at me, always asking the same question. I know what you want to know. Would you like to read the letters first?"

Leonora shook her head again, afraid to speak.

The opera of grief and remembering accompanied his story. Perhaps he did not hear it, anymore than he saw her. He was speaking his thoughts into an empty space before his eyes, filling it with the shape and spirit of the girl he had loved.

"I was in New York trying to break into the advertising game. It was harder than I'd imagined. I wanted to show my stuff to magazine editors. I thought I could get through to an ad agency that way. I had a campaign aimed at women for *Ladies' Home Journal,* at men for *Esquire,* and so on. I'd get to meet the receptionists. They'd ask me for dates. I'd take them to parties and meet their friends. It was a stupid way to pass the time but eventually it led me to the job I still have at Johnson and Freid — and it led me to Margaret Bradshaw."

Leonora understood the initials on the delicate water colors in the front room. She realized, too, that the feminine touches — the lamp shades and curtains — were probably chosen by a woman. His woman, whose suitcase she had discovered and on whose shared bed she now crouched.

"I saw her standing beside a handsome middle-aged man who looked familiar. She was the most beautiful thing I'd ever laid eyes on."

"And he?"

"I told you — handsome. White hair, ruddy skin, fine clothes — turned out to be Joe Pederson."

"Who?"

"Joseph Pederson. The composer. Come on, Leonora! Everyone knows his songs. I grew up singing them. I managed to get myself introduced to him, and since the girl was hanging on his arm, he had to introduce her to me. 'She's my right hand,' he said. And she said, 'My name is Margaret Bradshaw, but Joe calls me Peggy.' I asked her what she'd like me to call her and she said whatever I liked and it sounded like a challenge. I wanted to think up something that would impress both of them, the perfect name for the perfect girl, but I took too long and Pederson pulled her away from me and toward the door.

"I hardly ever went to the theatre, but I knew Pederson was at all the opening nights, his name was in the columns. Sometimes he was with his wife. Very glamorous, older — his age, I guess — she's in *Vogue* a lot. You've probably seen her picture."

"Yes. I remember him now, too. They go hunting in Maryland. I've seen them in the *Tribune* rotogravure."

"Well he wasn't with her very often then, mostly he'd take Peggy to the theatre and to opening night parties at Sardi's. I found ways to get invited to the same places and after a while we all called each other by our first names. I asked other people about Peggy. I found out she was quite a girl. Old Joe Pederson wasn't the first love of her life. But she was crazy about him. Listened to him, obeyed him, laughed at his jokes no matter how often he repeated them. The best thing about him was his voice. Deep and" — Stephen thought for a moment — "seductive."

Leonora wondered if somewhere else in the city Mrs. Pederson had been listening to and possibly obeying someone else. Did a man like Pederson mind?

"At first I kidded myself that she wasn't really his mistress. Just a girl he took to parties," Stephen said, "but whenever I was here with another girl that goddamned Peggy would come into my mind and I knew I had to have her."

Here. Leonora repeated the word in silence. Here, where I am now. She was conscious of a sick feeling all through her body, a weakness in her limbs, but she wanted more than anything for him to go on. She wanted to hear everything, much more than he was prepared to tell her. She wanted to be with him when he was first with her, when he touched and opened the mysterious parts of her. Peggy Bradshaw.

"Everything about her was like silver! Pale skin and hair. Grayish eyes with pale lashes. The clothes she wore. I told her she was like a sexy nun."

"I can see her," said Leonora so softly that he did not hear her.

"Pederson was doing the lyrics for a musical — I can't think of the name for the minute. It closed in Boston and they renamed it and brought it in the following summer. It was about show business. He was at all the rehearsals in New York and then he went to Boston. He was there a month. And she was with me."

Here, thought Leonora.

"Did you say something?"

"No. Tell me more."

"You love it, don't you? Come closer." He pulled her up beside him, and held her tightly as he described how they spent their days. Peggy dancing for him, Peggy bathing in the big tub in perfumed, bubbly water, Peggy buying furniture for the apartment, Peggy inviting him to Joe's weekend cottage in Glen Cove.

"She swore *both* Pedersons were in Boston so I rented a car and we spent two days there. The worst days of my life."

"Why?"

"Everything went wrong. I asked her to marry me and we got into a fight about Pederson and his hold on her. I told her it was insane for her to spend her life waiting for him to call her. A man with an important career and a wife of his own. And I called her a name I had never called her before except as a compliment. She started yelling and screaming at me and told me things I can't tell you because they don't make any sense and she ran out and took the car and left me stranded in that god-forsaken place. I chased her back to New York, but she wouldn't see me. She said she was through. I'd heard on the radio in the taxi I'd hired that Pederson had suffered a stroke and was under intensive care in a Boston hospital. Peggy never read a paper or listened to the radio so I went to her place, but she wouldn't answer the door. I could hear the phone ringing in her apartment, she wasn't answering that either."

"She killed herself."

"Yeah." She did not hear him start to weep. He handed her the packet of letters in the darkness and turned away from her. She spent the rest of the dawn hours reading them. There was a final letter, a suicide note. Incoherent phrases in shaky handwriting. She must have been drinking or have taken the pills before she started writing it. Leonora learned of the abortions, the unhappiness during the Pederson time when he would forget to call or write her, her fear of meeting his wife, her unworthiness as his mistress because she felt she had no talent of her own. Then there was a real farewell to Stephen. Memories of a trip they took to Maine when they went sailing and he caught his first fish. How he nearly sank the boat in his excitement, how he used her gray silk parasol as a sail. Each incident was followed by a series of dots. It looked as if she could not bear to end the letter. On and on the sweet memories went and then suddenly in a stronger hand the words: "When this reaches you I shall be dead and our love affair will have come to its inevitable conclusion. I know you will think of this as an act of cowardice by a neurotic girl, but I have lost everything I prized and now there is nothing and I cannot even say good-bye to him. I should have been with him at the end. But no matter where you go, Steve, you will never be able to escape from your dirty little soul . . . no matter how many women you sleep with you will never be able to nurture your puny ego . . . or overcome the deep-rooted and fully justified sense of your unworthiness . . . nor will you ever be able to forget me . . ."

Leonora folded all the letters back into their tissue-thin envelopes and placed them on the bedside table beside the empty bottle and half-filled glass.

"Stephen, darling, let me talk now. Thank you, thank you, for every word you told me. I won't ever ask you about her again. I had to know, I needed to know, and now I understand what has frightened me even when I have been happy with you. From now on it will be different. I will be strong and good and make you happy and we'll have a lovely life together and tell each other everything. You are so dear to me, so wonderful, and I love you so and I'm so happy now, so happy." She whispered endearments to his sleeping body until she fell into an exhausted trance beside him.

The final record of *Butterfly* played on, over and over again.

Part Four

THERE WERE compelling qualities about Martha Ives that made strangers notice her when she came into a room and colleagues obey her willingly and without question. "Order! Let us have order," Lem instructed her. Her life was orderly, even as a child. And unlike Leonora, she had confidence in her taste and judgment. She knew what to do with the plain dresses and velvet bows and shapeless guimpes Nana chose for them. A sash of bright color cinching her waist like a cummerbund made her party dress look feminine, while Leo's hung straight. She never pulled her hair back behind her ears, knowing that it would accent her broad face and spoil the natural waves of her curls. Her stocking seams were straight, her gloves pure white. She knew how to take them off and fluff up her pompadour in a casual way that was charming to watch. The pointless rituals of life were artful in her hands.

The ugliness of the furniture that surrounded the Iveses — the clutter of the wicker chairs on the porch at the Camp, the knickknacks on every available surface — prompted Martha to look in books and magazines at other rooms in other times. The ridiculous portière on the piano, the variety of Japanese plates and vases and fans in the dining room, the Spanish shawl draped over the bulky divan, the fan light over the front door — she shuddered to recall them. It was wanting to rearrange things when she was young that formed the habit she kept throughout her life.

It was a pity that her imagination had not led her to designing houses. That concept was too large for her; she had to rely on others to build the rooms she would decorate and enhance. If she had had training she might have created original environments, but the opportunity did not arise. Lem felt that after high school she should not go on to college and she did not question his guidance. She was apprenticed to Florence Deane, a decorator friend of Aunt Clara's, who lived and worked in New York City. As Miss Deane's assistant, Martha found herself in the homes of the wealthy. She felt comfortable there.

Florence Deane was a taskmistress. Her clothing was uniform-like, as if a man's tailor had simply followed a pattern for a suit and made a straight skirt instead of a pair of trousers. The tweeds and gabardines were the best. Her buckled leather shoes were brown or black in the daytime, and in the evening she changed to velvet suits, patent leather pumps, and gunmetal stockings. Formal clothes to cover her slim, angular body.

Her intelligent face was dusted with powder and a trace of pink was on her lips, nothing more. No scent. No jewelry except her wrist watch and a single unexplained gold band on the third finger of her left hand.

She taught Martha how to judge antique furniture, and when she trusted her expertise, took her along on her yearly buying trips to London and Paris. They traveled second class the first time, but first thereafter; an unspoken sense that they were denying themselves the pleasure of a good time made them go over the budget the following year and change the bookings. In London they stayed with relatives of Miss Deane's, in Paris in a small hotel on the rue Chambiges.

Martha's French was not grammatical, but she spoke more fluently than Miss Deane and the older woman expected her to make their arrangements. Appointments, theatre tickets, and restaurant reservations became her province. She did not need to be told anything twice; what Miss Deane asked for, Martha supplied. The trips were invariably successful and the best part for Martha was the arrival weeks later of the furniture they had selected. She went down to the boat to receive it, followed the shipment uptown in a taxi, trailing the van to their warehouse to oversee the unpacking. She reported to Miss Deane, "We chose well. I mean, *you* chose well."

"*We*, my dear. The shop is as much you as me now and someday it will — you must know by now — be yours."

She did know, but the saying of it moved her. I have a career, she thought. It will continue and grow, and this woman believed in me from the beginning. I couldn't live without the work now. How does my sister fill her days? And her friends? Mornings at the hairdresser, afternoons at thés dansants, evenings at concerts. And what about her classmates? Girls who didn't have money. What did they do? Ill-equipped for the job market, they were husband-hunting. Pretending to be having fun with their girlfriends, longing to meet a man who would take care of them. Martha did not want that. If anything, she would want to be the one to take care of him. Was there such a person for her? She seldom thought about it unless some prying fool asked her what her plans were. Her plans were to work. She considered not getting married, living like Miss Deane. It could be done. Before she went to work in the shop she would not have thought so, but she had seen a single woman manage to have an interesting, satisfying time. Miss Deane never complained, she had been too busy.

Nearly twenty years later, at Florence Deane's funeral, sitting in the chapel of the Church of the Resurrection, Martha listened to the rector mouthing nonsense about her, "Her life was a full one . . ." Is a life without marriage and children full? "Her work will live on after her . . ." Martha doubted that. She had been with Florence Deane when they had decided how to redesign a house completely, and in so doing wipe out the surroundings the previous owner or even the present owner had lived with and enjoyed. A few photographs remained of some of her work, but they were poorly lit and the black and white contrasts gave no idea of the shades the walls were painted, of the delicately orchestrated colors of the rugs and chintzes, the quality of light from the chandeliers and sconces.

I have gone about my own life, she thought; the business of life has erased Florence Deane from my consciousness. I look back on the crossings to Europe and remember the boredom of certain evenings when all our conversation was repetition of the words we had said the day before. Martha felt ill with guilt and found a way to leave the chapel alone and walked to the shop. The closed sign was on the door. She opened a bottle of wine, which had been saved to celebrate some happier occasion, poured herself a full glass, and sipped it slowly, trying to erase the truth of her thoughts that had overwhelmed the ritualistic nonsense of the rector's philosophy. She cleared the papers and pamphlets off her desk and continued with the preparations for her sister's wedding. Nana had declined the chore.

"Is Miss Ives there, Elma? This is her sister calling. Yes, I'll wait." Martha came on the line and Leonora hurried her words, "Darling, could you do me a great favor? Could you get away from the shop an hour or so today? I need your advice about something."

"What is it, anything serious?"

"Well, no. Yes. I don't know. You'll probably laugh at me."

"Do you want to have lunch?"

"No, I don't want to take up that much of your time."

"Leo, what is it?"

"I want you to take me to your hairdresser and to Bergdorf's or somewhere and help me choose a dress."

"What for? A celebration, a party before the wedding?"

"For my life."

They met at Elizabeth Arden and waited in the crowded overdecorated salon where women were having their nails polished and feet massaged while they sat under the hair driers and looked at magazines. The smell of shampoo hung in the air, the buzz of the machines made it difficult to hear. Martha nudged Leonora. "Madame Pascal is ready for you." A handsome, perfectly dressed French woman glanced at Leonora.

"Oh! Come with me. Please." She handed Leonora a pink cotton smock.

The meeting with Martha was effusive. Vivienne Pascal had been a countess during her brief marriage before leaving France and she held on to the title with elegance. Leonora emerged from the dressing room and interrupted their bright chatter.

"Be seated, chérie. Oo! What can we do with this?" She raked her brightly lacquered fingernails through Leonora's freshly washed limp hair.

"Whatever you think best, my dear," said Martha. "You style it and it will be perfect. My sister is placing herself in your very capable hands."

"Alors . . . Oui . . . " Leonora saw the countess give a tiny shrug.

Martha put her hand on her shoulder. "I'll leave you here, Leo, while I do an errand. I'll be back before you're done."

Vivienne prepared to give Leonora's clean hair its second shampoo of the day. She did it swiftly and her strong fingers kneaded her scalp and twisted the hair dry with cruel efficiency. She used the scissors without a single wasted motion, trimming the still-damp hair around Leonora's face in a few moments, and in even less time she set the obedient waves with metal clips. "Venez ici," she ordered and led her into the large salon to sit under the drier. She adjusted the metal hood over Leonora's head, set the timer, and disappeared. For the first few minutes, Leonora was fascinated by the behavior of the other women. She studied the faces peering from the noisy machines. Boredom, pleasure, vanity, and in the case of the woman directly opposite her, greed. She was eating and reading *Vogue* as her fleshy foot was being massaged. She beamed at Leonora and mouthed the words "Heaven, isn't it?" The intense heat from the drier made it a hell for Leonora. She waved at Vivienne and called out, "Est-ce qu'il y a une façon n'importe comment, a ce faire plus froid?"

"Speak English," Vivienne commanded. Leonora, unhearing, went on. "Est-ce que vous pouvez m'aider, s'il vous plaît, de ce fermer un peu?" Her high school French sounded like gibberish.

Vivienne glanced at her, adjusted the timer at the top of the machine, and walked away. Ten minutes later Leonora slid down in her chair in a faint.

Martha wanted to get Leonora something at once. At Saks she found a soft pink suit trimmed with black velvet, a pink chiffon blouse, and some black Italian leather gloves and took them to the gift wrap desk to have them boxed separately.

"Will you want to put a card with them, ma'am?"

"What a good idea. Yes." She stood for a long time thinking. It was not easy to choose the words because she knew Leo sensed her distrust of Stephen and the forthcoming marriage. If she wrote something sisterly, it would be ignoring the most important thing that had happened to Leo. She wrote swiftly "For Leonora who is lovely," and slipped the card into the envelope before the ink was dry. "May I pick these up in about fifteen minutes? Please wrap them as presents." Nana had taught them never to say *gift*: "It sounds common."

Martha hurried back to Elizabeth Arden.

Leonora was not under the drier in the large room. Martha peeked into several booths before she found Vivienne. "Votre soeur se couche, Mademoiselle Ives. La chaleur du sèche-cheveaux la faite s'évanouir. Pauvre petite. La voila."

She lay pale and perspiring, with a cold compress of pink towelling folded on her forehead. The pink smock had circles of sweat on it.

"I'm so sorry, Mart. I've never been under one of those things before. It got so hot and I was sure they'd forgotten me, I just —"

"Do you feel better now? Well enough to go somewhere for a bit of refreshment?"

Martha felt guilty. Leonora's still damp hair looked less attractive than it had before Vivienne cut it. In place of her natural, auburn waves, glistening dark wet feathers framed her eager face. She hoped the clothes would be more successful.

"How much shall I tip Vivienne? And the girl?"

"It's all taken care of, darling."

"Oh, no, please don't."

"It's done. Now come with me. There are some things for you at Saks." They walked hand in hand, something they had not done for many years.

"Shall I try them on, in case —?"

"They'll be perfect. I tried them on and they were a bit snug, so they'll be just right for you. I want you to be surprised. A belated engagement present."

Martha knew without asking that Leonora's panic about her looks came from Stephen's harsh appraisal. The subject did not come up. Unspoken, it made the sisters formal and polite with each other.

"Thank you for a lovely afternoon."

"It was my pleasure. Let me know how he likes the clothes."

Leonora came into the apartment like a burglar, quietly twisting her key in and out of the lock. Closing the door with infinite care, she succeeded in getting the packages into her room without Stephen hearing her. Overwhelmed by Martha's generosity, she hesitated to open them. She decided to show him her haircut first.

He did not notice. Perhaps that meant it was a real success. After dinner while he listened to the radio, she made an excuse to leave him alone and opened her shiny Saks boxes.

In a folder marked "File," Leonora found a strip of negatives. "Shall I get these printed for you, darling?" she asked.

Without looking up from the sports page, Stephen said, "If you like."

He kept reading as she held them up to the spill of light from the lamp over his head. The shape of a woman in a straw hat, a beach hat? On a boat. No one else in any of the mysterious frames.

A week later she saw the loveliness. The hair looked silver, the skin ivory. The hat was a bonnet caught under her chin with a bow. In the two pictures without it her hair framed her delicate face in waves that reached below her shoulders. Peggy Bradshaw was seated at the tiller of a small sailboat. Her smile was dazzling. Her eyes, squinting slightly from the glare of the sun's reflection on the water and the whiteness of the sail, were open wide enough to reveal their almond shape.

She put the envelope with the negatives in the back of the desk drawer and decided to say she had forgotten about them.

Did he ever look at them himself? It was as if he had no memory. Or was it that he hid all feeling for the past from the people in his present? Surely there were times when they were together, joined, when he thought of the exquisite silver girl.

Leonora and Stephen Tannenbaum's wedding took place in a ballroom in the Plaza Hotel. There was no question of a church, according to Ermina Ives, since the groom was — as she put it — "of the Jewish faith." Stephen was Jewish but of no faith. He admired Leonora not for her beauty, which was bounteous, but for her bravery. He knew she was afraid of him and that she was leaving what Mrs. Ives reminded him was *status* and *money*, "and a thousand important things only 'minny' can provide."

"Name one," challenged Stephen. Nana had stared at him with dislike masked by politeness. He watched for the telltale tongue exercise. She did it.

Stephen understood her position. It was harder to understand how Leonora could be the way she was, so open to the uncharted life he offered her.

"I'll tell you, Stephen darling. It isn't only that I love to be with you and want to touch you all the time and be touched by you until I faint from it. It's much more wonderful than that."

"What could be?" he laughed.

"You're giving me a chance to be somebody."

"A Jewess!"

"No, I mean, somebody that *I* can like. I don't like myself very much now. I've gone through life — through school especially — doing exactly what was expected of me and I'm good at it. I studied hard and the girls and teachers liked me. I know my father loved me. But I have never had an original thought or done anything to be proud of in my life."

"You're still a young woman."

"If I were to die tomorrow that would be my life. Some of my friends really *lived* their young years. Martha did, I think. She certainly has some kind of a *real* life now. One that I admire. A few of the others. Natalie, *maybe*. And maybe some of their brothers. But since school I've done nothing. I'd still be nothing if I hadn't met you."

"You'd've met someone."

"Yes, someone Mother approved of, I'm sure. And I think I could make a life with that sort of man. Perhaps I'm surer of that than I am of being right for you."

"You are."

"I want to be, more than anything. But you've got to help me."

"We'll help each other, darling. Don't you know that men feel exactly the same way? I don't want to be a consultant. I want to run my own agency. We all want to prove ourselves — to ourselves — just as much as you do."

"It doesn't show." She smiled.

"I'm a good actor. And you're a bit of an actress, I think. The kind of marriage you might have had would have been like a part in a play. But we're going to exist in reality — in real time — and that's much harder."

It took a month to convince Nana, but only a telephone call to announce to the Tannenbaums that they were prepared to spend their lives together. He'd never asked them about any girl he cared for. He didn't bother to ask about Leonora.

Stephen's stepmother asked them to supper in Forest Hills at eight-thirty on the Saturday night before the wedding. He did not want to go and tried to think of a way to avoid seeing them, but Leonora said, "We must accept. I'd love to meet them, darling." What he did do, without warning her, was to make reservations for dinner at the Colony at seven, and by the time they arrived at the Tannenbaums', they were both tired and full of food and wine. It was difficult to make conversation with his parents who saw him so seldom they did not know what job he had or where he lived, and agonizing to try to swallow the quiche and drink the not-quite-chilled American champagne. There was no smell of life-giving food in Stephen's father's home. The photograph of his mother was no longer on the wall.

They liked Leonora and were delighted at her stories of her childhood. "It's like he is marrying a foreigner, if you know what I mean," said his father. "Not an alien, I don't mean — but — different, you know."

"Foreign, but *nice,*" said his stepmother as she kissed Leonora's cheek and handed her the tissue-wrapped portrait of Ida. Leonora hugged them both before Stephen pulled her to the door.

Arnold LeVine was Stephen's best man. He stood nearby and offered the ring and watched Stephen place it on Leonora's delicate hand. He felt out of place, too young for the small task he had been asked to do, and the bride's family, who represented the height of what was Gentile to him, scarcely looked at him. He wondered where the Tannenbaums were. Then he realized that if he felt out of place among the Iveses and their friends, how miserable Stephen's father and stepmother would be.

The Tannenbaums celebrated their son's wedding day by ignoring it. They went shopping at Bloomingdale's and took in a double feature at Loew's 58th Street. Mr. Tannenbaum slipped the invitation from his wife's handbag and put it in the locked box where he kept his son's diploma from Erasmus High and the Eagle Scout badge.

At the wedding something perplexing happened to Leonora.

She was in the boudoir furnished by the hotel for the bridal party and was changing into Nana's refurbished wedding dress. In the mirror she saw a robust, confident, and handsome woman standing behind her and searching her reflected face with large, liquid eyes. Without turning she lifted the freshly ironed dress out of its more-than-forty-year-old Bloomingdale's box and held it in front of her breast. "Natalie!"

"Such a long, long time."

"Yes. How are you?"

"The same."

The same as in high school? Hardly. She had come into her own, Leonora thought, as she struggled with the delicate organdy sleeves.

"Let me help you."

"Oh, no thank you, I can manage —" But Natalie pulled the dainty fabric out of Leonora's hands and with skill began to fit the tiny buttons into their holes, all the while talking quickly and softly. "I'll never forgive you. I can't forgive you. You took what I wanted without even wanting it. I think of it still, although I was told envy and jealousy diminish with time. It's not true. And I think of you all the time too, Leo, and you never call me. I didn't even know you were in New York until I got the invitation. What happened to our friendship, to our life, to the Camp . . ." Natalie put her head on Leonora's breast, making muted whining sounds. Leonora was sure Nana would come in and find them. She rose quickly and Natalie lost her balance and fell to the floor. Nana strode into the room. "For heaven's sake, Natalie! Leonora! What's going on?"

Natalie's pain was lost in her confusion of trying to rise with some grace. Leonora felt helpless. "What have I done?" she said, but no one heard her. She followed Nana into the room where the wedding party assembled.

At the ceremony everyone concentrated on Leonora and the attractive, intense young man who was to be her husband. But just as the vows were being repeated, Martha saw Natalie, tears falling down her cheeks, her eyes riveted on Stephen. Martha was astonished to see what she could only think of as longing — or was it lust? — in that penetrating stare.

Leonora looked lovely but felt self-conscious in Nana's wedding dress. The organdy had been starched to stiffness and made the skin under her arms burn. The flounces on the skirt seemed to droop from her perspiration just as the flowers wilted in their vases from the steam heat. Dwight, flushed and bright-eyed, pretended not to mind having no part in the ceremony and paid off the musicians with a polite flourish.

Leonora changed into her traveling clothes in the boudoir. Stephen came in without knocking as she was folding Nana's dress into the precious, battered box. He held her in his arms and she responded to him.

"I'm only teasing you," he said.

"I know, let me get dressed."

He touched her breasts until her nipples stiffened but she did not move away. "I'll wait for you in the car. Hurry. Don't spend any more time with these fiends."

"My family?" she said, meaning it to be funny.

"Who else? Hurry, Leonora, girl, woman, wife. Hurry!"

Nana and Martha took the boxes of wedding clothes back to Riverside Drive in the rented limousine. It had started to rain.

"Not my idea of a wedding," said Nana.

"It's what Stephen wanted. Leo said he hates ceremony."

"Well I like it and I miss it. Your father and I had a lovely wedding."

"I know. I love the pictures."

"No photographer today. No record of the event."

"We'll all remember it."

"But everyone remembers differently, Martha." Nana wanted to get on the subject of her elder daughter's private life. It was past time for her to settle down with a nice man. "We'll certainly do all this elegantly for you."

"I'm not going to get married, Mother. I'm happy the way I am."

"And how is that? You're no better off than that Natalie! She can't stay married and there's something very *odd* about her now."

Nana described what she had seen in the dressing room and asked for Martha's opinion. Martha thought of the naked look she had seen on Natalie's face such a short time ago.

"I think Nat's always been a little jealous of Leo, Mother. And people seem to get emotional at weddings."

"Will you at yours?"

"Mother, please. I told you, I'm happy the way I am." Nana heard in the repetition of the phrase a plea for silence and did not press Martha for anything more.

"Well, good-bye, my dear. Thank you for all your help. Evans will get the box." He was waiting at the curb and helped his mistress out of the car at the same time he greeted Martha.

"I hope it was a nice party, Miss Martha."

"It was, Evans. Thank you," she said and gave the driver her address. She asked him to hurry.

When Martha was not actually working or taking part in a social event she preferred to be at home. In the comfort and privacy of her apartment she waited for word from the partner of her life.

What would Larry Parrish, who loved ritual and ceremony, have thought of Leonora's wedding? He would have seen the tiny lines of panic that framed her smile and heard the soft note of terror in her voice when she made her replies. But he would not have mentioned these things until Martha did, he was so careful of her family feeling. He knew that except for him and the half-real, half-imagined world they shared her mother and sister were the most important people in her life.

The call came and Martha described the wedding.

"You sound tired, darling," said Larry.

"I'm not tired. I'm sad." She told him the truth without expecting to. The event had left her drained and unhappy. She feared for her sister's happiness and felt more than ever that she must guard her own. Her lover's dear and familiar voice comforted her. They talked of ordinary things and before the call was over Martha felt warm with love.

Stephen wrote "Mr. and Mrs. S. Tannenbaum" in the register of the lodge in Connecticut where they spent their wedding night. They were treated with mild contempt by the proprietor. Leonora wanted to ask Stephen why they were being ignored by the staff and found the answer in his expression. She knew he had lived through all this before but surely not here. He could not have stayed with other women at this place with its perfect lake and lawns.

Their first night as mates had been uneasy. Her thoughts were constantly returning to her childhood, to Lem, to Nana. She was anxious to get to Maine and tried not to think of her secret plan to have had their honeymoon at the Camp.

On their arrival at Kennebunk the woman who owned the white-shingled boarding house greeted Stephen by his first name. Leonora looked away. He must have forgotten she had seen the letter. If he had remembered, would he have brought her here, driven along the same roads, stopped at the same restaurants along the way? Later she wondered if she, sitting next to him on the front seat of the rented sedan, was studying the same map and perhaps giving identical directions. There were not many variations to "the next left after the traffic light" or "ten more miles on this road and then right at the intersection."

The letter had said, "I'll never forget the funny way you tried to make a sail for the rowboat and how you taught me how to pole since there were no oarlocks and the oars made blisters on my hands."

"We'll hire a rowboat if there aren't any sailboats left," he said to Leonora. When they were on the water, he suggested making a sail out of her skirt. "You've got a slip on haven't you?" he asked when he saw her shocked reaction. She took off her full peasant skirt and he made a ridiculous mast and bright sail — like a parasol — and she rose unsteadily and began to pole the boat out from the shore.

For lunch they ate lobsters: ". . . the little kind, like langostinas in Portugal . . . Sweet, tender . . . We nearly got sick because we ordered seconds and felt we had to finish them even though our appetites were sated . . . Do you remember?" Would he order seconds? No. They ate and talked easily and it was one of the best times of the trip. Exhausted from the sail, they rested on the separate beds in their room, then bathed and dressed leisurely and were tired and hungry by the time the dining room was open for dinner.

For several hours she forgot the blueprint of the letter. He talked about himself in a detached, fascinating way, describing a childhood that might have been lived by a character in a book, except that no fiction could catch with such accuracy the stabbing details of the poverty of his boyhood. The illness and death of his mother had damaged everything he remembered about his father. "He liked Arnold better than me. 'He'll be somebody,' he used to say. Arnold was the good kid and I was the bad one."

"I can't believe that."

"Believe it. I'll be bad to you, too, one day, you'll see." He had been bad to the silver girl, driven her out of his life through some unpreventable perversity. But it would not be the same for her, Leonora vowed: I will give him no reason to turn against me. I will be good to him and believe in him and stay with him for as long as he wants me.

But they were married now. "For as long as" was not the right phrase — Until death do us part. Unthinkable. She knew they would die, yes. But death separating them was not conceivable that evening or that night as they explored each other as if it were their first night together. They did not sleep until daybreak.

The weather changed. The third day was too cold to take the long walk he had planned. He was restless. "Maybe we'll cut the trip short by one day and return to the city? Would you mind?"

A day of driving around the deserted Maine countryside unnerved her. There was a demand for conversation in the car that was more difficult to fill than in a dining room or their bedroom or even just walking.

"Talk," he ordered gently. He liked word games and they played them.

Geography and Categories and a game of his own in which whatever he said she must translate into another language. Bluffing was allowed if you didn't get caught. He soon realized that two years of French and a smattering of Latin was all the store she had to chose from and the winning was too easy so the game was dropped. Had the silver girl played it brilliantly?

One game was easier for Leonora: Essences. It took a long time to play and silences were permissible. Obviously she was thinking of a color, smell, texture, piece of music, or book title that suited the unknown person she was attempting to identify. A man or a woman? Living or dead? What color? What time of day? What food? What flower?

"You choose," he directed.

"I have someone. Thought of it last night."

"All right. Here goes. Color?"

"White."

"Material?"

"Linen — no! Sharkskin."

"Period in history?"

"Modern times."

"Charlie Chaplin!"

"Oh, Stephen . . ."

"Flower?"

"Sunflower. No — uh — daisy!"

"Which one?"

"Either."

"No good. Choose one."

"No, a chrysanthemum!"

"That's stupid. Now I've got three flowers in my mind. You've got to choose *one* essence, one thing. Don't speak until you're sure. O.K.?"

"Yes."

A silence.

"Well?"

"Oh. Sunflower."

"You sure?"

"Yes." But she wasn't. Should she suggest dropping this one, passing her turn and using this person some other day? No, he wouldn't let her off that easily. He was playing to win.

"Music?"

"A brass band. A little brass band."

"A *little* one," he sneered.

"Well . . ."

". . . no matter. What kind of a room?"

"Oh, outdoors."

"What kind of a *room,* dummy?"

"A gymnasium."

She had given it away now, she knew it and didn't care. Something had gone wrong with the game and the sooner it was over the better. Perhaps he would suggest stopping for a cup of tea.

"O.K. Let's review. Color, white; material, linen — no, sharkskin; modern times . . ."

"Sunflower," she put in quickly.

"Yeah, and little brass band whatever that means and —"

"— gymnasium."

"Right. I don't have a single goddamned idea. Are you sure it's someone commonly known? If it's too obscure it's not fair."

Because she knew, she was sure he would. The person had been in the papers many times, photographs, interviews, reports of activities.

"You'll know."

"Man or woman?"

"That's one question."

"I *know,* goddammit. Man or —"

"It's a woman."

"I *knew* it!"

"But that still counts as a question."

"O.K. O.K. What animal?"

"A coach dog."

"Dalmatian, you mean?"

"Yes, a Dalmatian. Darling, could we stop somewhere for a cup of tea?"

"Now?"

"Well, sometime soon. Wouldn't you like something?"

"Not especially. But if you do, we'll . . ."

"Oh, no. I just thought you'd like a rest from driving."

"Driving relaxes me. It's this lousy game that's making me jumpy."

"Let's stop playing then."

"We can't now. I've *got* to win — to guess, I mean — the lousy name of this lousy . . . Oh! I know! Babe Ruth!"

"It's a woman, darling."

She thought he was going to strike her. His face darkened and his hands clenched the wheel.

They had driven over thirty miles, the highways were no longer smooth. Past winters had split the tar and macadam surfaces. Roots of trees were encroaching on the shoulders of the roads. His frown had deepened. Surely the game could be postponed if not ended.

"It's getting late."

"Don't talk to me. I'm thinking. I'm thinking. It's, it's —"

She prayed he would think of the person. She thought of her so hard that her head ached.

"Ask me another essence," she begged, forgetting his edict of silence.

"All right. What kind of wood?"

"*Wood*?" she said incredulously.

"Yes, dammit, wood, and just tell me, don't comment. The game is just supposed to be that I ask you an essence and you give it to me. Nothing more."

"Birch." She wished she had said white birch but it was too late.

"Well, that does it. I don't give a damn who it is. *Who* is it?"

"Shall I tell you?'

He made a sudden turn. They both were lifted off the seat by the force of the car jerking to the left. She had not seen the teahouse. She arranged herself more comfortably on the seat preparing to open her purse, comb her hair, and add a little lipstick to her dry and bitten lips.

"Tell me," he growled.

"Alice Marble."

He stopped the car. She neither succeeded in freshening her appearance nor did they get out for tea or anything else. His amazement that she could choose a person he did not know made him angry, amused, impatient, embarrassed, and childish by turns. He kept repeating the name and as he did, she would insert the few facts she had based her choice on: ". . . she was the most famous tennis player in the world when I was growing up . . . she won at Wimbledon, dear . . . many times . . . singles . . . doubles." She could see the newsreels, the photographs in news magazines with the strong, tall, blonde woman squinting in the sun, grinning in triumph and she wanted to tell him how she almost chose Helen Wills Moody, the great champion Marble had defeated. *If* she had, would he have known? He probably knew of Marble, but it just hadn't interested him. Why did she choose such a person? She knew almost nothing of the world of competitive sport. She wanted it to be interesting for him.

He searched for a cigarette, she lit a match for him. His anger eventually subsided, but she knew he would not forget what had almost developed into a quarrel. If she had said what she felt, that it was too bad he didn't know, but after all wasn't that the point of the game, to trick the other person? If she had uttered those words, there would not only be no tea but surely no dinner and no lovemaking and no sleep — for her — that night.

Inhaling slowly, he began to relax. He took the map from her, looked in his pocket notebook and announced as if nothing had happened, "There's a splendid restaurant on Route Four. I'll take you there and we'll have an early dinner — let's skip the tea idea — and we'll have a lot to drink and then drive home."

"To the city?"

"No, donkey, to our little love nest."

The phrase, "Your silly sweet games . . ." had been in Peggy's letter, too. Leonora thought it meant private sexual games and wondered what they were. But after Essences she let herself believe that it referred to the car games. It was not any easier to deal with. She felt that the ghost of Peggy haunted his lovemaking from the beginning, before he had let her see the letter, and now there was another arena of competition in which she was sure she would always come out the loser.

But she was alive and Peggy was dead. She knew she would get stronger and banish his ghost from her present, but what if he was not able — or did not want — to banish it from his past.

A blizzard was forecast and began precisely when the chocolatey voice on the car radio predicted. They rose early, exhausted by loving combat, and decided to drive back to the city and beat the storm. He was in good spirits, planning and directing the packing and the timing of possible lunch and dinner stops if the snow was not too heavy. They were on the road at 6:10 A.M.

"Coffee."

She found the thermos and poured him a small amount.

"More."

"It's going to spill."

"My hand is steady. It won't spill." She filled the cup to the brim. He did not spill it, but sipped it carefully. They drove for an hour with the radio playing and the noisy heater warming the car. He opened a window and the knife blade of air cut her face.

"Mrs. T?"

"Yes, darling."

"Would you mind telling me where you got what you're wearing?"

"A present."

"Not from an admirer, obviously."

"Martha gave it to me."

"Oh." He concentrated on the road and quizzed her about the next turning-off place.

"Is there something wrong with this suit?"

"Some things."

Perversely she wanted to know his opinion. She wondered why he said nothing when she put it on for the first time that morning. She waited more patiently for what she hoped would be a compliment than for what she knew now would be criticism.

"The color?"

"Awful."

"The fit?"

"Worse."

"Hah! How can you tell. I'm sitting down after all."

"You were standing up when you put it on weren't you?"

"I didn't think you'd noticed."

"I was too stunned to comment."

"Are you joking me?"

"Of course I am. You look beautiful. Now, don't cry or you won't. It's a great suit. You shouldn't waste it for traveling. Save it for best."

"This is the best, darling. I'm so happy."

She watched him furtively. He hated to be stared at, yet her eyes found him again and again as she tried to look at the road, the signs, or the map. He was immaculately shaved, his collar clean and starched outside his cashmere sweater, his fingernails perfectly trimmed and clean. His trousers had a clean press mark in them, his boots were shined. How and when did he take care of all those things? Would she do some of them for him? And why was it, she mused complacently, that her clothes never seemed neat after she had ironed them, her hair always slightly uncombed, her nails though clean never quite the same lengths? His skin, too, was perfect. Not a blemish. Hers was clear, but under the powder there were often marks of former outbreaks and an occasional unruly single hair grew from her nose or chin. Did other people see these things? Did he? Did he have tiny imperfections she did not see? She could not let her glance stay long enough to find out.

He shut the window and glanced at her. "Start the game. Choose someone, have you got someone? Let's go."

"Oh, please. You go first this time. Let me choose someone carefully . . .You go."

It was fun. He enjoyed her thoughtful queries. They took their time and another person seemed to be there in the car with them. For several questions before she guessed, she was sure she had the correct name, but because it was such a happy time she prolonged climax with the additional essences.

"What sort of jewel would personify this person?"

"A diamond."

"What sort of material?"

"Burlap."

"What time of day?"

"Bright morning."

He said the words so gently, reverently that she blushed. "Oh, I know, I know, my darling."

"Guess, then."

"It's *me*. It's me, isn't it?"

"No." Now the blushing included her entire body, the blood in her legs and thighs and chest and temples seemed to pulse and throb.

"That's one. You want to ask some more questions or guess again?"

"I'll try again. Then, it's not a woman? No? That's two."

Flower, food, time in history, style of painting . . . she asked but could not register his replies. Her concentration had been split and she was not able to pull her thoughts and focus them. She gave up.

"Tell."

"Albert Einstein."

The rushing of blood again, worse this time, as he pronounced the name of the genius.

Of course; diamond, burlap, bright morning, edelweiss growing wild, Mondrian, and to her last question, "Where would he live?" he had replied, "In space." Without meaning to, he had humbled her. She had no need of it. If only she had laughed, seen how funny it was, but there was no going back to the moment even in conversation. She missed the moment when laughter would have saved the day with him.

The snow thickened. He cursed it as it clouded, then obscured the windshield. He got out of the car five or six times to remove it and returned, furious and shivering. The urgent voice on the radio reported the conditions of the storm. He decided that they would find a hotel in New Haven. She wondered if the room would have a double bed.

There was nothing available at the Taft. He stopped at a drugstore and made some calls. "They told me the name of a fleabag. It's downtown. Sounds awful."

"We don't mind. Just for the night."

"You don't mind. I do."

"Sorry, darling."

"Don't keep saying that."

"Sorry. Oh —"

The lobby — a cramped hallway — was lit by a grime-covered bulb. The drab clerk offered them the last room, at the same time warning them, listlessly, that there was no other available space in town.

Stephen insisted on seeing the room. "We may have to sleep in the car," he muttered as they let themselves in.

"I can't sleep here," he said. She could not imagine his fine clothes hung on the pole in the open corner that served for a closet, or his perfect body in the dingy bathroom. She waited for a moment and then suggested, "We'll just rest here, won't even turn down the bed — the sheets are probably gray, too — we'll stay in our clothes and get an early start."

He agreed and went down to sign the register while she used the bathroom and inspected the bureau lined with six-year-old newspapers and tried the bed lamp with its bulb as dim as the one in the lobby. But it was their first double bed.

They found a Chinese restaurant and had a quick supper, trudged back to the hotel, went through the motions of getting ready for bed without performing any of them completely. Depressed, cold, and annoyed by the circumstances that had brought them to this ugly place, they were of no comfort to each other. The noises from the other rooms were plaintive groans and an occasional few words muffled by the thin walls. The daylight woke them accompanied by the banging of radiator pipes. They hurried down to pay the bill and shovel the snow off the top of the car. It took four hours to reach New York.

They played Geography until they both got stuck with too many countries and cities ending in A; then a long spelling contest which Stephen won; and one more try at Essences, which Stephen used to make Leonora laugh. His parody of their earlier attempts was as close as he could come to an apology.

A copy of the *New York Times* was on the seat between them and he asked her to read him the news of the Market.

"It's getting dark. I don't think I can make out the figures."

"There's a flashlight in the compartment." It slipped from her gloved hand to the floor. The paper was awkward to hold, and she misread the prices several times.

"Just give me the *changes*, just the last column," he ordered, and she read him Con Ed, Mobil, US Steel, and Western Union as he directed. They were all her mother's stocks.

"Down a fourth, down one and five eighths, up three fourths . . ."

"Not what you'd call 'bullish,' is it?"

"I don't know the terms. I don't understand half of what I read you."

"You have a highhanded attitude toward money, Leonora. I suppose that's because you've always had it. But you can't live your life as if you *will* have it. Or will you?"

"You mean from my father? I guess there'll be some income from that. Most of it is invested in the same companies as Nana's money. Her second husband did that for all of us, and I hate to admit it but he chose well, as Nana keeps reminding me."

"And what about the land?"

"The actual acreage in California and New York State belongs to my mother. We get it when she dies, I think."

"You think?"

"People change their wills, don't they?"

"And if we have a child?"

"That might be a reason."

"I should hope so."

"But I'm sure Mr. Dennison has charge of all her finances now."

"I think you should make it your business to find out just exactly where you stand. I mean, all three of you, in case something should happen to your mother."

"We never talk about money —"

"It just isn't done?"

"Oh, I don't mean that. But it's handled by her lawyer, and Andrew, and the check comes from them."

"And when do the checks come?"

"Every two months."

"On time?"

"Usually."

"Will they be the same amount now that you're married?"

"I have no idea."

"Why don't you ask her?"

"Oh, I couldn't."

He looked angry. "Why not?"

"Well, we never talk about money . . ." She repeated helplessly.

"Whose name are the checks in?"

"Mine, of course." She wished she had not added the "of course," and tried to think of a way to change the subject.

"Will they continue to be?"

"Stephen, I don't *know.* It's her money, her way of doing things."

"But it's your money, too. The family money." Now it was his turn to regret a phrase. He could never be family to that arrogant, prejudiced tightwad and he knew it. He felt Leonora shudder. "All right, forget it. As long as they keep coming. But I do think with the price of everything rising —"

Leonora surprised him by laughing. "Oh, Stephen, I wish you cared as much about me as you do about money!"

Stephen continued to think about the Ives fortune as part of his future. It spurred him to work harder at his office and he surprised Leonora by his good humor and his renewed interest in his career.

"I'm going to prove to that family of yours that I'm somebody," he told her.

"You don't need to, darling."

"I want to." As they made preparations for dinner he brought up the other — related — subject that had been filling his thoughts.

"Listen, Leonora, it's time for us to have a child. What do you think?"

"Oh — I love the idea of being a parent, because I want to be the best mother in the world, and I know I can't be, but I think I could be a sort of teacher and guide as a parent. I'd want to take care of a baby. But later, when the child grows up and I'm judged for what I am, for what I have done as a parent, I am afraid of what starts to happen then. I'm sure my mother tried in the same way and yet she lost my respect and love. One year it was gone and she could never woo me back as a daughter. There was a scary atmosphere among all of us when my father was dying. Even my sister wouldn't relent. No tears, no regrets, and, it seemed, no memories. I think one of the reasons Martha never married and had children of her own was that she felt Nana had been such a failure."

He said, "Take it easy, darling. You're not like your mother any more than you are like your sister. There's no reason to think of family life in terms of repetition. You have an absolutely fresh chance with your own child."

"I wish I could believe that. I think that with friends I've been able to make lasting relationships, but that isn't as demanding as a child or a lover or a husband. There's always a time when you can close the door. Or the friend can close a door."

"Why can't a child slam a door? I did, many times."

"I don't think I could bear it."

"Then that's what you can spend your child's childhood learning how to do."

"Will you help me?"

"Goddamn right I will. You'll be a lovely mother."

His compliment thrilled her. But she wondered about him as a father. He was too impatient to deal with the endless detail of a child's life. Much more troubling was his possible indifference. Leonora was made so miserable when he rejected her, seemed to have no need of her, how would their child endure his remoteness? The times Nana had turned away from her left wounds that had not healed. Still fearful that she had been the cause of her moody mother's displeasure, Leonora often relived incident after incident, playing her part differently each time, hoping to enchant and amuse her adversary.

As a mother could she help a child — especially a boy — to be tough enough for the world he would live in? "I know I'm a mass of weaknesses that I try to cover up with sophisticated behavior," she said. "But that isn't good enough for a child. Maybe I'm too childish to be a parent."

"Childlike." He corrected her. "I'll be the grownup."

Leonora thought she was pregnant and was afraid to tell him. Why? He was the one who wanted a child. She waited another month.

"Go and have a test," said Stephen. "Find out for sure."

"I am sure," she said, but she went to a laboratory and had the test. The technician called her the next day and said, "The rabbit survived!"

"I don't understand."

"No baby this time, my dear," he said in mock consolation.

"It's just as well," said Stephen. "We can't really afford a family now."

"Stephen," Leonora was trembling, "you were the one who said we should. You said —"

"Don't start the 'you said' business."

"But this is so important. You did say you wanted —"

"I said for you to think about it."

"I was sure you wanted a baby. We can't have one if you don't want it, really want it, want it —"

"Stop it, stop that. If you're sure then we'll have it."

"But a child has to be wanted."

"The child doesn't know a damn thing about it."

"But someday —"

The lab had made a mistake. The child was growing inside her and Leonora was happy. She started to talk to it, she imagined her belly heavy with it when there was still no outward manifestation of her inner joy. This one thing, this part of her life, would be perfect.

Dr. Richard Scanlon's office fronted on Park Avenue. The entrance was on a side street in one of those anonymous buildings where well-off, sensible people lived. His nurse was a slender, pretty woman, a silent rebuke to the bulging, carelessly dressed future mothers who waited in the crowded anteroom. Time with Scanlon passed quickly. His interest in each patient was complete. Leonora disrobed and put on a short white shirt that opened in the back. When she was ready, she called out and Scanlon led her to the leather examining table and covered her upper body with a cold white sheet.

With the touch of an adoring, curious lover he went about

the business of preparing her for the probing of the impersonal instrument he held in his rubber-gloved hand. She did not make a sound the first time or the second, but on her third visit she sweated hearing her soft cry of pleasure, knowing he heard it. She never looked at him, lying still with closed eyes. When she was dressed and sat opposite his surprisingly disordered desk — personal letters, medical reports, snapshots lying in careless piles — they were eye to eye.

Were all the women in the outer room as attracted to him as she was? Probably. It was a tale they told each other. You fall in love with your obstetrician. But she was not in love with him. She was loving the time and attention he gave her and felt proud that she had banished her fear of him at the same time she almost conquered her fears of having and raising the child that was to be born in so short a time. Stephen's child, who would be whole and strong and good. It was her part in its life that she questioned, never the completely separate existence of the new life itself.

When she got home she did not report her visits in any detail. What worried her was the knowledge that the secret rendezvous would end, except for an occasional note or card at Christmas he would drift out of her life the way her favorite teachers had. I can't hold on to anyone, she thought. We're not supposed to, but I want to. If the only person I can own is myself, life is not enough for me. Will this child be the person I can own? That was not to be asked. It was not hers, it was theirs. Would he want to own it, too? Or would they tear its life apart, each needing to say, This is *mine*?

Part Five

THEY NAMED their daughter Nell. Leonora thought her perfect in every detail and loved her utterly. The birth was overwhelming. Never such pain, never such joy. It took forever; it was over too soon. She remembered the sound of her cries, so violent, so primitive she was sure they came from some other woman. She wanted to have another child.

Stephen beamed at his daughter. He touched Leonora's damp forehead and made her feel blessed. Later that morning he went out to lunch with Dr. Scanlon and when he reported it she was jokingly jealous. "Oh, why didn't you wait for me to come, too?"

"Men want to be alone sometimes," he said like an English colonel in a clubroom and made her laugh. She wanted to ask what Scanlon had said about her, but it seemed girlish. "He thinks you're the best patient he ever had and our child the best baby!" What more could she have asked for?

Before the week was over they left the hospital. Feeling strong and well, she clutched the baby and Stephen carried her suitcase, a bag of presents, and the remaining fresh flowers. During the drive home they were quiet. He realizing that her new responsibilities would certainly change her, she wondering if he would love her more or less because of the child sleeping at her breast.

There was no way to tell. There was too much to do. He had not wanted to have a nurse, assuring her she could manage by herself and promising to help.

They came into the apartment and there was a sound, regular and piercing, not like the ringing of a bell, more human. The Siamese cat had been shut in the hall closet. "Don't worry, darling, just let him out and I'll warm some milk for the baby and give him some." She set about making Nell comfortable and hurried to put a bowl of milk on the floor for the shivering cat. She stroked its back tenderly. It was painfully thin. The time in the closet must have been — what? — the length of her stay in the hospital. Stephen had not been there.

The apartment gradually became their home. Peggy's water colors remained on the walls, but the sounds and smells and tastes of life in the rooms changed. They were a family.

Stephen teased Leonora gently, "I've turned you into a Jew, haven't I?" The welcoming warm aroma of his favorite foods cooking made coming home from his office unexpectedly pleasant. Leonora had a talent for preparing the foods he described to her, the simple chicken in the pot, the more complicated tzimmes, blintzes, dumplings, and matzo pancakes. He brought home gefilte fish from the best delicatessen in the neighborhood and on Sunday mornings they shared smoked salmon and whitefish on seeded rolls she had baked the night before. While Nell napped, Leonora cooked. For her, too, it was a joy she had not looked for and it created a bond with Stephen, connected with the mother of his memory and dreams.

"You've changed, Leelee. Being a mother has changed you. You're softer and calmer and sexier and sweeter. I hardly know you."

"Was I so — white bread — before?" She dared her little joke and he accepted it with a bright grin.

"I don't care what you were before. I like what you are now. And I love to watch you eat. When I first knew you, you just moved the food around your plate. Now you devour it."

Being hungry for everything was the best part of being married. Her straight body remained gently rounded for months after Nell's birth.

Stephen was proud of it. But as the first year of their marriage came to an end, his pleasure in her flattering greediness to share his tastes was tempered by his envy of her behavior with Nell. Leaving him, her eyes and ears were ready to give themselves to the slightest movement, the softest cry from the baby.

The baby. "Call her by name, will you?"

"Sorry." She tried to remember. She tried, too, *not* to answer Nell's every need, but her baby became her day, her night, her life.

When Martha suggested that Leonora leave Nell with her over a weekend, she had every intention of taking her four-year-old niece with her to Sand's Point and showing her off to her friends. There was something so beguiling about her gentleness and Martha was afraid of missing key moments in her development. She was the first one to give her ice cream, she was there when Nell's first steps were taken, and she hoped that some fortune would make it possible for her to hear her read her first words.

"Come and spend the afternoon with us on Saturday, instead," said Leonora. "We'll sit in Washington Square park. It's lovely."

"No, no. Why don't *you* come to the country, too."

"Oh, I couldn't go without Stephen."

"Ask him."

"Well, I mean, the fact is, I'm not sure what he wants to do this weekend. He hasn't told me, so I don't want to plan anything."

What seemed simple became complicated because of Leonora's attempts to keep Martha from knowing that she was increasingly uneasy with Stephen and deeply troubled about her daughter's progress.

Leonora wanted the chance to be alone with her sister and

Nell. If Martha saw what she saw, then perhaps they should consult a specialist. Once when Arnold was visiting she had questioned him about it, asking him if he thought Nell's reactions to heat and cold were slower than normal. They tested the child's hearing, too, for it seemed that often Nell did not respond instantly when her name was called. Arnold said he saw nothing at all unusual.

"Come with me to the park, tomorrow. Look at the other children her age. Then you'll see."

That afternoon of watching was the beginning of Arnold's involvement in Leonora's fears.

"What does her pediatrician say?" he asked her.

"He says she's fine. I don't ask him much when I'm there. He seems so busy and when I do say that something worries me, he just pats my hand and says I seem nervous and should be sure to get eight hours sleep a night."

The following week she arranged to meet with Martha. Sensing Leonora's need, Martha rearranged her plans and met them in the park. For a long time Leonora avoided mentioning anything specific but she urged Martha to throw the ball for Nell to catch and to help her dress and undress her doll. She wanted to let her see her do as many physical tasks as possible. Nell was happy. She acted the part of a concerned mother as her doll fell out of her hands to the grass. She mimicked parental concern and sucked in her breath the way Nana did whenever Nell spilled anything on her visits to Riverside Drive. When they returned to the apartment, Leonora put Nell on her bed for a nap, then made tea and sat with her sister in the living room.

"I bet you'd love to get your hands on this apartment, wouldn't you?"

"Why did you say that?"

"You're giving the room that *look*." They laughed and out of the laughter Leonora found the courage to talk to Martha about Nell.

"I'm so grateful to you for including me, Leo. I want to help. I want to be more than just an aunt. Don't leave me out."

Because the rhythm of Nell's actions and needs was at variance with other children's, all her activities seemed syncopated, off their beat, disjointed. Reaching for a cup, opening a window, rising to greet a new arrival — each effort always a beat or two late. After the moment had passed, she was ready to seize it. This handicap of which Leonora was unaware at first and only partially conscious during her first years, was to become so much a part of her outward personality that it became her refuge in a life of her own: a taking of time, a loving of time, that was to give her her happiness and her rest. It was also to give her the reputation of being funny, just as a comedian who is expert at delaying his reactions to an obvious joke can reap the greatest laughter by his careful unhurried response. Nell learned how to use this in speech and action and she provided for her friends a different kind of world where serenity and calm prevailed.

Her dark hazel eyes, straight nose, and her soft, round chin and high absolutely unlined brow were restful to contemplate as she listened and observed. The portrait she sat for as a little girl showed a daydreaming countenance, hands folded one over the other, shoulders sloped with relaxation, lips slightly parted as if the figure in the canvas might speak or sing.

When Nell was ready for elementary school, Stephen decided to give up the 12th Street apartment and move out of the city. He started to re-read Thoreau. He told Leonora he was going to change his way of life.

How he made himself believe this plan she could not fathom, but she knew that if he saw even a flinch of doubt cross her face it would infuriate him. She did not say what she thought: that in a short time he would tire of what he now longed for. He had said to her the first time they ever made love, "You'll get tired of this you know. Of me. Everyone does. It's foolish not to prepare for it now when everything's good."

"I'll never get tired of being with you, never."

"You will."

From that moment she was fearful that *he* would tire of her. And from the first musings about a life in the country, she wondered why he was not able to apply his fixed rule of diminishing happiness to that. Surely they were close enough now that he could read her thoughts. Where did he find the power to avoid facing what was true? Was it that life in the apartment had become unbearable and she was the blind, dumb one who did not see that?

After dinner Leonora and Arnold washed the dishes while Stephen made telephone calls from his desk in the front room.

"I know this move is a beginning for you, Leonora, but for me it's the end of something. You'll live up there and I won't see you anymore."

"Oh, Arnold. Of course you will. I'll have to come in to the city for the dentist and all those dreadful things. And occasionally I'll be staying over at Martha's. We're not going to lose touch."

"But things will change, won't they?"

"Yes, dear. And I hope for the better. We'll have a chance to live more simply in the country and I think Stephen will be happier there."

"But Nell will grow up and I won't see it happen." He was looking at the sleeping child, the blanket pulled up into the shape of some comforting creature in her arms, her face glowing with peace. He reached over and smoothed the pillow, inhaling the scent of the powder and oil and clean linen that surrounded Nell whenever she came out of her bath. "*She'll* change and I won't be there."

"You'll come and visit us."

"I don't think so. I have a feeling Stephen won't ask me."

"What an extraordinary thing to say! You're his best friend."

"I'm his only friend, Leonora, but I'm no use to him anymore. When I was younger, I could make him feel good by just hanging around him. After that, when he started to work at Johnson and Freid I ran a lot of errands and stuff. But now —"

"You are 'useful,' Arnold, to me and to Nell. So you're useful to him. You make everything easier for us, I don't know what we'd do without you. In fact I wonder that you don't need more time on your own. What do you do when we don't see you?"

"I'm writing a lot now. Sending articles to magazines. And my job on the *Journal* seems fairly secure."

"Getting ads?"

"That's what I'm paid for, but usually when I leave here I go to the office and help rewrite stuff for tomorrow's paper. I think they'll take me on full time before long."

"That's wonderful. I'm proud of you."

"Nothing to be proud of yet. I want to write a book for you — and Stephen. I'll dedicate it to you."

"Dedicate it to *him*."

"No. I couldn't. For the last year or so I have had the feeling he resents me."

"You're inventing. You're part of our family."

"No. Leo, we both know why."

"Tell me what you think, what you feel."

"It's because I love his daughter more than he does."

Leonora wanted to protest but could not. Arnold's care for her daughter had made the experience of being a mother wonderful. He exulted in every change and nuance of the child's existence, and when Leonora realized that Nell was developing in a special way and she sought a doctor to counsel her, it was Arnold who went with her and to whom the doctor addressed himself after the interview with Nell and Leonora. Stephen had refused to come.

"Take old Arnie with you," he said. "I don't have a free minute this week."

"You don't mind?"

"I hate doctors' offices and I hate waiting. Take Arnie, the Jewish martyr."

"He's a saint."

"Like your nutty brother, right?"

When they came home with the doctor's report, he did not ask to hear it.

"It's good news, darling, we have nothing to be upset about. When the tests are completed he'll write it all down for us, all the terms and so on, but in plain English it's simply that some things will take longer for Nell to learn and accomplish. Otherwise her health is perfect."

He did not look at her when she told him, nor comment on her news. Arnold suggested they have a drink and the liquor loosened the tensions in all of them. Arnold wondered what the child thought of her adventure in the white tiled room with the strange man.

"I liked him," said Nell, when he asked her. "I think he's trying to help me."

Madison Avenue was gleaming in the strong noon light. Leonora looked in each window as she came nearer to Deane-Ives. She was early for her date with Martha. When Elma came to the door she said, "Sit down and rest, Miss Leonora. Miss Martha's on the overseas telephone." She brought her some sherry and a plate of Carr's biscuits on a silver tray.

The large room was crowded with furniture, lamps, chandeliers, candelabra. Leonora loved sitting beneath the crystals and looking up at the light refracted through the bluish-reddish glass. The consoles and tables were covered with complete sets of antique china, the walls with paintings, mirrors, and sconces. Although most of the things could be exhibited, it was not like a museum, but more like an elegant storeroom bursting with life — the life of the past with a promise of the future. Who would live with these fire screens, these vases, clocks? Who would purchase the walls of the room that had been brought over from England and installed by Miss Deane? Who would walk on the Bessarabian rug patterned with the heads of blackamoors? What child would play hide-and-go-seek behind the Chinese lacquer screen near Martha's desk? What windows could be beautiful enough to be framed by the damask curtains glowing pink in the sunlight?

"Sorry I took so long." Leonora jumped up, and put her hand to her heart. She had not heard her sister coming toward her.

"Easy, Leo, easy. Sit down again. There's no hurry. I'm free for the rest of the day. Where's Nell?"

"With Arnold."

"Nice man."

"Yes. Very. Can we stay here awhile? It's so lovely, so peaceful."

"Certainly. Elma will fix us something for lunch. We'll eat at my desk."

"I'm tipsy on your sherry!"

"All right, I'll have some, too."

"Stephen wants to leave New York. He can't take the life here anymore. He's thinking of Long Island or Connecticut and — oh, Mart — I'm so afraid to leave the city. I'm used to life here." She did not want to betray Stephen. She knew he was sick of the competition in New York and that he wanted to own a house, but she was sure there were other reasons for leaving — some restlessness rooted in his past and present unhappiness — that she did not understand.

"Has he started to look?"

"I think so. He's been leaving us alone on weekends. He rents a car and goes looking."

"Why doesn't he take you?"

"He senses, I guess, that I don't really want to go."

"Darling, why don't *we* go? We could take Nell with us! We could find you a place. You'd like that wouldn't you?"

"What would Stephen say?"

"Darling, he's your husband. You've got to be able to share things with him. If we find something nice you'll just tell him about it and see how he reacts. Do you want to try?"

"What is the alternative?" said Leonora quoting their father.

"What will you do about your apartment?"

"It's all arranged. Stephen's subletting it to Maury Crandall — the vice president of Johnson and Freid — with the understanding that he can have it back with six months' notice."

"He thinks of everything."

"And he's getting more than we pay, because of the furniture and the location. Maury told him he wanted a quiet place. He's tired of midtown hotels."

"What on earth are you suggesting, Leo?"

"Nothing. Oh! Martha — don't be silly."

While, unknown to Leonora, Stephen and his secretary covered the territory on Long Island, Martha, Leonora, and Nell explored Westchester. They did not find anything on the three Sundays they looked. They took picnics and had good times together, but the houses were run-down places, too near the road or else so expensive and well cared for that they were out of the question. Then one day Martha was working in Putnam County and drove herself home. At a gas station she asked about houses for rent near the Croton Reservoir, and when she drove up the road and saw the gray Victorian house, she knew it was the one for her sister. It could be as beautiful as Hopecroft, the house she was decorating in England for Laurence and Sarah Parrish.

Part Six

ELM HILL PROVED to be a difficult house to live in: drafty, badly lit by ancient chandeliers that hung too low over the dining table or too high in the living room, plumbing that was older than the lighting fixtures with pipes that rattled and shuddered as the water went through them whenever it was used in any part of the house. There was no view from any window although from the bedrooms on the second floor the glimpses of the red roofs of the barn and outbuildings shaded by tall trees was lovely in the summer and even lovelier in the fall when the leaves were changing. On the first floor, the porch darkened the family rooms. A giant elm was the only impressive tree within sight and the stone-walled garden could be seen from the two chairs at the dining room table facing west. All the rooms were square, each with its door to another. The hall was the finest space in the house. The curve of the banister, the rich color of the uncarpeted stairs gave promise of something more interesting behind the series of painted doors.

Leonora missed the city and longed for her sister's eye in her large, gloomy house. Martha would not roam through the dark rooms day after day, wondering what to do to brighten them. She would be able to transform the spaces and make them beautiful. Naturally it would cost a great deal and Stephen did not want to spend their invested money on Elm Hill. They had used Nana's wedding check as the down payment, and her present at Nell's birth for the expense of moving. Stephen had expected Nana and Martha to offer to renovate the place as a housewarming present to Leonora.

The house remained in its original condition for over a year and, as Arnold had predicted, Stephen did not invite people to visit.

Stephen liked to touch the stones by the front door and tell Leonora, "It will outlast us, this place, outlast everything."

Our lives or our marriage? she wondered.

Even though he was rarely at home, it was Stephen who made the household decisions. When there was a need for repairs of any kind he would mention it to Leonora and wait a few days before reminding her. Was she capable of acting on his suggestions?

"I'll only have to *un*do it and do it again, dear. That's why I'd prefer that you make the call."

"But it's your job to do things like taking care of the house. I have my work at the office." Stephen usually made the call. Leonora followed his precise instructions and more often than not the results were what he had had in mind.

In the case of her sitting room it did not work out as planned. He told her, and she remembered his telling her, that she might do with that room as she wished. "I never go in there, make it your own. Get someone in to help if you want. What about that chap at Pauline's party the other night?"

A small, perfectly formed young man in neat clothes had been the extra man at Pauline Reinhardt's sit-down dinner and Leonora had found herself on his left. He talked with enthusiasm of creating atmospheres. "For you, I see a house full of curtains and veils, dear lady, in the softest colors of the rainbow. The bedroom . . ." She thought Stephen might overhear and interrupted him. He did describe a sitting room that caught her and she remembered it now.

"Oh, Stephen, that would be grand. His name is Peter Holczer."

"Hungarian?"

"I have no idea. He's a sweet man. He's a friend of Martha's."

"Sweet. That's the word."

His disapproving question and brief statement told her Mr. Holczer's plans would not be acceptable. But she went ahead anyway. "When shall I ask him to come?"

"Don't ask me. See him when I'm at the office. Show him the room, get exact estimates, and we'll see."

"We'll see" could mean anything. We won't do it, we will, we'll do something about it but not what you expect. Her anxieties made her hands sweat. She rubbed them on her dress.

"Don't do that."

Peter Holczer was delighted when she called. He arrived the following day with a Vuitton case full of samples: chintz, velvet, taffeta, satin. She wondered if he could design dresses as well. The color combinations of the swatches delighted her. How did his clients ever decide on a single shade? She would have to let him guide her. They had a cup of tea and chatted, picking up and dropping the colored squares, considering possibilities for curtains, a cushion cover, "or perhaps a tiny footstool covered in pale yellow velvet." She asked him for an exact estimate and he giggled girlishly as he wrote down the figures, then kissed her hand in farewell.

When Stephen came home she was still playing her game with the samples, delighting in the various combinations of colors. She had the room all pale yellows and greens when he handed her his hat, gloves, and briefcase.

He noticed that she was trying not to interrupt him as he commented on the day's doings at the office, and to tease her, told detail after detail of transactions, letters received, deviations in the daily routine, until she could bear it no longer.

"I'm teasing you! Come on, out with it."

"Peter came and he has thrilling ideas. He's going to make the little room into a bower of yellow flowers —"

"Ye gods!"

"Oh, I don't mean that! I don't know why I said that. Wait. I'm going to get the swatches."

"Later, when we have coffee."

"Oh, please, I can't wait." She jumped up and disobeyed him, hurrying until she had gathered up her new toys and spread them out on the table before him. "Look!"

"Oh, definitely a *bower*."

"And he has a way to widen the window so that there'll be sun in the room more hours each day."

"Is he a contractor, as well?"

"No. I don't think so. But he studied to be an architect. He went into business with a friend when his family hit bad times."

"And how much will all this cost?"

"He wrote it down. Here." She handed him the list.

"He's just a little twerp, an opportunist. We can do it ourselves for half the cost. It makes me so goddam mad, sycophants like that, attaching themselves to women, making them feel inadequate, and then cashing in on their weaknesses."

"But we asked him, dear. You told me to call him. He didn't try to sell me anything."

"They all do. They have no real lives, so they live for a short time in other people's. I've seen it happen, don't tell me about it. They can take you for thousands."

There was no use arguing. She never would have thought of having any room in the house "done" by someone else, even Martha. She was sorry she had let herself imagine drinking her morning coffee in a glowing yellow sanctuary.

Stephen found a local painter who worked by the hour and dates were set up. Promptly one morning he arrived and asked for a place to change his clothes. He emerged from the spare room in white overalls spattered with white paint, a clean white shirt, and white cap. Beneath its visor his eyes gleamed bright blue. She could not remember what he was dressed in before he changed and wanted to look at him again when he finished work for the day.

While he was in the house Stephen telephoned. "How's it going?" She reported that all seemed well. "I've been thinking. The bedroom and the library could use a coat of paint, too. And the front hall. Look around. Make a list. Might as well use him while we've got him."

"And Nell's room? Please."

"O.K."

"Shall I ask him for an estimate?"

"What? Oh — no."

He was conscientious and there were no splattered clues he had been at work. Only the clean, smooth walls of varying pastels throughout the house. He arrived each day a half-hour to the minute after Stephen left. She prepared a second pot of coffee and offered him a cup as soon as he had descended from his dressing room like an actor prepared to play his part. He drank standing in the door of the kitchen, filling the space with his easy, tall body, seeming to hold up the doorjamb with his strong left arm. He spoke quietly, smiled often. She was sorry when he handed her his empty cup. At noon he would stop and get off his ladder, clear his throat, and squat in the corner of whatever room he was painting and unwrap his sandwiches. Hearing the cough, she would appear with fresh coffee, invite him down to the kitchen, but he always refused. She watched him eat tenderly, as one watches a child.

He had been in the house four times when he mentioned that in two days he would be finished with the last wall. "I'll leave the bill, or should I send it to Mr. Tannenbaum's office?"

"Oh, send it to us here." She wanted to see his handwriting. She wanted him to keep talking; he had a nice, calm voice. She knew he had no interest in her, and it alarmed her to feel drawn to him. If he had stayed to talk it would upset her and yet she was forlorn watching his van disappear behind the trees.

How could she be lonely? She had a husband and a child and in time they would make friends with other people who lived around Elm Hill. The painter was the first stranger to come to their house. Good-bye, good-bye, she whispered. A year later she could not remember his name.

"What's this package?" asked Stephen as he pulled a small parcel out of the post office box.

"It's for Nell, dear."

"Nell?"

"She has a new hobby. She sends away for samples. And, Stephen, I've let her use your typewriter. She's taught herself to type. She's much faster than I am already, and what's much more important, she doesn't make mistakes."

"Maybe she can be a secretary?"

"*Don't*. Listen, will you look in on her sometime when you hear her typing and praise her? It would mean so much."

"You don't have to tell me a thing like that, Leonora."

The soft clattering of keys gave him his cue and Stephen went straight to the study without helping Leonora unload the car.

"What are you doing at my desk?" he asked in a mock-angry voice.

"Dear sir, I am writing to answer your advertisement of the thirty-first. I enclose, etcetera, etcetera." Nell pulled the neatly typed note out and showed it to him. She had copied the form of a business letter faultlessly.

"Well, Miss Tannenbaum, how many words per minute can you type? I am in need of secretarial assistance."

"It could only be part time, sir. I have another job." She showed her father her spiral notebook with each ad pasted on one page and the date she had sent away for the sample and the cost on the other.

"So this is where your allowance goes."

"Yes! But wait, wait until you see what I've gotten already." She pushed the desk chair back, stood up, put the cover on the typewriter, and started out of the room. Stephen sighed. No matter how sweet his daughter was her careful slowness irritated him and he was not good at hiding it. He decided to make it up to her when she came back with her miniature boxes of soap powder, small tubes of toothpaste, and an envelope of something he had never seen.

"What's this?"

"Instant coffee."

"What do you mean?"

"You just pour it into hot water and it's coffee."

"Show me."

Nell beamed at him. "Do you really want to see? Can I make you some?"

"Have you got enough?"

"I'll send for more."

"Here," said Stephen and took all the change out of his pocket. "Use this for your collection."

"Oh, thank you. I'll get lots. Come on."

"Where?"

"The coffee."

He had forgotten.

"I'll bring it to you. It will only take an instant."

As soon as Stephen and Leonora moved to the country, they had invited Nana and Andrew to come, but weekends were not convenient for Nana. Those were her days with Andrew when they made no other plans. Some holidays they hardly left their bedroom.

Now that their need for each other was diminishing, their meetings less violent, they arranged for their young servant, Evans, to drive them to Elm Hill. After years of inventing excuses, Nana accepted Leonora's invitation and decided to be her most charming, hoping to regain her daughter's affection and thereby find a way to Nell's. Her granddaughter was a stranger and Nana was concerned about her future. She sent a check every month after Nell was born. Since her sister Clara's death the amount was slightly more, Clara having left her money to Nana with a proviso that until Nana's death half of the legacy was to be split three ways among Dwight, Leonora, and Martha. Later, Nana put her share in a savings account in Nell's name.

The drive took two hours because, in spite of Stephen's neatly drawn map, Evans got lost and the Dennisons were not paying attention. They were holding each other in complicated, inventive ways, hiding from the driver's mirror and the windows of the passing cars. By the time they reached Hawthorne Circle they were unkempt and glowing with pleasure.

As they turned up the dirt road to Elm Hill, Nana smoothed Andrew's thinning hair and he attempted to straighten her frilly collar and cuffs.

The leaves were crisp from the early frost and the sound of the gravel under the tires was grating. The car skidded to a stop directly in front of the long porch.

"How stupid to have the driveway in front of the house. The road should turn under this huge elm," said Nana.

As they got out of the car, Leonora watched from the bedroom window, thinking: I'm going to let them wait a few moments on the porch. They took long enough to get here, I'm in no hurry. She went into the bathroom and combed her hair, wiped away the remaining lipstick she had applied ten minutes before, selected another shade, and pressed the moist rouge twice across her mouth, clamped her lips together, grinned, blotted the color onto the same smudged tissue, and admired the result. Her mouth looked wide and hungry. She found Nell and they went down the stairs slowly, Nell's hand smoothing the banister.

Leonora called, "Stephen!" There was no answer. He was closeted somewhere. The study? As far as the barn? She ran down the last steps in case Nana and Andrew were looking through the torn screen door, and arrived on the porch to find them with their backs to her, examining the garden.

"Hello, hello at last. Three years to get here and I'm late to greet you!"

"Not at all," said Andrew. "There's so much to see." There was nothing to see. The garden, like the trees, looked curiously abandoned, even though the life of the plants was gathering force under the fallen leaves.

"Come in, come in," said Leonora, "we'll have some coffee or tea or whatever."

"Whatever for me," said Andrew. "I need something strong and neat." His handshake was surprisingly limp.

"Stephen will be here in a moment. He'll make you anything you like. Would you *both* rather have *drinks?*" Her invitation implied a criticism. Nana gave her an unforgiving smile that said yes, both of us and soon. They followed Leonora inside.

"The air is wicked, isn't it?" said Nana.

"What?" asked Nell, offering Nana a platter of sandwiches. She shook her head.

"I mean *chilly.*" Lem's word. But when they were settled around the empty fireplace she said, "I feel a draft, Andrew. Will you get my sweater. It's in the back seat in my carry-all."

He left the room obediently and Leonora was about to comment that she had never felt a draft in her life when Nana grasped her hand. "He's not a bit well. Something wrong in the digestion department. We can't stay long. Don't make his drink too strong. It's been a ghastly day."

Leonora was ashamed of her unfeeling reception of her guests. She had hardly looked at Andrew's face. She touched Nana's shoulder. "Mother, go whenever you like. I mean *stay* as long as you can. I mean, I'm so sorry. Is there anything I can do?"

"Nothing."

When Andrew returned, Leonora applied Nana's information to his gray visage and lethargic behavior. She saw a sick man where a healthy one had stood only a few minutes ago. She handed him a drink just as Stephen came in. Having heard nothing he played the welcoming host without surcease. He insisted on showing them each room, the attic, and cellar.

They regrouped in the living room under the Venetian chandelier, Martha's housewarming present. Nell escaped to the car and sat talking with Evans and chewing her Milky Way chocolate bar that he had waiting for her in the glove compartment.

In the house conversation spluttered. Attempts to bring in the news of the world or reports of Nell's grades in school were disappointing. Relief soothed them all as the first attempt to leave was made by Andrew who remarked that the pale sun was "paler than a moon, don't you think?" and they all made gestures of preparation, smoothing hair, adjusting cuffs and collars that were in their correct places. Nana investigated her handbag as if it were going to reveal a hidden treasure.

"Don't you want to —" What was the phrase? Leonora paused. In the Pringle household Nana had been taught to say, "Excuse me, I have to write a letter."

"No, no. We're on our way," said Nana. But Andrew did want to. He went to the upstairs bathroom and did not reappear for what seemed longer than ten minutes.

"Whatever took you so long?" Nana inquired.

He'd been sick but he did not say so, though it was clear from his awkward avoidance of all good-bye embraces. Nell met them under the big elm. She held Andrew's hand, kissed her grandmother, and stood waving and watching until they turned toward the main road.

"Thank God *that's* over," said Stephen and took the remainder of his highball back to the barn. "Call me when dinner is ready." Leonora did not answer.

"I will," said Nell.

Although her mother and Andrew had merely walked through the house, Leonora set about to put each room in order as if they had spent the weekend. With a soft cloth in one hand and a feather duster in the other, she caressed her possessions as lightly as Nana used to dust her freshly powdered face with a brisk touch of a swan's-down puff. When she came to a mirror, she looked in it. She tried each faucet, flushed each toilet, opened and shut the drawers of desks and doors of closets no one had touched in months.

In a cabinet in the guest room on the second floor, she discovered a packet of letters tied with string. They were instantly recognizable as little love notes she had written Stephen early in their marriage. He had not saved them; she had. He read them, and left them open on the top of his bureau or the bedside table and at the end of the day she collected the page and put it back in its envelope and then added the discarded letter to the packet she kept in her lingerie drawer. She wondered when she had changed their hiding place. Now not only had he forgotten about them, but she had, too, and was moved to find they still existed. Perhaps she should throw them away, but to do that would be to erase the evidence of her devotion and obedience to him.

The painter in white had covered the dark gray of the room in robin's-egg blue with a border of soft brown around the baseboards and in the squares of the doors. To surprise Leonora he decorated the furniture, too: a drabber blue-gray with an olive tinge. Flowers were painted on each drawer and on the headboard of the bed. It might have been a pretty room, but it lacked comfort. Stephen insisted on having a Ping-Pong table upstairs — because the attic was too hot in the summer, too cold in the winter — so it stayed in the guest room, the oversize green table with the paddles lying on it embraced the free space in its ugliness. The closets and bureau drawers were full of the odds and ends of country life — bathing suits no longer in fashion, espadrilles with worn soles, faded by the sun so that they appeared to be dusted with sand, a broken beach umbrella, towels laundered so often there was no nap left on the faded stripes. All to be given away or thrown out, but Leonora did neither. She went to her sitting room and re-read the love letters. She wondered if she would have had the same sort of marriage with another man. Did the things that kept going wrong between them happen because they were mismated or would she have been as irritating to whatever man she had chosen to spend her life with? If she had been brave enough to chance a love affair — or many love affairs — might she have found a man with whom daily living was as easy and natural as her life had been before she married? It was useless to speculate, she realized that; and yet her fear of self-examination was so great that whenever she was strong enough to look at her own life she forced herself to look longer than was pleasant. She saw a difficult, high-strung woman who demanded more of a man than he wanted to give her and was not able to give that man as much as he needed. No matter how she vowed to change, to relax her rules and standards, she could not do so. She irritated him by the lift of an eyebrow, the lack of a smile. She was unable to apologize when she was wrong and unable to accept his apologies when he came to her to make up after he had retreated to his room in the barn with a bottle of brandy for half the night.

The ten-year-old letters written in her slanted, neat script frightener her. She felt she knew less about the person who wrote them than the Leonora who was reading them. And Stephen, the object of her fascination, was still a puzzle to her. What kind of parents were they for Nell? Unable to answer her own questions, she put the letters in a cardboard box tied with the same frayed string and went downstairs to the kitchen to prepare dinner.

Nell's door was open and, looking in, Leonora saw her daughter sitting cross-legged on the straw rug next to the little painted chest where she kept her outgrown toys, her shell collection and her aunt Martha's letters. The book she was reading had a bright dust jacket. It was not Nell's, nor Leonora's. It had belonged to Nana and Lem and with the law books and forestry journals had found its way to Elm Hill and the bookcase in the lower hall. Had Nell discovered it just as Leonora had one afternoon at the Camp? *Marriage Manual.* Diagrams and charts, line drawings, one or two photographs. How vividly Leonora remembered the mixture of repulsion and fascination the pages held for her. The text seemed to warn: If you do not obey the lessons in this book, you will commit sins that cannot and will not be forgiven. Do not have intercourse unless you wish to have children. A calendar prescribing the times to procreate. Long before she wanted to touch a man Leonora shuddered at the information, doubted and questioned it. But there was no one to share her stolen knowledge with. She knew she should engage Nell in an effortless, comforting talk about what Nana called, "Growing Up." She had not forgotten how she and Martha found out what it meant.

When Martha was twelve, Nana decided it was time to tell them. She didn't want to, but it seemed wrong for Lem to speak to them about private matters. They rarely spoke of them between themselves, how could they manage this situation together? Neither knew that earlier in the year on a warm spring day the girls had been riding in the Hammel's Chevrolet when Natalie turned to Martha and whispered, "Have you had it yet?" Something in her hushed tone made both girls realize "it" was mysterious and perhaps wicked. Martha took the lead in answering, "Have you?" They all giggled and Natalie described something that confused Leonora: bleeding, not knowing when, underwear, protection, staying home from school for a day, breasts and nipples hurting, stomachaches. And only for girls. For boys it was something else. "What?' No one knew. The conversation turned to kissing and having dates in dancing class — laughter drowned out words. The subject of "it" was ignored, but not forgotten.

Martha waited impatiently, Leonora with dread. For Martha the acceptance of her bodily functions was a natural and easy thing. Neither digestion, elimination, nor menstruation held any fears for her. But when Leonora "grew up" three years later, it was a nightmare for her. Unable to discuss her secrets with her sister who had gone far beyond her in what she thought of as the real world, and fearing confidences with Nana who now no longer seemed interested in anyone's body except her own, Leonora faced each period of staining and bleeding with shame. She wondered how she could ever share her life with anyone else. How did other people manage? That was the only question she wanted to ask Nana and it was Nell's question for her, but instead of asking her mother she consulted the index in the black book. Nell needed a friend.

Of all the friends Martha and Leonora shared in childhood Natalie Hammel was the most vivid. She was the smartest — in school and out — there was no question about that. It was foolish to compete with her in conversation or homework. The Iveses found her more stimulating than their own children and she spent holidays with them as a matter of course. Vernon and Dale Hammel were pleased with the notion because it was never easy to have her with them, and making the arrangements, bringing her to the Iveses, and picking her up gave Vernon a chance to flirt with Ermina. He never said anything that could not be overheard or touched her without propriety, yet every word and gesture he exchanged with her excited him, and when he made love to Dale he imagined she was Ermina and that the children from his seed would turn out to be like Martha and Leonora. He did not care for his own daughter.

"Did you have daydreams of being 'someone' as a child?" Stephen asked Leonora.

"No. I think Natalie did. Maybe my mother had dreams for me. I'm not sure."

"Do you know what they were?"

"Not sure. I think she would have been happiest if I had entered into the life of the community, been a sort of leader, you know. She once showed Natalie's report card to everyone she knew because the history teacher had written 'A natural leader' in the margin. After that *I* tried to be a leader at school. It was an obsession in high school. I wanted to win every relay race, get A's in all my classes, get elected to every possible committee. I made quite a good stab at it, but when it was time for me to graduate I decided I didn't want to compete for anything ever again."

"So you did learn something without being *told,* didn't you?"

"Yes. Different though. Not really what you asked me. I had

to go through those years wasting my energies on something I didn't want, to find out I didn't want it. I couldn't learn it from watching the other girls who were driven by real ambition. I never knew how they felt about winning or losing, I know I lost one of my closest friends. She started avoiding me the day I won that election. She made me feel that I had betrayed her."

"Natalie Hammel?"

"Yes. Nat."

"The only smart person you've ever known, except me." Stephen grinned.

"And the most complicated."

Natalie was competitive and industrious. She loved to win at games and tests and invented them so she could win. She knew her looks were not going to attract people to her, she was too odd looking for grownups to compliment and at school the boys were not interested. The people she felt close to were the Iveses. All of them. She was attracted to Lem's quiet sensible fathering of the brood, she knew she could please Nana because she carried out each task with greater skill and speed than any of her children, who all had qualities she envied. She thought the girls were beautiful. The vividness of their coloring, their luxuriant hair and clear skins were magnetic. Natalie wanted to touch them. Martha returned her caresses with smiles; Leonora usually pulled away without saying anything. Each visit Natalie would plan a way to be alone with Leonora and work out a game — a private test she must pass — and to win the game Leonora would have to return whatever touch or look or word Natalie had chosen as the code. She stretched this game across the time from their first meeting at the Peebles and Thompson School in New York, through the years at Miss Wetmore's School where they both were fascinated by the art teacher, Molly Brigham, and more daringly in high school and at the Camp. As Vernon Hammel simply followed the plans Ermina Ives made for her girls, Natalie found herself in the same dancing class, the same clubs, invited to the same parties. She brought her problems to

Nana who enjoyed advising her, she chose dresses that would make her look like a sister to the Iveses even if her features and stature betrayed her as an outsider: too plump for her five-foot-three frame, her purplish pale skin always had some blemish on it — a pimple, the birthmark on her brow that face powder would not hide, the ugly blush that suffused her cheeks when she felt rejected.

In high school she signed her assignments "Nat," expected and received A and A-plus in history and English, and listed so many references in her bibliographies that Mrs. Rumson, the history teacher, sent for her and warned her not to "pad" her list. Natalie shouted, "I've read them all. Test me, test me!" They sat together and talked for over an hour interrupting each other with facts and data. The history teacher did not doubt her again. She had established her reputation as a "brain." She helped Leonora and Martha with their homework, and introduced them to authors whom they were afraid to read. "It looks so *hard,*" Martha complained and Natalie would begin the book reading aloud in her precisely inflected voice, mesmerizing the sisters and making them understand what the teachers could not: the thrilling discovery of someone else's life story. Natalie planned to write fiction based on characters in history. She was the first young person Leonora knew who owned a Remington typewriter, and one Christmas Vernon Hammel bought them all — the Iveses and Natalie were to share it — a duplex phonograph with two horns and two vibrating diaphragms in the sound box. It arrived at the Camp in a crate from the factory in Kalamazoo, Michigan, and had a place of honor in the main room. The unmusical Ives family was lulled into an appreciation if not a love of sound by the diligent Natalie who would sit listening to the music and chewing Chiclets all afternoon if Nana did not order her to stop.

Once when Leonora was dancing around in her Japanese kimono, she swept by Natalie and said, "Please put Geraldine Farrar's 'Un bel dì vedremo' on the Kalamazoo, will you?" They all laughed and that became the name of the machine from then on. And Natalie noted with pleasure that Leonora had taken the trouble to learn the name of at least one of the singers and the songs. "It's *by* Puccini," she prompted softly as their giggles ended and the melody filled the room.

Natalie introduced the forbidden cigarette to Dwight and the girls. She took a supply of Vernon's Turkish cigarettes with her when she came to stay and one by one she taught the Iveses how to inhale without throwing up or choking.

It was Natalie who, having so little regard for her own looks, became the fascinator of both men and women. Her eyes were large, intelligent, and kind. Her skin, which gave her so much trouble as an adolescent, took on a glow that made it look ivory, surrounded by her hair, which she learned to cut short and straight as a perfect ash-blonde cap for her serious, appealing face. Natalie, who without knowing what she wanted attempted childish seductions of Leonora and several other girls, was the first to have a love affair with a man and the first to marry. She sold her travel agency and married a man she did not love and stayed married to him until he left her for someone he did. He gave her a great deal of money in stocks and bonds and Natalie started to write articles and to be published. Her field was European history. She doubted if anyone she knew ever read her in journals and magazines, but she corresponded with scholars all over the world.

At school it seemed to her that everything she really wanted she could not have. Even more than admiring glances and friends she wanted power and worked hard to achieve it. In high school there was a student government, and in her senior year, Natalie was the obvious choice to be its president.

She planned new ways to conduct meetings. Informal on the surface but with a strong guiding mind — hers — ready at all times to lead the discussions along productive lines. She took out all the library books listed under "Utopia."

Toward the end of March, midterm examination panic was

replaced by election fever. On a hot May afternoon the elections were held. Natalie made more of an effort with her hair and school uniform that day. Leonora, whose name was also on the ballot for president, did not. She wanted it to be over.

The students who were not running for office became unruly until the results for the highest position were brought in an envelope and handed to the secretary pro tem, who ripped it open and read in surprise, "The next president of the high school is Leonora Ives."

Natalie closed her eyes. She would learn later in the day from Mrs. Rumson that she lost to her friend by one vote. Shaking with disappointment, she found Leonora and confronted her.

"You didn't vote for me did you, Leo?"

"It's a secret ballot, Nat."

"Tell me the truth."

"Nat, I voted for myself. Didn't you?"

"I don't ever want to talk to you again."

"Natalie, it's not that important."

"It is to me. It was."

Natalie's thick lashes were studded with tears that did not fall until Leo left the room. Mrs. Rumson waited for her to leave, walked toward Natalie with open arms, and said, "It should have been you. Everyone knows that. In ten years this won't matter. Be strong."

One night Stephen asked Leonora if she thought Martha was as interested in women as she was in men. She answered the question at length, enjoying the consideration of her sister's tastes and social preferences. He did not interrupt her, but when she finished, she realized that she had completely misunderstood the question and was ashamed of herself and blushed. "Does it embarrass you to consider it?"

"No," she answered. "I'm flustered because I had no idea what you meant until a second ago. What do I know about her personal life? How does it affect me anyway? The only reason to ask such a question about anyone, it seems to me, is if you are interested in someone that way."

He laughed.

"Are you?"

"We're all interested in what goes on with people when we're not permitted to observe them, aren't we? Why else do we read and go to the theatre?"

"And gossip?"

"Are we gossiping about your sister? I just asked you a question anyone might ask."

"Well, I can't answer it. Now I *am* embarrassed. Do you suppose she has such conversations about me with . . . well . . . with . . . a man?"

"She'd know what to answer. You're all woman, Leonora, and you're all mine."

There was an uncomfortable silence. His statement had been made without feeling, and it threatened her. He was waiting for her to speak.

"Life began for Martha the day she threw away her high school diploma and went to work for Miss Deane," said Leonora.

"Pushing the tables and chairs."

"You can call it that if you like. She sees it as a way to make life more — well — livable. She enhances the settings for people's lives."

"*Rich* people, very, *very* rich."

"Yes. Her clients are rich. Working people don't think of decorating their rooms, they just live in them."

"And the rich can't live in them, so they make them pretty and expensive-looking and for *my* money — which is never enough — uncomfortable," he said.

"You should talk to her about it. It's her subject. She'll make you understand."

"I wonder."

"Do you think women who prefer their own sex are less womanly? I wouldn't agree. The lesbians I've known or seen closely seem intensely feminine to me. In fact that's what makes me feel apart from them. Not that they avoid men, but in their search for what's perfect in women they have a kind of apartness, a mysteriousness, that I've never been able to penetrate. It was certainly that way with Natalie when we were all young and at the Camp. She was so much more curious than anyone else our age, so sure of herself with the grownups and in her odd way so elegant."

"Did you love her, Leonora?"

"For God's sake, I'm not talking about that. I can't talk about that with anyone but you and with you I can only speak of what we know together and even then I feel shy."

She was about to mention Natalie's odd breakdown on their wedding day when Stephen chortled. "I think your sister was crazy about Natalie then and has always had a woman or two on the side."

"Stephen!"

"Lots of people live their lives that way."

"I don't mean the way of life. I mean the way you say it. You make her sound like —"

"A man?"

"I don't understand men, I don't really understand you. I'm frightened when I think that most men need far more than a simple relationship with a wife to keep them content."

"And a woman? Your sister?"

"Martha doesn't tell me much about her personal life. She works hard and meets a lot of people through her work whom I'll never know. Very social —"

"Very rich."

"Yes, they pay her well to decorate their homes."

"But she has affairs, doesn't she?"

"Stephen, I don't know. The only time she told Nana and me about someone significant, it all ended in tragedy."

"You mean the Wyman Walters thing?"

"Yes! How did you know?"

"I heard the gossip."

"She met him through his brother, Jerry, who was the lawyer for one of her customers. Someone out in Sand's Point, I think. She must have lived with Wyman for a while because she told Nana to keep any mail or messages, not to send them to the shop or to her apartment."

"Why didn't she marry him?"

"But you know perfectly well why. He was mixed up in that murder case. Never had an alibi but got off because his brother was a big lawyer. No one remembers it now but it was a scandal at the time. Wyman was just as handsome as Jerry and much wittier. He was the one everyone was interested in. But he stayed too late at a party one night. He was discovered in the bedroom with the hostess. The husband came upstairs with a gun and the husband was found dead from a bullet wound . . ."

"And the woman?"

"I don't remember the details. She gave some sort of deposition and they let her off. She said the gun went off and he shot himself. Martha didn't believe a word of it, but I know it ruined Wyman's life. He left New York and tried to make some sort of career for himself in Chicago with a meat-packing firm. He kept his name and some people remembered. It was awful, a complete mess of a life."

"And now, how does Martha feel about him?"

"He's dead. He died of influenza before there were miracle drugs. He just got sick and died and that's the end of his story."

And your sister? he wondered. Martha seemed to be a happy woman. Something serene and warm in her face, her eyes. The grasp of her embrace in their occasional meetings was so — human. Leonora knew that Larry Parrish filled her life, but she did not want to discuss it with Stephen. She was jealous of the hidden source of her sister's contentedness, just as she was of her profession and her freedom. Once more she asked herself why her marriage was not answering the needs she dreamed it would. Unable to face her doubts she tried to ignore them, but her look held the question.

He smiled at her and patted her hand. He was enjoying a

satisfying flirtation with Jeannie Flynn, a rich debutante who worked in the suite of offices adjoining his, and felt sure that within a few weeks she would become his next mistress. It excited him to talk to his wife and think of the girl. He kept her on the subject of her sister's sexual life as long as he could, feeling the desire for Jeannie rise in his groin. When Leonora rose abruptly and made an excuse about preparing dinner he wanted to grab her and slap her or take her to him, but he was given no choice. She moved swiftly to her tasks and he was left sitting on the couch pressing his hands deep between his thighs.

Stephen's envy of the rich had started early. Even at school, where most of the teachers and students were part of what was called the middle class (but appeared to him to be lower class in terms of money, comforts, and opportunities), there was the Top group and the Bottom. And being in the Top meant not only that you had money but that you were good-looking and wore newer clothes than your classmates. Exceptions: You could be unattractive, your skin covered with acne, kinky uncombable hair, skinny, fat, if you could afford to treat the class on your birthday. One boy took them all to the circus in hired limousines and they went back to his parents' house afterward and had soda and chocolate cake. He was accepted simply because his parents were able to spend their money to buy him approval. Stephen felt it keenly. He saw it with the girls, too. Certainly the really pretty ones were asked everywhere and treated like princesses, but after that the segregation into cliques came about depending on what businesses their fathers were in and where they lived.

In adult society, it seemed much the same to him. The Negroes were granted lip service, the Jews were tolerated if they were talented or did not look too Jewish, and the rest — for the majority of people he saw and knew what mattered was how much money they had in the bank. But just to have land and savings and investments was not enough, you needed money to spend. That was the kind of money he wanted.

That he had married a woman who seemed to have no awareness of the cost or value of things surprised him. That he had married a woman without real wealth — spending wealth — surprised him even more and he would daydream about another woman, another wife with lots of ready money.

Where would he find her? At a party probably and Leonora could get him asked to those parties. But she made no effort to do so. "I'm perfectly content with you here," she would say. Or, "Let's go to a restaurant if you're restless. We probably should get out more, but parties are so . . . exhausting really, don't you think?"

"It depends on how long you stay, who's there. They can be inexhaustible!" She laughed. "No, I mean it. Other people are interesting, not exhausting. Think of it that way."

"I'll try to."

"If we gave some parties, we'd be asked back."

"Who'd come?"

"We'll make a list."

Won't it be the same list of the people you have contempt for? she thought, but did not say.

It was. They were pardoned for a time. They were to be called and asked and she would plan the food and he would order the liquor and find someone to serve. Candles for the living room, a new welcome mat perhaps? New wineglasses, an ice bucket . . . The list grew longer as the day approached.

They found a woman to help with the party through an advertisement in the Mahopac paper. Leonora called and a severe voice answered demanding, "What? What? Speak louder!"

"My husband and I," she began.

"Who?"

"We're . . . I'm . . . giving a party for about twenty people next Friday and I was wondering if you would be free to help."

"About twenty? Where d'ya live? Will your husband come and get me and bring me home?"

It took longer to make arrangements with Janice Brewer than

to order the food and liquor. She questioned Leonora, who felt it was better to go ahead and deal with her than to start over with someone else. Toward the end of the conversation Leonora heard herself ask, "Don't you *want* the job?" and was immediately sorry. The answer came slowly.

"I'll consider the job. Give me your number and I'll call you back."

When Janice Brewer was ready she called back and accepted the evening's work. Leonora hoped she would approve of her house, guest list, and husband.

The evening was a rare one, the air clear, stars visible, moonlight making the elm loom imagined, unreal. Dinner was served from big platters on the dining room table, which had been pushed toward the wall to make a buffet. The cooking had taken Leonora two days and was, on the whole, successful, in particular the cold salmon and the apple pie. Janice did not stay to help clean up. She had said she worked from seven to eleven, and at ten twenty-five she gave Stephen her first warning. At quarter of, another, at ten of she disappeared, returning at precisely eleven in her street clothes, a good-looking felt hat pulled over half her handsome face. She towered over Stephen as he preceded her to open the front door. Leonora was left to serve the coffee and slice the pies.

The coffee had not been made. Had Janice forgotten? It was time for hot coffee with the pie and cheese. In the top kitchen cabinet Leonora kept some instant Nescafé which she often made for herself in the mornings after Stephen had breakfasted on tea and toast. If she measured carefully there might be enough for sixteen demitasse cups. She and Stephen would pretend not to want any. She boiled the water, poured the coffee into the silver urn, asked him to help her carry it in to the dining room, and began to ration it out. One of those party silences fell and the sharp voice of Mrs. Weldon, chairman of the Putnam County Garden Club, was heard solo and strong, "This is ersatz coffee!" In the hush, Mrs. Weldon put the cup down on the marble-topped table in front of her and concentrated on the pie.

When Leonora was washing the delicate blue and white cups Stephen asked, "For Christ's sake, what the hell was all that about the coffee?" He insisted Leonora find a couple to work for them. She was no good at managing alone.

When Plez Mooney was hired he was told his duties would be to drive the car and keep it in perfect condition, to weed the garden, and to do the heavy cleaning. His wife, Louise, was to cook, wash, and sew. It was an ideal arrangement. They could live on the top floor. It meant Leonora could join Stephen in the city and there would always be someone at Elm Hill at night with Nell.

There were no complaints. The quiet couple did their work and lived in the house with dignity. Whenever Stephen was not using the car on a Sunday or Thursday he urged Plez to take it, and he and Louise would drive away for several hours and come back with bags of fresh fruit and flowers. Where in the country did they go, that they could bring back such vibrant, tangible proofs of their journeys? Stephen suggested they drove to the Ninth Avenue markets in the city.

The door to Nell's room was kept open, a family habit, easier to look in on her. She was not the kind of child to cry out for attention or from pain. No one noticed when the doorknob fell apart. The useful part of it was left in the door, but one knob — the inside one — was missing. If Nell wanted to close or lock the door it was not possible.

Louise fell ill. She did not cook or clean for several weeks. She lay in her bed with a low-grade fever, aching bones, and dry throat. The doctor prescribed aspirin, fruit juices, and rest. Plez managed to do some light cooking. The family made few demands on him. Plez appeared ill, too. Distracted, he moped and would not accept the car on his day off.

Leonora was aware of Plez's restlessness. She thought she heard him on the stairs late at night, but his footsteps did not seem to go farther than the family floor. Without turning on the light she went to her door and opened it noiselessly. She saw Plez leaving Nell's room. Too frightened to speak, she waited until he had returned to the top floor and the latch of his door clicked. Then she went to Nell's bed.

"Are you awake, darling? I thought I heard you call me. "

"I'm wide awake."

"Why? It's so late, it's nearly morning."

"Mother, can I ask you a favor?"

"Anything."

"Can I have a lock on my door."

Leonora reached her arm under her daughter's sleep-warmed body and pulled her to her breast. "You can have one tomorrow. It should have been taken care of weeks ago." She waited hoping Nell would say more. Then she decided to joke with her. "You don't want to keep me out do you, Nelly?"

"No. Just Plez."

"I feel so guilty," said Leonora. "How could we have let whatever happened happen?"

"Servants feel they can take what they like after a while. He wanted Nell."

"He didn't 'take' her, for God's sake!"

"No, I don't think so. I guess he just fooled around with her."

"Oh, my God, Stephen!"

"But to Nell that might mean the same thing as being raped to someone —"

"I know, I know. Do you suppose I ought to try to talk to her about it?"

"Someday. Not now. Maybe she'll say something to you. But let's not take any more chances. Let's get rid of them. Both. Louise is such a drip. Let's try it without anyone."

How was she going to keep the entire house in order? "You mean, no one living in?"

"Yes. Wha'd'ya think I meant?"

Leonora spent most of her days and nights in the country at Elm Hill with Nell. Stephen found use for the apartment his company now owned.

Symka Bjetzki was born in Salzburg where she lived until she was fourteen years old. She met Lex Woolf when he was a private in the 11th Infantry in the First World War, came to America as his wife in 1920, and settled in a little town called Purdys in New York State, not far from Brewster. Leonora met her at the Garden Club.

The melody of Symka's native tongue played through the banal Americanisms she had incorporated into her everyday speech. She spoke faster than anyone Leonora knew, and although the words did not always mean exactly what the hearer thought, they meant what Symka wanted them to. She read little, listened carefully. She could use three or four words, a shrug, a gesture of her tanned hands, and a widening of her eyes, and the thing described was clear and often funny. But when tragedy touched her she was more eloquent than ever. Without the vocabulary of grief she could communicate all its hurt and some of its healing qualities.

Leonora had seen Symka deal with terror. One day she and Nell had been at the Woolf's for lunch. It was a bright August afternoon and Nell and Symka's daughter, Sylvie, were leading the Woolf's horse down to the paddock. The heat made the air vibrate like a shining curtain. Through it came a cry and Nell came panting toward the patio. Symka leapt up and ran. She got to Sylvie first. The horse had kicked her in the face, the mark of the metal shoe was on one cheek and her eyes were covered with earth and blood. She was screaming.

How they got the doctor, how Symka was able to telephone Lex and describe the indescribable, how the child was capable of the pain, how Nell somehow stopped shaking, were things Leonora never did sort out. Time healed the memory and Sylvie's adorable face, but the thought of Symka that afternoon haunted Leonora.

She felt guilty. If Nell had been quicker, could she have pulled Sylvie away from the horse? Shouldn't they both have watched the children more carefully?

In addition to admiring Symka, she now felt she owed her something. For that reason whatever she asked of her — and it was little — Leonora tried to do.

She enjoyed being with her not only because Symka's energy gave her energy, but the foreignness, the European qualities of her look and sound and temperament fascinated Leonora. "I feel like a piece of white paper next to you, Symka."

"Why?"

"I can't explain it. It's partly — well — you're in touch with important things and I spend most of my days trivially."

"Trivially? Listen, my Leonora, we all do the same, no? I get up and waste most of the morning doing things I should have done the night before. It is not interesting to anyone how I bathe and dress and clean the house and shop the food —"

"But it is. That's exactly what I mean. The things of the day seem more interesting for you than for the other women I know. We all look and talk alike. Our husbands treat us in much the same way, with a kind of offhand friendliness. But when you meet Lex at the station I have to look away when he kisses you."

"Yah, but then we get in the car and have the same conversation the rest of you are having. 'How was your day?' 'Fine.' 'How was yours?' 'O.K. Nothing special.' 'We need a new whatdyacalleet for the kitchen sink —' "

"And Lex knows what you need and gets it and puts it in and the sink doesn't leak anymore!"

"You are not jealous, are you, Leonora?"

"I think so. A little. I'd love some of your color."

"Get out in the sun! Make that patch behind your house into a vegetable garden! It will be hard in the beginning and you will curse me for suggesting, but I tell you sometimes I leave all morning tasks and just go into my garden and the garden tells me what to do! That's what you need. Then when he comes home you will not have conversation. What you say will not be so important all the time."

Then it must be true: Symka and Lex make love all the time. Every day or every other day?

"What are you thinking, Leo? Something about me and he?"

"Yes."

"Well, you are probably right what you are thinking. He is wonderful to me that way."

"But Symka, don't you think it's possible to have a life with colors in it, even if you don't have that — that perfection — with someone else?"

"I do. I think that way is how it was for my mother and father. May not be so, but it's how I see it when I remember, they move in waltz time. Half-time." She shrugged. "Ragtime?"

"Harmony?"

"Harmoniously!" she said, smiling.

Leonora vowed to herself to make a vegetable garden.

Leonora had not wanted to go to the Woolfs' party without Stephen, but the constant urging by telephone and teasing notes full of Symka's descriptions of the guests and menu made her feel that if she didn't go, it would hurt their feelings. So it was arranged that Bill Donahue would pick her up and bring her home, since his house was on the way.

It was an outdoor supper and Lex had strung lanterns from the porch to the trees making the place look prettier than she remembered it. Only once before had she been there late at night, with Stephen, and it was then that they had met Bill. He seemed to press his good looks and charm on everyone and did not appeal to Leonora. But he had good manners and had a lot of easy small talk and consequently was a popular extra man. After several casual meetings, she and Stephen grew used to him and discussed him without cruelty at their after-party gossiping.

He was surprised to see her alone. She knew, because he had a habit of purposefully widening his eyes which at first she had thought absurd but now amused her. Without his asking she said, "Stephen had to stay in the city for the weekend. Appointments both days so it didn't seem worth it to take the train four times." It sounded rather lame. He took the train every weekday, but she let it go at that and wondered why it troubled her to report on him. She rarely went out by herself, because she had no desire to make the arrangements and follow up on them: A kind of social laziness.

Now she was glad to be among the chatting, drinking crowd of friends standing in line for Lex's hamburgers cooked over an outdoor grate and Symka's salad, made with the youngest, freshest vegetables from her garden.

Food, hot and iced coffee afterward, and plenty of wine. A few people started to say good-bye and suddenly Leonora felt trapped. She wanted to leave at once for no reason she could explain. Bill was still eating dessert — another of Symka's miracles: fruits cut up and marinated in white wine and chilled in separate glasses with sprigs of mint. She went over to the wicker chaise longue where he was holding court, surrounded by three women, and tried to get his attention. He saw her, she was sure, but did not widen or narrow his darting eyes. He did not exactly ignore her, either. She wanted to raise her hand like a schoolchild to distract him; she caught herself clearing her throat. It was useless. She went back to the house and spent another half-hour with Symka and several other women discussing the price of food, servants, and the education of their offspring.

Bill left to go to the bathroom. From the window she saw him rise and found her way to the door. "Oh, excuse me, do you want to use this first?" he asked.

"No." She stepped aside. "But whenever you're ready, I'd like to start home."

"Something wrong?"

"No. I'm just ready to go whenever you are."

In a few moments he was beside her, with her sweater and handbag, the perfect escort. "Oh, thank you, Bill. I hope you don't mind. But I'd like to be home in case Stephen gets a chance to call."

"Couldn't he call you here?" he asked pleasantly.

"Yes, but —"

"Say no more." He widened his eyes.

The car smelled like a tool shop. Old oil and grease mixed with the softer odor of the upholstery. Even though he drove with his window open it was musty, male, not unpleasant but unsettling. She imagined that the glove compartment was full of soiled rags, faded maps, and stale cigarettes. The car and everything in it looked and smelled gray. His bright yellow summer linen trousers and clean white sport shirt and her flowery chiffon dress were out of place.

She should have dared to wear slacks as some of the other women did. She was slim enough and, with a Cuban heel, tall enough to look well in them. But Symka always dressed like a hostess and as her guest, Leonora felt more comfortable in what Nana called party clothes.

In the front seat of the moving car she ironed her dress over her breasts and knees with her hands.

"Need any help?" She couldn't suppress a foolish giggle. He had caught her so completely off guard, and what was she preening for anyway?

"Thank you, no," she answered in an artificially high voice and looked out the window. He was driving so slowly that the world seemed to be moving along with them at the exact rate of the wheels of the car. It made her sleepy, and she had had how many glasses of wine? Two certainly, perhaps a sip more. She closed her eyes. He stopped the car.

"Good Lord, are we here?"

"Where? No. I thought you'd like to stop for a moment. Do you feel O.K.?"

"You asked me that before. I'm fine. Please let's keep going."

"I asked you because you look so tense. What's bothering you? Why can't you relax a little on a Saturday night?"

"I'm relaxed. I just want to get home, that's all."

He started the car again and threw it into gear, as if he had been reprimanded.

It occurred to Leonora that she was going to have trouble getting out of the car and away from him when they stopped. It made her pull closer to the door on her side of the car, and as she did so, she knew it was a mistake.

"I'll have you home in five minutes. Take it easy. I'm not going to rape you, cutie."

A bad pause, then lamely she suggested he put on the radio. He did, and they finished the trip with music playing.

Now after wanting to get home she hated the moment of the car stopping and she knew he would turn the engine off, which he did.

"Thank you for taking me, and bringing me home. I'm sorry I wasn't better company."

"You're just on guard all the time. Do you know what I'd like to do" — she started to speak as he said — "to you?" Then she mumbled, "What? No." He began to talk in a rough voice, low with urgency, and he told her exactly what he intended to do, using words she had only heard Stephen say and all the while releasing his belt and the buttons of his trousers with one hand and grabbing at her breasts through her dress with the other. It was all over in a minute or two and by the time it was, her dress was torn, and her underthings pulled away. Her back and neck felt broken. She heard herself moaning, but it was an unfamiliar sound, and at first she thought it was Bill. She pounded him with her fists trying to hurt him wherever she could strike. She heard him groaning as she pushed her way out of the car and rushed toward the house. He started the motor and drove away.

She ran a bath. The telephone rang. "Change of plan. I'm at the station. I'll be home in three minutes."

She bathed and threw all her clothes into a paper bag and hid it at the back of her closet as if she were placing something secret out of Nell's sight at Christmastime. She put make-up on her face and was perfumed and combed and smiling when Stephen's car took the place of Bill's gray one under the elm tree.

Magically the memory of the incident had for the moment been washed off her body with the soapy perfumed water. She had the strength to keep her mind off it as she described the party to Stephen. He drank his drink, smoked a cigarette, and listened with polite interest. The evening ended simply and easily as they prepared for bed and he fell asleep comfortably, without touching her, in their wide warm bed. Lying beside him she stared at the ceiling, and as if she were watching a piece of film on a spool, she reviewed the evening. Not just the time in the car, but her preparations for the party, her acceptance of Bill Donahue as an escort, and then the climax of the dismal experience in his smelly, alien car. She tried to start the memory earlier, to remember when she had first talked to him, to find a way into the evening that could make some kind of sense. She wondered if he was doing the same thing. Probably not. From the way he talked and behaved, she felt that she was simply one of many women who had borne his angry sexual assault in that unseemly setting. He did it all so mechanically, his anger was distilled, without feeling.

The days went by and she was able to forget, little by little, as if the frames of film were blurred in certain places.

The blurring came into focus one night. Half-awake, thinking, not dreaming, another film was superimposed on the reel. This one was unremembered for so long that it returned to her in the old browns of the rotogravure section of the Sunday paper. But this series of pictures was not of suburban women in chic clothes, it was rural: a two-hundred acre farm near Plattsburg, where Lem had sent his surviving children the summer after Harrison drowned. Rows of boys and girls in a wide field harvesting the potato crop as part of the outdoor program. Dressed in overalls, working as hard as the boys, Leonora saw herself — body bent toward the earth — stopping only to wipe the sweat away or to scratch an itch it caused, and finally hearing the whistle for the end of the day.

Dwight liked the farm and sang the songs he learned there for the rest of his life. Leonora hated it. It seemed to her a punishment for Harrison's death. Why should they be sent away from home? The hot, dusty fields, the plain food, and sharing her sister and brother with strangers made her angry. Her letters to Lem were brief and it was not until he reminded her that she sent Nana her love.

Because Leonora was the youngest girl in the group of eighteen children, she was chosen to sit in the front seat of the farmer's truck on the trips to the fields. "Oh, please, let me stay in back with my sister," she pleaded, but the farmer squeezed her hand and lifted her up onto the hot leather seat.

He was a huge man — she had never seen anyone as fat — and marveled at how he found clothes to fit him or rings that would go over his fat fingers and huge knuckles. He wore five rings studded with diamonds. He gave himself a ring to celebrate each five-year period of his marriage to a woman he called "the wife." The stones were large, he boasted the number of carats and how many "simoleons" each cost. She thought they were the ugliest of jewels and vowed never to wear them. As she was thinking this, he offered her a diamond ring. Knowing he was joking, she joked, too, but it sounded like a bargain.

"What's that you're humming, little Leona?"

"Leon*ora*. It's the song we learned yesterday. You're supposed to sing the chorus as fast as you can to make it funny. I'm going over the words in my head."

"Out loud," he commanded.

" 'Silviculture I will master I will put out fires faster I will learn to use the compass and the ca-li-pers . . .' " she rushed through the words to the end, " '. . . and the names of trees will never bother me, when I have studied forestry!' "

"What does all that mean?"

"I don't know. I like the Gilbert and Sullivan songs better."

"Then sing them to me."

"I don't feel like singing." She moved nearer the door. The skin on her legs was damp and stuck to the seat.

During the third week of camp he put his hand on her leg at the after-dinner song hour. The following morning instead of taking her to work in the pick-up truck he helped her into his Reo town car, dusty outside and in, smelling of potatoes and cigarette smoke. She missed the uncomfortable springless seat of the truck. She tried to remember the words of "The Nightmare Song" she had practiced with Martha when they were falling asleep, but could not.

He called himself the Potato King of the Valley and for three weeks he bragged to her of his wealth and strength. He complimented her on her score in the contest with the other campers: more bushels per day than anyone. "You're the Queen of Potato Pickers and I'm the King," and he squeezed her thigh. He continued to drive the Reo and refused to have anyone ride with them, making some excuse that he had deliveries piled in the back seat.

During the last week, he pressed his fat mouth on hers and she tasted his wet lips and felt his thick, soft tongue and was sick. He kissed her when he picked her up and when he took her home. She closed her eyes and held her breath. She hated it, hated him, and most of all hated herself for allowing it to happen. When she thought of the summer and how Lem and Nana had praised her for behaving so well at a difficult time, she had felt like a cheat and a whore and never told anyone, not even Martha.

Forgotten. Then remembered. Sordid and unimportant, it now became mixed in with the humiliating evening with Bill. She blamed herself, sure there were young girls and women her own age who could take better care of themselves in such situations. Yet each time the film went through the spool of her memory there seemed nothing else for her to do but to be passive and to accept what happened without protest.

Natalie Hammel wrote a letter asking Leonora to meet her on a Wednesday for lunch. She copied it out several times, changing the phrase "I have something to tell you" to "There is something I know that will interest you." She changed the "will" to "might." In her first draft she signed her first name and nothing more. By the third and final draft she wrote: "With every good wish" and her initials.

She knew it was a stupid thing to do. No good could come of it, but she did not resist the impulse to summon this friend of many years, the person who haunted her life and her thinking, to see her face to face and let her feel some of the pain that others — that she — had lived with over the years. Why should Leo be exempt? How satisfying it would be to see that serene, mercilessly calm face flinch and that even, soft voice break in anguish. That anguish I will share with her. That pain, partly of my making, will bring us back to friendship again.

Waiting for the day to come, deciding what to wear, and practicing what to say became a fascinating task Natalie welcomed. Day and night she planned how she would play her role in the sour comedy she was rehearsing with such care.

Stephen read Natalie's letter over Leonora's shoulder. Her look questioned him.

"I think I know what it is about. I can probably tell you better than she, and I should have told you long ago."

After Nell was in bed, they sat together drinking coffee and all he said was: "I guess it's about the night Nell was born."

"I don't understand."

"Relax. It's not life and death. Just listen to old Natalie, and then we'll have our talk."

"That's not fair, Stephen!"

"Fair? What's fair?" He spent the next three days in the city, and bought Jeannie Flynn a charm bracelet at Lambert's.

Arriving at the restaurant ten minutes before the appointed time, Leonora sat in the foyer and watched the couples meet, greet, and parade into the dining rooms. There were three. One was small, the owner called it intimate; the other two were larger, darker, noisier, and more popular.

Natalie was late. It meant that Leonora waited for her over half an hour. The anger stuck in her throat and mixed with her words of greeting. Natalie slapped her on the back, "What's wrong? Sore throat? Frog? What?"

"Nothing at all. I'm glad to see you."

Whatever Natalie weighed ten years ago she had added at least twenty pounds. Her seal coat and the batik dress under it were loose fitting so that her waist was not visible at any time, but a glance at her cheeks and neck was enough to hint at the heaviness elsewhere. Leonora wondered how she appeared to Natalie. Her weight was the same, she knew that, but surely she had lines on her forehead and at the corners of her eyes and mouth. Natalie barely glanced at her.

"Where are we sitting?" Leonora asked.

"Is the Candlelight Room all right?"

As she turned to find him, the headwaiter in charge of the Candlelight Room came up to them, checked Natalie's name off his list, and directed them to their table. She sat down heavily and shrugged the coat off her shoulders revealing her arms. They were rounder, fatter certainly, but wonderfully beautiful. The shape of her forearms as they joined her wrists, the hands, the fingers rounded and without visible veins to mar their whiteness. Her perfectly manicured nails were polished with a translucent enamel. Leonora had never looked at a woman's arms before and considered them an asset. Legs, yes. She had been envious of other women's legs, and had once called Martha's "eloquent" which had made Stephen laugh. I'll keep looking at her lovely arms and she won't see how appalled I am by what she has let happen to the rest of her, she thought.

"I'm going back to France soon. I'll go on a diet there."

"A diet in Paris!"

"Not just Paris. All over. I'll hire a Peugeot and go, *go*!"

"Shall we order? A drink?"

"Food *and* drink. Lawks! What an elaborate menu. What're you gonna have?" Was she slurring her speech to be modern? Had she already had a drink somewhere else?

"I'm going to have white wine —"

"I'll have a vodka martini, please," Natalie said to the young waiter who hovered by her side. She continued talking as if he had asked her to lunch. "On this diet you drink a vial of protein each morning when you wake up. Then you drink water all day and afternoon and in the early evening you give yourself a shot of glucose."

"I'm losing my appetite!"

"I'm not." She glanced at the adjoining table and asked the waiter, "What's your name? What's that lady having? I want some of that."

"Ray," he answered. "That's the Special Lunch today, striped bass."

"I'll have that with a baked potato."

"With sour cream?" he asked. She looked at Leonora and said quickly, "*No,* no. And a salad, bring anything that's fresh and nice. Now you order."

Leonora was ashamed to choose fattening things, feeling that to ask for what she wanted might be taken as criticism. While Ray was writing her order she heard Natalie whisper to him, "Sour cream, *please*."

The lunch was long, the food good, the talk saddening. Natalie felt restless, unhappy with herself and her life. "I drink too much, that's how I solve the messes in my life."

"Solve them?" Leonora wondered if the messes were her marriages. It puzzled her that Natalie still wore a wedding ring.

"Well, *you* know," said Natalie vaguely and went back to her food.

Glancing at Natalie while she ate, Leonora could see herself through the same critical eyes. I *have* changed, too, as much as she, but perhaps not as obviously. Where she has grown fat through her voracious appetite, I have grown thin by straining for things I cannot reach. She must see under the careful colors I have painted on my face, the shadows under the eyes, the network of intricate wrinkles not quite hidden in those shadows. The brown marks on the backs of my hands, the gray hairs near my temples. The things I see in the mirror every day and some days do not even attempt to hide. And did I remember to tweeze the stiff black hairs on my chin, the stray ones in my brows? Oh God, what's the use? I will never take care of it all and here I sit studying Natalie as if I were an appraiser. They had cared for each other as real friends long ago and now the texture of that relationship had been stretched and creased and neglected like their skin and hair and waistlines.

"Are you well, Nat? Is your health as good as it always was?"

Natalie hiccoughed. "What a funny question. No one but my mother has ever asked me about my health like that. I guess I'm okay. I sleep like a log. But then, I should. I drink shamelessly at night. And I eat too much, too, as you can plainly see. I'm sure there are reasons why and I don't want to know them. I just eat and drink until I stop thinking."

"Thinking?"

"Well, living. Oh, don't look shocked. I'm not contemplating ending it all. I'm just filling my gullet and my belly with liquor and food until something better comes along. How's your sex life?"

Leonora blanched. "Normal, I hope," she said lamely, hoping the subject could be avoided. Talking about sex with women embarrassed and bored her. She did not want to know about Natalie's private or sentimental hours any more than she wanted to share hers. What surprised her about herself was that she was fascinated to hear or overhear a man talk about his feelings and never tired of reading novels about marriages, affairs, liaisons, casual encounters. Lately magazines had started to include more daring stories and articles about men and women and how they felt about each other sexually and Leonora bought them, read the articles, tore them out of the magazines, and ripped them to shreds before disposing of them in the trash. Natalie would never do that. She'd read everything and leave it around wherever she was and talk about it with whoever would listen. She was going on now about a man, younger than she, a decorator, possibly homosexual, whom she was attempting to "turn into a — you know — man."

"Can that be done, I wonder," mused Leonora.

"My dear, I've done it," boasted Natalie and described her bizarre, brief adventure with Peter Holczer, whom Leonora pretended not to know. As Ray mixed the salad, Natalie flirted with him openly, adding to her order and discussing each dish to keep him involved until she dared to find out his last name and where he lived. Leonora made an excuse to go to the bathroom and when she came back Natalie was folding a piece of paper into her pocket.

As their table was being cleared, Natalie continued her seduction of Ray. By the time she had chosen her dessert, she knew his age, where he was born, and that he had a girlfriend. She did it so artfully it was difficult to know whether embarrassment or admiration was the suitable reaction, and looking for a moment at Ray's sweating face, Leonora could see a mixture of both. He did not seem to hurry, yet he lingered only long enough to murmur "Anything else?" and for some unaccountable reason all three of them laughed like friends before he turned and went back to the serving pantry.

Flirtation was a habit, formed early for Natalie, and so was gossip. She loved it and fed on it as greedily as she did the food.

"What're ya gonna have for dessert?"

"I thought I'd skip it."

"No, don't do that." Ray brought two desserts. For Leonora,

rum cake. He assured her it was a "speshiallity." It remained in front of her as Natalie gulped down her blanc mange. When he returned to take their coffee order, Leonora pushed her dish toward him, but Natalie reached across the table and touched the edge of it with her lovely, fleshy hand, indicating that he could bring it to her. She ate it carefully, pushing little bites aside on the plate to save, chewing, chewing like a pleased cow.

"I want to talk to you about Stephen's promiscuity, Leonora."

"Natalie, for God's sake —"

"I have to. Part of it is out of guilt, which I will explain later, and part of it is because I think you ought to know."

"I know everything I am supposed to know about my husband, Natalie. I don't ask you about your marriages —"

"And a good thing, too, my girl. Sham, absolute sham! Past history, anyway. But you have a child and you're trying to make something out of your life and I thought we should have a little talk."

"Why didn't you tell me a long time ago?"

Natalie smiled. "You seemed so defenseless, Leo, I simply didn't have the courage."

"And how do I seem now?'

"Furious."

"Well, I am."

Ray brought the coffee and served it with flourishes, fresh napkins waving, cups swooping down between them. Leonora reserved some of her fury for him but he did not meet her angry gaze. He concentrated on Natalie's constant approving winks and blinks.

"Let's get this over with, Natalie. What do you want to say?"

"I promised myself to tell you what happened the night your Nell was born. Let me tell you and it doesn't matter if you don't believe it."

"Tell me then."

"I'd had quite a lot of wine with lunch that day. Too much, I guess. I was not drunk exactly. But I felt hazy."

"Fuzzy?"

"Yes. I was tired and wanted to sleep, but when I lay down I felt sick. Really dizzy, waves of nausea, you know, disgusting. I took a bath. For once I didn't hang up my clothes or put anything away. I just sort of drifted around the room until I was ready for bed when the telephone rang. It was Stephen telling me you'd gone to the hospital and asking me to have dinner with him."

"And you accepted."

"For God's sake, Leonora. If you anticipate the whole thing there's no point in my telling you and it's hard to remember. Will you *shut up* please?"

"Nana said never to say that."

"We're adults now. Screw all that affectation. Screw Nana!"

"Natalie! Please!"

"O.K. Where was I? Oh, yes, I napped for a while and then another bell —"

"Doorbell?"

"Yes. So I pulled on my flying Josie." She imitated Nana's name for her dressing gown. It irritated Leonora to hear it from Natalie's lips. "All right, my negligee, my prettiest pink negligee . . . and groped around for the doorknob and there was your Stephen smiling at me as if it was the most natural thing in the world for him to be in my front hall. He waited there on the little bench while I got dressed and we took a cab to the Plaza."

"Did you choose the place?" said Leonora, remembering her wedding day.

"I don't remember. It's where I met Steve in the first place," said Natalie innocently.

"What did you talk about? He hates hearing about my childhood. Did you do that cruel imitation of Nana for him? He must have loved it."

"Let me tell it. I don't remember 'he said and I said,' I remember what happened. We had dinner and then he took me home. This time he came in and we had more drinks and sat in front of the fireplace as if there were a fire there, looking into it instead of at each other. He told me about some woman in —

I'm not sure, California? — and then he made what I suppose is called a pass." She stirred her creamy coffee. "He tried to touch my breast. I thought it might have been an accident. I didn't exactly pull away but I moved over toward the arm of the settee. I guess it's all going to sound exactly like two kids in the back of a car. But it wasn't. It all seemed quite formal and only when I realized that he was actually kissing with his tongue —"

"I'm sorry I can't bear to hear any more. Let's stop this."

"Leonora, don't be silly. Let me finish. I stopped him. I pushed him back. By then he was excited and he's a hell of an attractive man, so he's probably not used to that and didn't pay much attention, and he kept on until I got up and moved away. I was afraid he'd get angry but he didn't. He seemed to be suddenly sober and he started talking about a sort of 'relationship' we could have and the more he described it, the more I thought it must be the sort he'd had lots of. Don't get mad, I mean, he must have always had plenty of women, don't you think? And even though I know that shouldn't have been the reason I made him leave — *you* should have been the reason — anyway, my pride got all burning and I told him I could never be one of many. He pretended not to understand, so I was in the position of telling him what I thought his private life was, and since he was married and had just become a father, it was all a bit bizarre." She pronounced the word "beez-*ah*."

Leonora winced in irritation and asked, "Did he keep trying to —?"

"Yes, I suppose he did. Part of the time he was on top of me and I could feel his body moving and changing and I must have gotten away from him again because I swear —"

"— nothing happened."

"That's right."

"Oh, yes, yes, yes! That's what you've waited all these years to tell me and I'm supposed to believe it's hilarious. You must think I'm an absolute idiot!"

"Why?"

"To believe you."

"Why don't you believe me?"

"Because if it were true, you would have told me ages ago."

"You *are* an idiot. It isn't what happened or did not happen that's hard to tell. It was finding a way to tell you anything about it at all. Don't you think that's the trouble with most secrets and misunderstandings? That the moment to tell just doesn't happen or happens and goes by without anyone knowing it?"

"Is that all?"

"Unless you want to know about current events. Miss Pretty Young Rich, Sarah Lawrence's first —"

"Stop."

"All right, I will. It's just a typical office romance, I guess. But you should tell him to be more discreet. Lindy's isn't exactly a private club."

"Are you finished now? Because I don't want to start until I know you are damn well finished." Natalie shrugged. "All right. Now, listen to me. I'm talking to you out of anger, but I'm going to try to say something that will end this idiot quarrel — or whatever name you have for it — forever." She paused to take a breath. She took too long.

"*Well*, go on!"

"Shut up!"

"Leonora Ives!"

"Oh, I can say worse than that, my dear! I know all the words you spice your talk with. I know them all and how and when to use them. I know you think I'm a prig for *not* using them. Don't interrupt for a minute, will you? I think you're going to *like* what you're about to hear."

Natalie started to speak but wisely stopped herself. Leonora's deep breaths had calmed her and for a moment she thought, I *am* going to enjoy this.

"Listen. I *knew*. I have known for a long time that I am not the *one*, the only one. It killed me when I realized it. Killed my joy in everything. And what it damaged most is what I hate worst about myself and what *you* hate, too — my pride. I thought

I was the most important part of his life. I'm not. I thought I would die when I realized I wasn't. I didn't. If I had behaved any worse than I did when I found out, he would have let me drift out of his life taking Nell with me, and we would be utterly alone now and — keep still — it would have been my own fault. What I had to learn, and what I know you cannot teach anyone else, is the difference between a man and a woman. Not *all* men and *all* women, I'm not clever enough to have that figured out, but by studying him and really trying to understand him I found I loved him more. I didn't mean to use that word. *He* never does, doesn't say it about anything. I change it without changing the feeling: *Cared* for him more. Much more.

"I survived not being the only one, and the other — I don't want you to say her name and I'm not going to — is gone. I hoped he had forgotten her, for a long time I think he did. That was the time when I thought I had no rival, but I've learned humility. Maybe he *hasn't* forgotten her. Maybe he thinks of her when he is with me, sometimes. But I am still with him. And why you want to destroy the only happiness I have by telling me something you thought I didn't know, I'll *never* figure out."

"Don't try, my girl."

As Natalie pulled her coat on and took care with each finger of her suede gloves, she thought, I did it because I hate you. Hate your composure and stillness. Your remote politeness. Your skill at avoiding the horror and mess of everyday life. I did it the way people pick up guns and kill and are later told by experts that it was an act of passion, a once in a lifetime loss of control. Was it that? Could she have avoided it? If she had, there would have been no resolution to the long play of her life in which Leonora was always crowding her off the stage and into the wings. This easy act of cruelty killed in Leonora the awful composure that made her a perfect target. "I told you because I thought it would help you," lied Natalie. "You act so sickeningly complacent all the time, I don't see how any real man can stand you."

"I don't need your help. I want you to leave me alone." She

stood up and started to walk away. Natalie pulled at her sleeve.

"Leonora, you need friends. You need the truth. I am your oldest friend."

"I don't want any more friends. I'm free now. You've done that for me, Natalie. Good-bye."

She went into the powder room where a mouse of an attendant was reading a comic book. The little gray face poked itself toward her, "Can I help you, madam?"

"Yes. Do you have a cigarette?"

The mouse gave her one in exchange for a five dollar bill.

Whenever memory began for Leonora there was a dark room, a bed, sounds of night — a light from the sky or a streetlamp — and the endless going over and going over again the happening in the day that had damaged or betrayed her. Sometimes the rehearsing of the event was so strong that later on she felt sure she had acted on it. Confronted the teacher who had humiliated her, spoken directly to the boy (Karl, blond, thin, beguiling) who had ignored her. And time and time again faced her parents — one or the other or both together — with *her* side.

This pattern was so strong that as she grew older she came to know it would take the place of actual confrontations and betray her greatest weakness: to let the moment pass without dealing with it, to avoid the unpleasant, to be unable to see clearly her side of the argument until the argument was over.

And so it would be that evening, of course. Going home in the train she made plans to prolong her waking hours, for it would not be pleasant to stare at the ceiling and imagine her silent voice saying what she should have said at lunch, should have acted on months — perhaps years — ago. How could she have waited until she was an adult to look openly at the needs of a man? It was not surprising, considering how seldom she dared think about her own needs or her sister's or her mother's or even her friends'. God knows, she thought, what Natalie needs. It isn't food. It isn't telling me something that will shake me and make it hard for me to breathe and want to run away.

Cowardly. But I will not be with him. I won't confront him. I will lie down in my bed in the dark and think through what I must do to find peace and a way to breathe quietly again. I will not cross-examine. I will keep my questions in my heart.

Stephen left her alone in their bedroom. Excuses were easy and a life of pretense had made him a skilled dissembler. But he had never had an audience like Leonora. She knew him, read him, saw into him. When what she saw troubled her, she remembered her promise and did not question him. The pain in her breast tightened, the lines of a smile were on her face but the smile was not there to fill up the design. She, too, began to act. It was something she did not do easily or well.

It was at moments like these that he rose uncomfortably, mumbled an excuse, and left the room. Books became his refuge. He who had not been a reader as a child now sought out the books his friends and teachers had recommended. Titles that were on the summer reading list at the end of each school year now appeared on his bed table. The adventures — yes, that is exactly what they were to him — of Robinson Crusoe, Alice in Wonderland, Moby Dick, filled the time that used to be spent with her.

"Read them at the same time I do," he urged her.

"I've read them."

"Twenty years ago? You couldn't have understood them. Or appreciated their style."

Do you share them with someone else? she wondered, never having heard him use the word in reference to a piece of writing before.

Don't ask questions.

If it were true, if she were able to confront him with Natalie's information and ask him "Is it true, is there another person, an important person?" would he tell her, and if he did, what then? How would it be easier to live with the knowledge of its truth than it was to live doubting it or not accepting it.

Days went by, then weeks, and time calmed the panicky breathing, smoothed the frowns from her brow. How demeaning for both of them if she had been defiant or even pleading. Wasn't his duplicity a part of his personality that intrigued her? Because of his volatile nature, his curiosity and hunger, there was a place for her with him, too. She had a sense of sharing him with this other woman. He was divisible. He was more than most men were able to be. He had made her happy, and if he made her sad, that was always part of her life with him. She caught herself wishing that she might create in him the same kind of passionate interest, but she knew she could do nothing consciously to provoke it. Stillness. Waiting. That is what she knew how to do. Calm breathing. Clear brow. And time passing.

She lay on her bed and remembered his touch. She let her hands move over her body and at length, breathing gently and evenly, found herself wondering — as she often did — about her sister Martha and her lover.

Christmas meant little to Stephen. His father did not celebrate it. They exchanged only perfunctory Chanukah greetings as he got older. He hated the shopping and parties and made a point of avoiding both, so Leonora did his gift-giving. She wrapped their presents for the Woolfs and Nell ten days early. She loved the season. The Christmas story was the only part of the Bible she believed in, and when Stephen questioned her about it she defended her position. "I know, I *know*. It doesn't matter whether it happened! If the angel flew through the window! I can *see* it, Stephen. Don't spoil it for me." She hoped they would act out the Annunciation at Nell's school.

Nell spent the holidays with the Woolfs. Stephen and Leonora drove up to Purdys to be with her on Christmas Eve. The plan was to have dinner and go with them to the elementary school for a candlelight service where Sylvie was going to read her poem about the winter solstice, and Nell was part of the heavenly host. Leonora was as excited as a child. She missed Nell, even though she knew it was fun for her to spend some time with Sylvie Woolf, and in spite of Stephen's resentment of all the fuss about

Christmas, she hoped he might be swept up in the holiday happiness.

Leonora enjoyed the preparations. It was not often she went to much trouble with her clothing and grooming. She made a ritual of it, spreading out her clothes like costumes on her side of the bed. She polished her patent leather slippers with Vaseline, and put Nana's pearl and opal clip in a jar with ammonia to clean the stones. She selected her prettiest underthings, her most delicate stockings. She washed her hair and set it in loose curls. She examined her brows and plucked them. She cut her nails guiltily: Nana told her, "*file* and shape them, *file* and shape. Never use a scissors." She cut them too short and it hurt to use the file so she simply pushed back the cuticles and thought as always after such care how pleasant it was to be a woman.

Stephen walked into the bedroom and sat down on his side of the bed. She rushed to rescue her things. He grabbed her arm, then her hand, and moved himself over toward her, crushing the dress as he pulled her near. She hated herself for thinking of her clothes and it was not until he entered and spilled himself in her that she forgot them and tried to make her own pleasure equal to his. The time she was going to spend adorning herself with lotions and make-up was gone. Her preparations for the party were rushed and haphazard.

The familiar drive was brightened by the decorated trees glowing in the windows and in front of the houses on the road. She hummed the Annunciation carol, "Lo, How a Rose E'er Blooming."

"Don't hum."

"Sorry."

"There's something I want to tell you. I won't feel right if I don't. So listen."

"I'm listening," she said.

"It's over now, but I've had a little — well — fling with someone, a girl at the office."

"What do you mean, it's over?"

"She's going away. To Europe."

"Why?"

"A better job, I guess," he said with a rueful smile.

"And will you miss her?"

"No."

"You don't love her?"

"For God's sake —"

"I imagine she must feel terribly unhappy."

"And how do you feel?" he asked.

"I want to laugh. I mean, is this my Christmas present? Why did you decide to tell me now?"

"I thought of it when we were in the hay just now." The rueful look again, as if he expected her to comfort and forgive him. "And I suddenly knew it was time to tell you."

"Do I know her?"

"I don't think so."

"Has she ever called you at home?"

"Once or twice."

"I know her voice. She's asked for you just before you've picked up the extension. Is she nice?" She wanted to ask is she pretty, is she young, do you make her happy, but is she nice is what she said and it was not what he expected or wanted to hear. It was odd that her straight precise lips did not curve and twist into that ugly ridge across her face that meant she was trying not to cry. She remained in control and for some reason it made him furious. She supposed it was because he had prepared himself for a "scene" that did not occur and he felt let down. But it was more than that. The event itself had not been important enough to move her and it angered him. He teased her, taunted her, but she would not rise to his excited state. Finally she asked her name, "Will you tell me?"

"No." His tiny triumph.

"I think I'm going to be sick. Could you stop the car?"

"We'll be late."

"Oh God, Stephen! What the hell do I care if we're late? Let me out, please."

He stopped the car and as she opened the door on her side he gave her a rough push.

"What are you *doing*?"

"Sorry. I meant to help you."

She made herself stand outside the car for as long as she could bear the sting of the wind. She thought she heard his voice calling her through the closed window. No. He was humming a Christmas carol. She got back in the car. They drove to the Woolfs' in silence.

They drank too much champagne. It helped them behave easily toward each other and generously to their hosts and the other guests. They put Nell's and Sylvie's presents under the Woolfs' tree and promised to pick her up in the morning. She hugged them good night. Snow was falling. Leonora thought of their wedding trip as they got into the car.

"Aren't you going to say anything else about it?"

"Are you disappointed in my reaction? I'm sorry."

"Oh, Jesus. What does it matter?"

"*Does* it matter?"

He drove away without slowing or stopping, even though he knew Nell was standing on the terrace and calling their names. "Merry Christmas, Merry Christmas," cried Leonora through the closed window, wishing she could see Nell's face.

The silences grew. And when she could bear it no longer, she attacked him with a rush of words that would not stop. Sleep would interfere, but her tirade would start again the following day. He could not escape the sound of her voice or the dread of it in the silences.

There was no solution. She did not want to leave him. He did not have the stamina to leave her. He thought about it, of course. Even at their happiest times there was something in his head that made him consider being as happy with someone else, or perhaps happier.

The marriage continued and they were more and more lonely

together, while Nell watched and listened without judging.

Stephen started to plan his trip to Europe. He thought of hiring Janice Brewer on a full-time basis so that Leonora would have someone around to help her with the shopping and cleaning. He called her from his office and offered her the job with a good salary and the use of their car. Janice said she would think about it and took a week before she replied that, yes it would suit her. Having employed her, he then went to Leonora and suggested it to her. It took her a while to get used to the idea but after a day or two she agreed. "I'll call and tell her, then."

"Oh, I'll do it. There are some things I ought to ask her."

"No. I'll do it from the office in the morning and you can talk to her later in the day. I'll make the deal." So he called her again and simply said how pleased his wife was and spent the rest of the morning planning his itinerary. Spain — Barcelona and Madrid — then Paris, then London for a week, and then home. Twenty days counting the trans-Atlantic flights. He invented work to do in each city. His office arranged for the tickets, he would choose the hotels himself. He wanted to be free.

Stephen flew to Spain and did not write or cable for two weeks. His office did not seem to know where he was staying or on what day he would return. His secretary had taken her vacation at the same time.

Janice left after the twentieth day. A great deal of liquor, a box of stale chocolate mints, and a string of artificial pearls disappeared with her. She thanked Leonora graciously, if formally, for the extra ten dollars added to her final check.

Leonora and Nell were alone at Elm Hill.

Part Seven

AT THEIR annual birthday lunch — just one for the two birthdays — Leonora found herself half-listening to Martha's voice. Her own thoughts made hearing difficult and the crowded restaurant was noisy. She thought of how Martha was able to sustain a relationship through the years and across thousands of miles and she was not able to make her marriage work. How did Martha wait? Certainly her work had something to do with her strength. Her contact with things she loves, and sharing them, fills up so much of her life. But not all. She is so civilized, so quiet, but there must be times when she aches for love as I do, even from Stephen when he has been terrible to me. I will forgive him anything if he will call me to his side, to his bed.

"I do envy *you* sometimes, Leo. I'd like to have someone to come home to at the end of the day. I'd like to have had a child, I think. I know I make Nell into my child when she's with me, but I don't try to 'unmake' your motherhood."

"You want to possess her. You want her to be one of your splendid things."

"She's not a thing."

"No, but you see the world in terms of things that can be bought and sold, moved around, replaced. That's your job, isn't it?"

"Hardly. When I was with Miss Deane in the beginning I

used to wonder how she could bear to part with certain paintings or pieces of furniture. When we were on our searching trips the ecstasy she felt when she found something was so complete, so personal, it astonished me. Her pale face would get all flushed and her hands would shake when she wrote out the orders. I realized after a time that this was, of course, her way of communicating. *Through* the things she discovered. And that's why she selected her clients so meticulously. She couldn't bear to think of her things in the wrong places. When I figured this out — about her, I mean — I started to understand myself. I could have that joy, too, as soon as I was the one who made the choices. And that is what has saved my life. No matter how sad or lonely I am I have this game I play with matching the splendid thing to the splendid person. The people let me down sometimes, but the things don't. And they don't die. They live forever and I see them in my mind's eye. I don't forget anything I've chosen, no table or chair or mirror or rug. I see them all and love them all."

"And your face looks the way you said old Deanie's did. Oh, Martha, is that what it's going to be for you then? And nothing else?"

"How can you ask me that? I can't say to you, is it your marriage to Stephen and nothing else? Life isn't like that."

"But you think that anyway. That for me there is nothing else?"

"I don't know."

"How can you bear the long separations? I think I'd rather have nothing than have to wait so long."

"It's not always such a long time. I've learned how to wait and when I'm not with him I can *see* him. What made it possible was Hopecroft. I don't know how he got Sarah to let me do it, but every room in that house is *mine*. The colors, the furniture, most of the china, even the kitchen things. She gave most of her family things to her sister and wanted to start over with Larry and have new things."

"New antiques!"

"Oh, Leo, not everything I do is a thousand years old."

"I know it. I wish I could see Hopecroft."

"You might not like it. It's a bit formal for your taste."

"I have no taste."

"Don't keep saying that. It isn't true. You have marvelous instincts, but you just don't care enough about the way things look to take any real trouble. Lots of people are like that. But the first thing I do when I meet someone is to imagine a room or a house for them. In the beginning Larry used to let me describe rooms to him and the lovely part of it is that he lives in those rooms now."

"And Sarah didn't mind?"

"She is a mystery to me, Leo. She should hate me and she treats me like a friend. When I was working on the house it was the same mixture of business and social life I have with my other clients. And she likes me to be around her sons. She says I teach them what Americans are like. And another thing, she told her friends I was the best interior decorator and it is entirely thanks to her I have a reputation and a clientele in London. And Paris. And once I designed all the staterooms in a Greek millionaire's yacht in Monte Carlo. It's all because of Sarah. There's quite a lot of money in an account in Barclay's Bank as a result of the work she's gotten me. I leave it all there. It seems to belong to another life."

"It's fortunate you can support yourself. I mean, makes it easier, doesn't it?"

"For Larry? I don't know. We don't talk much about money. He's odd about it, just the way everyone else is. He's incredibly generous and easy about it sometimes and then he gets in a sort of panic about every farthing. It usually has to do with the morning's headlines. I had no idea how much a banker's career was mixed up with politics and what Mrs. Rumson used to call 'Current Affairs.' I wish I'd paid more attention to her classes."

"Nana's so smart about 'minny.' Why are we so dumb?"

"She *cares* about it, darling. That's the secret of everything: what you think of my taste, her expertise with the long green, and your —"

"I don't have any passion, do I?"

"I think you do. But I'm the last person in the world you could tell about it."

I want to, thought Leonora, oh, God, I want to tell someone, but instead she sipped her wine and asked Martha what she thought of Nana's health.

"It's Nell's health that interests me," said Martha. "Does she have any idea what is happening to you and Stephen?"

"What? *Nell*? I don't know how much she sees and hears. I try to be careful. But she has always known things without anyone telling her. It is almost impossible to surprise her."

"Not even Stephen? Oh, sorry, I didn't mean it to sound funny."

"When she says something subtle, Stephen's thrilled, but I think he liked her best when she was tiny and pretty and just smiled at him. But then he got jealous of her taking my time, and — I hate to say this — he's been so impatient with her slowness, he's beaten her."

"I can't believe that! Oh, no!"

"Yes, when he's unable to divert or astonish her — as he can me — he strikes her. And the next day, he's forgotten it. It is never mentioned. Even now when I want to run away from him, I am still fascinated by him, you know. *He's* never boring or dull. But he lives on people's reactions to what he says and does. He has a wife who exists in his existence and a child who can exist without any part of him. He can't understand her."

"Does he know what's wrong with her?"

"The slowness?"

"Oh, Leo, call it by its name. She's retarded, isn't she?"

"*No.* Absolutely not. They wouldn't have her in school with the others if she were. She's only a year behind, Martha. My God, some of the children in her class are bigger and older than she is."

"That's probably because their birthdays come at the end of the year." Martha meant to offer comfort, but it was no use. Leonora could not hear. She had started to gasp for breath. Martha held her hand until she had calmed her sobs. "Listen, Leo," she said, "who is the most important person to you in the world?"

"Nell. Of course, Nell."

"Then leave him."

Martha spoke with a sense of urgency that caught Leonora at once. Leonora drank her wine and listened.

"Go to a lawyer. We'll go now, after lunch, and see Jerry Walters. Find out what you can do. Get out of it before it's too late. Before he injures her. Or you. Or worse, before he makes himself so miserable that he does something more dreadful."

Leonora knew she was betraying Stephen but she could not stop. She heard herself tell Martha about the first time he had hit Nell — when she was young enough to believe him when he said, "I've never hurt you, have I, Nell?" She told about trying to hide her own bruises from her daughter — and it seemed a more terrible betrayal than the idea of escape. She watched Martha check the bill and pay it.

"You don't have to tell me anything else, Leo — honestly — I know a lot more than you think I do. And so does Dwight. I don't think Nana does because she wants to believe we're all just perfect so she —"

"— can tell the world," added Leonora and pulled her coat around her.

It was snowing. They could not find a cab and walked against the wind to 43rd Street, turning left on Fifth Avenue, and left again — as Martha directed — into the Bar Building.

The marriage ended. Leonora knew it, Stephen did not.

Jerry Walters prepared the documents and mailed them to Stephen's office. They were not forwarded. He came back expecting to find Leonora as he had left her.

"I'm not the same. I tried to explain it to you in the letter, Stephen."

"I didn't get any damn letter. Tell me what you mean."

"I mean I don't feel the same. No, that's not it. I do feel the same in many ways, but it is as if I were anesthetized. I'm existing without feeling, so I'm existing without caring."

"For me?"

"For our life together. I do care for you. I just know things won't get better. You'll be happier, too, when you get used to the idea."

"You are not going to leave me," he shouted suddenly.

"I've left you."

"No you haven't. I won't let you. We've got to talk about it, think about it more. We can make some arrangement, some way of managing. Come *on*."

"No."

"We *could* try again, if you want to," said Stephen.

"I haven't got the strength."

"That's ridiculous. You're as strong as a horse."

"You always say that and it makes me furious. I am not talking about physical strength. I don't have the character to make it work any longer. It saps my strength, whatever kind it is."

"Oh! Spiritual, certainly."

"Let's not quarrel. You asked me if I thought we could try again and I said no."

"I knew you'd say no."

"Then you shouldn't have asked. I don't want us to be angry all the time when we are separated and I want you to feel happy about Nell."

"A bit late for that isn't it? You've turned her into my enemy."

"That's a lie! My God, Stephen, have a little understanding of what I want for her. I know she needs a father —"

"— and she's never had one."

"I didn't say that."

"You think it. Well, Jesus! You're right. I kept waiting for her to grow up so I could talk to her and have fun with her. But it didn't happen."

"She grew up. Differently from other children, but in her way she could have been the best friend you ever had."

"That's what I wanted *you* to be."

"Then why did you destroy what I felt for you?"

"Leonora, I told you I was rotten when I met you. I can't be any better than I am. I wanted to make it work as much as you did. I am deeply sorry and I know you don't believe me. I know I'll never find anyone else like you. And if there were a way for me to change, I would. But I don't know how."

"All right, Stephen darling. That's enough. We can't say any more. But Nell is yours, too. She'll need you. Don't let her down."

"I can't talk to her."

"She thinks you're bored with her."

"I am, sometimes."

"Then we'll have to wait until you need her. And when that time comes, she'll be there."

Nell had watched her mother and father pull away from each other, without understanding the reasons. When Leonora told her she was not going to be married anymore, Nell said, "I know."

All the care, the trying not to shout or quarrel in front of her, the holding back of unsayable things until both of them were sure Nell was asleep, was for nothing.

"Will it make you sad, darling?

"Yes. Will it you?"

"It's sadder this way."

"And now — no more fighting?"

"That's right."

It was Symka Woolf who helped Leonora give up Elm Hill. Stephen refused to go back to the house; Martha was in Europe on one of her working-and-with-Larry trips; and Nana, who had offered to send Evans to give whatever assistance he could, had fallen ill with bursitis. She needed Evans to fetch and carry.

"It's perfectly all right, Mother, I'll manage. I have a good friend here who will help me."

"The foreign woman?"

"Yes. My friend."

Stephen moved his things out of the apartment, while Leonora, Symka, and Nell chose what to keep and what to sell, what to pack away for storage, what to take back to the apartment that would now have the front room for Nell and the big bedroom as a studio for Leonora. Arnold had encouraged her to write. She did not respond to his idea.

"Because you're a writer, you want everyone you care about to write. But a writer has to have readers. I couldn't write to be read, Arnold."

"It doesn't matter if it's published. If it's something you'd like to do, it will be good for you. Yes! I know you think I'm joking, but you'll feel better. Self-expression is like medicine. You've never had enough of it."

"I'm not sick, Arnold," she said, knowing she would not be able to put her private thoughts into words.

"You know I didn't mean that. It's simply that everyone has a story to tell. And yours seems to start when you went into that room and your father didn't answer you."

"For the first time."

"Call it that. See, you've got a title already. What is it, Leonora, that makes the relationship between a father and daughter so enduring?"

"Most men disappoint women, most fathers don't."

They changed the subject simultaneously, neither wanting to think about Stephen. The divorce had its effect on Arnold, too. Banished from the Elm Hill part of the Tannenbaums' life, he now was free to become a part of the fatherless family in the Village. He was pleased and shy the first time Leonora asked him to dinner, and brought Nell a bunch of carnations and Leonora a bottle of white wine.

Nell's reports at school were as good as most of the other students'. It was not possible to tell she was slower than the majority by the written comments or the marks she received.

It took her longer to accomplish the work; she played no part in the extracurricular activities but came home every day after classes to work on the assignments required for the following day. When Arnold was in the apartment, he discussed her work with her and Leonora was a careful guide and kept in close touch with her teachers. There was no question of doing Nell's work for her, but they both helped her organize her time.

Her friendships were casual but pleasant. She told Leonora, "You and Arnold are my friends."

"And your father."

"Yes. When I see him. But do you know, I'd rather be with the grownups *all* the time? I feel left out when you don't include me even when I know I don't belong."

"You belong, my angel."

"Not always everywhere." Her usually clear brow was tense with frowning lines of unhappiness.

"What do you mean, Nell?"

"Oh, nothing."

"Don't give that word as an answer, my darling, or no one will be able to help you. Tell me what it is — not now, later, if you prefer — and we'll talk about it."

"I think I have to talk to Arnold."

Leonora laughed softly. "Now *I* feel left out."

Nell touched her face. "Oh, Mother, Mother — you know I don't — I mean — it's about being Jewish."

That night at supper when Arnold asked Nell about her day Leonora took a chance, "While I get the dessert, why don't you tell Arnold something about —?" With Nell it was not necessary to finish a sentence. They often finished each other's thought.

"I will. I want to," said Nell.

Arnold reached for a cigarette. Nell gave him a cautionary look. One of her best subjects was science and health. She understood, without anyone helping her, the important relationship of the body and the mind. She did not take a pill or a sip of medicine unless the doctor insisted. She begged her mother to stop smoking and eventually Leonora did. She was having a harder time with Arnold. He put the match down. "I know you'll light it later," said Nell. "I can see you are going to distract me and then light it."

They sat on the couch and Arnold waited until Nell was ready to confide in him.

"At lunch today, three of the girls — Cynthia, Pam, and Yvonne — were sitting on one side of the table. I was opposite them. They were talking about the war and what Hitler did."

"Oh, *my* war?"

"Yes. We're studying it now. And Pam said, 'It must be awful for you, Nell, being Jewish.' "

"Awful?" asked Arnold.

"I don't think many of the other girls in the class are, but I never can tell anything about people until I talk to them. They sort of singled me out and I felt . . . so . . . uncomfortable. I know they think they are better than other people because they are all pretty and rich."

"Well, you know *that* much about them."

"They talk about money a lot. And about clothes. And boys."

"So do Jews."

Nell smiled. "Yes. But today, when Pam said 'awful,' I thought she pitied me. It made me want to go away. And I didn't know what to say to her because she hadn't meant to be mean. It's just, I've never thought this before, accept once or twice at Nana's."

"*Except.*"

She echoed the correction. "Yes, sometimes I think she feels the same thing about *you* as the girls do about me."

"Nell, it's a double problem," said Arnold, deciding to avoid the question of Mrs. Ives and her special kind of social anti-Semitism. "It's personal and general. Your personal problem will work itself out. Being a Jew — or part Jew — is like being dark or blonde or tall or short. You neither brag about it nor attempt to conceal it. It is part of what you are. But you have to know what it means."

Leonora brought ice cream and Hydrox cookies and sat cross-legged on the floor near the coffee table and listened, looking at their faces and loving them. His darkness, intensity, and concentration focused on Nell's eager, lovely face.

"What *does* it mean?" asked Nell.

He reached for his cigarette, ignoring the dessert plate and Nell pretended not to notice. She waited as he struck the match and inhaled deeply and thought that even though he was doing a bad thing he did it gracefully. He did not waste a motion. His fingers, relaxed and strong, caressed the cigarette tenderly. He loves it, thought Nell. I must not mention it anymore.

"I'll only have one, Nelly belle. And you can have my ice cream." Another puff, then smoke sneaking out between his lips and through his nose. Another, and he blew a perfect circle of smoke. She put her hand through it and he leaned back, grinning at her.

"What seems to you just an uncomfortable time at school is the result of centuries of superstition, which were revived in a way and made infinitely more dangerous by the man you are studying, Adolf Hitler. But all intelligent human beings know that almost everything bigots ascribe to a race or a religion is false."

"Is Nana a bigot?"

"No. I'll come to that." She did not let him off anything, this serious child, and he loved her for it. He looked at Leonora and caught the expression of tenderness still on her face. How happy it made him to be with them, to talk, to flow into their lives. He smoked again for a moment. "Listen, there are no basic differences among peoples, no ingrained or inherited tendencies to avarice or generosity." He felt himself getting to Nana before he wanted to. "There are habits of living that depend on the way one is brought up and educated."

"And for you?"

"My parents were Jews, but it was more a part of their social life than anything else. They lived in a Jewish neighborhood, their friends were Jewish. And at Erasmus most of my classmates were."

"And my father."

"Yes. We took it all for granted until we got hit in the head by a missile from a Gentile and then we threw something equally distasteful — a rotten piece of fruit if possible — right back at them."

"But I can't do that!"

"No. You're beyond that. It shocks and saddens me to think that children of good background and, as you point out, some wealth and education, should repeat the horrible racial obscenities on which Hitler rose to power."

Nell looked at him searchingly.

"What is it?" he asked.

"They called me a —"

"— kike? I thought it was something like that. It generally is. You didn't have to tell me. If your last name were Ives, they wouldn't have. They don't know what you are or who you are, but the important thing is that you do. You will never, will you, deny any human being his standing as a human being?"

"Deny?"

"Treat him less well. Avoid him. Call him names?"

"No."

"My own habit — which I practiced with your grandmother — is to let people know I am a Jew and then proceed to discuss anything they say. What is important is to get rid of fear. It is fear that makes people put up barriers to keep other people out in the name of protecting what they love."

"There are none here," said Nell and took Arnold's ashtray into the kitchen, where she washed the dinner things and thought about what he had said and how he had said it.

Nell asked her mother why Arnold never spent the night with them.

"We're friends, darling. Friends."

"I think he should be president."

The following Sunday Arnold took a long walk with Nell and connected what he had told her about being Jewish with being a survivor of a war and being part of the center of the experience of a time. "So few people are, Nell. That's why we are all looking for leaders. People want their presidents and kings and philosophers to find a path for them through the confusions of life. It's why I want to be a teacher, Nell. I've tried a lot of other things, but if I could help people understand what was happening in the world, I think I could have a better life."

"You teach me. And doesn't what you write teach other people?"

"Sometimes. How's the reading coming along?" Arnold had made a book list and posted it over Nell's work table. Her reading was slow, but her capacity to remember detail was prodigious.

"I'm reading some things for the second time. That's almost the best. Will you give me some titles tonight?"

"I'll give you some books."

"Thank you, Daddy — Oh, I'm sorry, I mean —"

"Do you miss your walks with your father, Nell?"

"I miss the walks. I don't miss my father. He took me with him because he felt he ought to, not because he wanted to and we both knew it but neither of us said anything, so it was funny, you know? It was better when he had a friend with him. They were always so nice to me and it was easier. I have always been afraid of my father, I don't know why."

Had she forgotten that he had struck her? That he had gone away for weeks without saying good-bye? That he had refused to speak to her when she had misbehaved? All that must have happened when she was too young to remember, but Arnold remembered it because Stephen had told him. Now it was his turn to pretend with Nell. He could not betray his friendship with Stephen and even if he did tell her what he knew what good would it do? Would it help to tell her the kind things he remembered Stephen saying about her?

"I think lots of children are afraid of their parents at one time or another. I think your mother is still a little bit afraid of Nana."

Nell laughed. "So do I! But it's hard for me to think of Nana as anything but my grandmother. And I always expect everyone in a family to love everyone else, don't you?"

"I did when I was young. I stopped thinking it when I began to read Russian novels."

Nell laughed again. "I'm serious," said Arnold. "And American and English novels, too. It was from books I learned about cruelty and unfairness."

"My father said nothing is fair."

Arnold had heard him many times.

The blizzard in March was the worst in fifty years. Traffic was slowed on all the highways coming in to the city and private cars were being towed off the side streets. Buses, subways, rented limousines were all off schedule. The city was quiet. Schoolchildren were sent home the first day of the storm and the following morning schools were closed.

"Why don't you stay here with us, Arnold? You'll never get your Jersey bus in this weather. I'll make up the couch for you."

"What will Nell think?"

"Nell?"

"Leonora, she's extremely aware of my being around all the time. If I stay here she'll think —"

"But there's nothing to think."

"Her imagination will provide a life for us. The life we don't have."

"Is it the life you want?"

"I want you to be happy. I love being your friend."

"You're the best I ever had." She left her seat beside him on the couch and began to move around the room as she talked. "I wish I — we — could have more. I know it's my fault. Since Stephen, I —"

"You don't have to say anything. I understand."

"How can you, when I don't? It's unnatural, the way I live now. Without anyone. But I changed after Stephen. I don't seem to want anything else."

"Do you mean you'd like him back?"

"Oh, no! That could never be, for either of us. He wouldn't come back and I could never live with him again. You have to *want* it more than anything. I remember feeling that way about him, even during the terrible times. And I don't remember when I changed. But if he came through the door now it would paralyze me."

"Couldn't you be friends?"

"Arnold, you are my friend. You are the most trustful — is there such a word? — person I have ever known. With Stephen I was always afraid he was lying to me. If he wanted to be my friend again I'd think he wanted something. You see, I've become suspicious. And I realize that in my time with him, I lied, too. It was easier. I agreed with him when I thought he was wrong, I did things I didn't really want to do, and it was only with Nell that I was honest."

"But he had a say in the decisions about her, didn't he?"

"Of course. I mean I risked his anger or disapproval when we dealt with the Nell part of our lives. And I think he trusted me as a mother more than he did as a wife."

"But you were faithful and trustful?"

"Oh, my dear, I was boringly, faithfully faithful! I didn't know how to be anything else. Martha and I are so stupidly old-fashioned we're afraid to do anything that will look wrong much less *be* wrong."

"Wrong?"

"We're not good liars or deceivers because we didn't get enough practice when we were young," she laughed. "We wanted our parents' approval and we wanted each other's, too."

"Do you, still?"

"Yes. In fact when I asked you to stay, it was Martha I was thinking about more than Nell."

They became a family during the three worst days of the storm and from that time on Arnold spent the night or the weekend with them in all weather, in many changes of season.

"I love it here."

"We love to have you, don't we?" said Leonora.

"Yes," said Nell, without looking up from the long scarf she had been knitting all week. "But don't you get scared you'll fall off the couch?"

Everyone laughed, but Leonora gave Arnold an odd look. He thought she was blushing.

"No, when I was in the Army the cot was narrower than this couch."

"You could always have my bed, couldn't he, Mother?"

"Or mine," said Leonora without thinking and then she blushed so intensely that she buried her face in her hands and made a sound so new and strange that Nell dropped her knitting and ran to her.

"Get me a glass of water, will you, darling? My throat is dry." Nell left the room and Arnold stood up.

"Oh, Leonora, you are a funny, unpredictable lady."

"I don't know why I said it! It was just sort of in the rhythm of the conversation, wasn't it? I wonder what Nell thinks I meant?"

"Ask her."

"Are you serious?"

"I don't know. Am I?"

Leonora knew she was depending on Arnold for her enjoyment of life. She shared Nell with him, the pleasures and problems of her life at school, the possibilities for her future. She felt at ease with him in every situation and, until the snowstorm, was not threatened by the possibility of changes in their future.

She was grateful to him for being genuinely interested in Nell's well-being without seeming to be troubled by anything that set her apart from other children. She had not resolved whether Stephen had held Nell's slowness against her, or was simply bored by all children including his own.

"I think I loved Nell too much for Stephen to bear," she said to Arnold. "I could not make him behave like a father and I have no idea how I seemed to him as a mother, but when neither of us was able to make the pretense anymore, I knew that for Nell's sake as well as my own we had to go away."

"And how did Nell react?"

"She saw him for a little while on a somewhat irregular, improvisational basis. He'd call and tell me to get her ready. Sometimes he'd come and pick her up and sometimes he'd call back and say his plans had changed. So, of course, the pretense went on. I'd try to explain to Nell about grownups and business and all that, but I don't think she believed me."

"And when he did come?"

"I'd get two reports. When he brought her back she'd tell me where they walked — he'd take her on long, long walks and was very proud of her stamina — and where they'd had lunch or dinner or whatever. When it started being in 'someone's' apartment I began to worry. He didn't try to hide anything. After he got home he'd call and tell me about how great Nell was and what a fine time they'd all had and then he'd describe to me the young lady he was with at the time. It was always someone young and pretty. I worried a little — but he assured me they were all 'crazy about Nell.' I don't know, I wanted it to stop, but I knew he'd never see her if I made a fuss and before you and I became friends there was no father figure in her life except her father."

"Well, I'm not that, anyway."

"No, you're — too young."

"I don't feel like a father to Nell. I love her."

"I know you do," said Leonora quietly. "I know."

On Thanksgiving Day Martha gave Nell a blue and white striped wool dress and a pair of red shoes. "I saw a little girl in Paris dressed this way last week and I have been so impatient to see you in them. Run to my room and change." Nell did not hurry, she moved happily toward the door with the packages in her arms and turned when she reached it. "Shouldn't I wait until Christmas? Or —"

"No. Now! I have other things for your birthday, you goose! Wait, I'll come and help you."

Martha was pleased with the fit of the dress and the shoes, but something was wrong. Of course! In Paris the little girls wore short hair and bangs. "Shall we surprise everyone?" she asked Nell conspiratorially.

"If you want to. How?"

"Sit down, darling."

Martha cut off the thick reddish-brown hair in handfuls and when the back and sides were trimmed to her satisfaction she said, "Think how comfortable you're going to be. And let's make one more change." She picked up the scissors and comb again and cut perfect straight bangs across Nell's wide forehead. "Now! Wait! Don't look yet." She found some witch hazel and dampened Nell's hair with it, shaping the new cut into natural waves. Then she patted her face and neck with the lightly stinging liquid and smiled with pleasure. "There!"

Nell looked at her reflection and saw a new person. The dress, of course, made a difference. But the shape of her hair — particularly the bangs across her brow — made her reach out and touch the glass. "Who is it?" she asked.

"It's you, my angel!"

They went into the living room and the effect on the family was stunning. Nana cried out, "Ye Gods! Mart! What hath you wrought?" expecting everyone to laugh. No one did. Leonora jumped up as if she had been struck, ran to Nell, and hugged her. Dwight was astonished. "Why'd'ya do that to her? She looked great before." Arnold watched Nell's face, looking for a true reaction, but found only her sweet grin, so he followed Leonora and put his arm around her. Leonora was shaking with rage. In a few moments it was time for dinner.

Leonora did not speak to Martha for the rest of the day.

In the elevator Nell felt her mother's hand patting her shorn head.

"How come there are flowers in the winter at Aunt Martha's house? *We* never have them."

"Ask *her*, why don't you?" Leonora answered.

There were lots of taboo subjects, but why flowers on the mantelpiece of the prettiest living room Nell had ever seen? It seemed important. An answer to a small riddle, or a door into the adult world.

As the months went by, Nell's hair grew back, the lush mahogany waves reappeared around her face and she formed the unconscious habit of pushing the bangs to one side. It was something she did for the rest of her life, a languid circular motion of her wrist and fingers as if she were washing her face or putting aside her cares.

Part Eight

TO CELEBRATE the completion of work on a sixteen-room Fifth Avenue apartment for a member of the French diplomatic corps, Martha called Poll's and had an afternoon tea party catered for her assistants on the job. They assembled in the sitting room of the ambassador's suite. Elma, her maid, came in to serve. Champagne, chicken sandwiches, chocolate cookies, and tea. It was remarkable to see the men and women who had painted the walls, placed the furniture, and wired the electrical appliances move so gracefully and naturally in the setting prepared for visiting royalty and leaders of society.

The beauty of the objects in the room gave it life. Martha looked at each thing longingly, remembering where she had first seen it, how she had bargained for it, when it was shipped back to the United States. One of the vases was found in Aspery's in Bond Street. Larry had seen it and said, "It is like you," and wanted to give it to her. It was too fragile, too expensive, and far too special for her to own. Her pleasure was to place these splendid things in the sight of others. And until she met this man who selected the ruby fluted-glass vase, her craving for love had been satisfied by her connection with the craftsmanship and imagination of artisans of the past.

"Let's finish every drop of this nectar," she said, and between sips of tea her guests emptied their wineglasses.

Elma packed the boxes with the Deane-Ives silver service, and the glasses and dishes to be dropped off at Poll's. Martha took a last look through the rooms to be sure that everything visible was welcoming.

By six o'clock Martha was too tired for her usual brisk walk to her apartment, so she hailed a taxi. The traffic jammed, tempers short-circuited. Her driver was yelling at other drivers, trying to make lights that had already turned red. She was pointing to her awning when the screech of his brakes made all other sound go dead. The cab crashed into a truck. Martha was hurled against the front seat. Her doorman heard the noise and ran up the block toward the car.

"You go in Miss Ives, I'll take care of this," he said.

She obeyed, trying to hide her face with her scarf. The pain was less troubling than the sight she knew was there. She did not want the elevator man to see it.

The doctor came and went. There was nothing to do but wait for the bruises to heal.

Nell did not want to look. It was worse than a black eye. The left side of Martha's face was still swollen red, and the purple marks, splotches of ugliness, were too painful for her to cover even with her pink swan's-down puff smothered in talcum. She tried it, but the powder stuck to her skin like flour to dough and she could not take it off. Her face was raw and both eyes bleary as she watched her niece tiptoe hesitantly into the room.

"I know it's hideous, darling. I should wear a veil. It's dear of you to come. No one else in the family has the guts."

"My mother *told* me to come," said Nell, innocently, unable to think of a polite lie.

"Did she! Well, I'm lucky. The only accident I've had in my life and I'm grateful to it. You were brave to come today."

Nell smiled. "I feel quite sick looking at you! I'm an awful coward, hate the sight of blood. The scent of the flowers is — so strong."

"Oh! I put some perfume on the light bulbs. The doctor just left and the place smelled like his medicine bag. Poor darling, it's like an opium den. Musky."

If her aunt Martha's taxi had not crashed, the series of Saturday tea parties in her apartment would not have started so soon.

The child was full of questions, the woman wanted to tell her story. Martha knew things about Nell's mother and father, about her own mother and father, and even their parents that she wanted to tell. Someone should know this family's story. Why not her sister's child, the only child she'd ever loved? Maybe it will help her to understand living better than we did. We haven't made a good job of it. Will she? Martha used to beg Nana to tell, explain, remember, but she was always too busy. When Martha talked to Nell, she tried to tell her the truth. What she couldn't figure out were the causes. If there is a choice between cruelty and kindness, or between sensitivity and foolishness, why had the people in her family behaved so carelessly? she wondered. But if she were given another chance, she would make all the same mistakes, and she had had more chances than Leonora, even though she'd never had a child.

It was spring. There were lilacs on the mantel, forsythia and pussy willows in the hall. But it was the aroma of the bouquet of pink carnations near the chaise longue that overcame Nell. Like an aphrodisiac, it made the shape of time change and communication simpler. It was part of the story.

"I asked my mother something. She wouldn't tell me. Will you?"

"Ask me."

"I will someday," said Nell.

"I won't live forever. Ask me now!"

Nell got up slowly and went to the mantel and fixed the flowers just as she had watched her aunt do. It was easier to change the subject from another position, and perhaps the answer to her question would be in one of the stories. That was always her hope. Or was it, as she sometimes caught herself wondering, that the answer was the one thing she did not want to know? A key to a door she might *not* want to open?

"I'll tell you whatever I can," smiled Martha.

"When I come to see you, when you open the door, the first thing I notice is the smell of the flowers from your room. It's like a garden here, and I love it."

"Yes?"

"So I said to my mother how I loved it and wondered why you always had flowers and we didn't."

"Ah." Martha reached over and took her hand. "I said I'd tell you, so I will, but —"

"What?"

"Nothing, dear. The flowers are a present."

"Every day?"

"No. Once a week the florist brings them."

"Oh. The florist?"

"Let's have some tea? Or cocoa, that's what you still like isn't it?"

"Yes, please."

They shared the making of the sweet, hot drink and sat in Martha's flower-filled room for the rest of the afternoon, occasionally returning to the kitchen to refill their cups. Martha began her story. The one she had waited so long to tell, and long after Nell had left, she stayed in her chair, holding the black lacquer box filled with her diaries and datebooks, looking at the pages she knew by heart. Even the blank ones, she knew exactly where they came and why. And the pages crammed with names and places and codes and initials. Private, personal, with meanings too secret to speak. She rested in her chair and let the memories of her life with Laurence Parrish flood her senses.

For Martha Ives, the day she told Nell her story would always be one of those days set apart in memory. She had lived so long with her secret — her love — and having it secret seemed to sustain and protect it. Then suddenly one afternoon looking into the face of a young girl, an impulse deeper than she could control rose in her and she began to confide her inmost thoughts. She felt no embarrassment and no sense of time. Shy about being the one who talked in almost all her other relationships, even with Larry, Martha was made bold by the unquestioning gaze in Nell's dreaming face. She felt like a teacher and her subject was the secret of happiness, of perfection. She wanted to share what it was like to stop asking questions about life, to receive answers. Laurence Parrish was her answer. If she were able to tell the truth, to say how hard it was some of the time to make their life balance, perhaps her Nell — Leonora's Nell — might dare to look for something, someone to fill her need for answers.

When she was not much older than Nell, it had been difficult to keep her private life private. She had chosen to love men who were not legally free to love her. She had rarely lived with a man. She had had delirious weekends, afternoons, mornings, but seldom a day-after-day lover, friend, or partner. As she approached her thirties she stopped questioning that part of her life and decided to live without looking for someone to share her life. At that moment she met Laurence Parrish. They were at the same party. She was there because Natalie had asked her to join her in renting a sedan to drive out to Sand's Point on a Sunday in September.

They arrived in time for a lavish lunch, and when that was over, the guests were taken to various rooms to freshen up. Before dinner they were served wine and liquor and hors d'oeuvres of many varieties by servants appearing and reappearing only when they were needed to take away one glass and reappear with another. Martha did not get tight, but she had trouble remembering the exact sequence of events of that afternoon and evening. It was easier to remember four days later, and sweetly sober, the sensation of being held gently in Laurence Parrish's arms and being kissed. The brief space of time with him had led up to that perfect moment and the rest of her life, her own choice of a life, was planned and arranged so that she could be near him. The possibility of another kiss was always between them.

She could not write a poem, a book, a song. Knowledge of color did not mean that she could paint, a sense of design did not prepare her to draw. Her sketches were an embarrassment to her and the moment they had been seen by the carpenter or an architect's assistant she would retrieve them and throw them away. She had not written a letter, even to Larry, that had any worth beyond the connection with him it recorded. He saved them and returned them to her — "with more than gratitude," he said, "they save my life" — and when she looked at them, reports of unimportant happenings, the only thing she loved to see again and again was his name.

It was his strength as a man and as a lover that gave Martha a new identity. She began to think that what she did could have importance for others, her behavior, her work might make a difference in the world in which she existed until then without true confidence.

He listened. She wanted to express her thoughts to him. "Write them down," he said. She obeyed. It was not an order, a suggestion, but nothing could prevent her from sending him a letter every day.

He talked. He had led more lives than she. He had traveled, read more. He had loved more, learned more.

He remembered. He was able to tell what had happened yesterday or twenty years before and it was newly minted. He took her there in the telling.

He invented. He made not only her life but the life around them full of possibilities.

He knew what things were worth. Ideas, time, thoughts, personalities. He took nothing for granted. Even himself. There was a knowledgeable pride in him. He had worked hard and long to achieve the life he now led and shared.

He had no God. Neither did she. Yet she was often moved to

thank, to pray to something beyond what she knew, because he was in her life.

They were together whenever, however, possible. Parties, luncheons, card games. Looking across tables, rooms, sometimes a glimpse from across a street, getting in or out of a taxicab. Waving hello, waving good-bye.

Early in their loving, after her first voyage across the ocean to be with him, Martha became ill. She was furious with herself, frightened that her nose blowing, coughing, spitting, and general sick-ugliness would make Larry turn from her. On the contrary, it drew him to her. He was fascinated by medicine and read all the journals he could find. Two of his closest friends were doctors with offices on Harley Street and each day he greeted her with a new cure. "You can try it or not," he said, offering her pills, elixirs, powders.

They continued to touch and explore each other with a special gentle pleasure. "I never want to tire you."

"You never do. And talk to me. Tell me things . . ."

"When did you know?"

"That I wanted to be with you?"

"Yes."

"I saw you get out of the car. I watched you say hello to our hosts and then the most extraordinary thing happened. I felt a pang of jealousy that made my head ache."

"But I —"

"No, nothing like what you're thinking. You were alone for a moment in the living room and you looked at the things in that room the way other women look at faces and hands and eyes. And bodies. You took in the colors, you listened with your eyes. And I saw that look of rapture on your face for a room full of splendid things and I wanted it for myself."

"And you said, 'May I be of any assistance.' "

"And it all began."

She fell asleep breathing irregularly.

He watched her lying in the bed with the moisture shining on her brow. He had promised her once to take care of her if she were ill, but it was a joke between them as she never seemed to flag in energy or spirit. Now she was parted from him no matter how close he stood beside her or how gently he touched her cheek. The noise of the traffic woke her from time to time and reminded him of Belgravia forty years before. The driveway was gravel and macadam. When it rained the street filled with mud. At the corners there was a "crossing sweeper" who was tipped a penny for clearing a path for a passerby. The carriages got splashed and muddied, their polish ruined. When Larry was young, lying awake in bed, day or night, he could identify the cabs from the sounds of the horses' hoofs: the hansoms were quick clip, clip, clips, the "four-wheelers" much slower, and the dog carts were faint and fast. When an important person fell ill in the neighborhood the whole block would be covered with fresh straw to deaden these pleasant sounds. He would miss them in the night when he was trying to fall asleep and would wonder what kind of illness had struck and where. The freshness of the straw would last only a short time and it would have to be raked up in a soggy mass and carted away by the crossing sweeper. The following morning at the breakfast table his mother would report to his father the precise details of the invalid's situation and Larry wondered how she had found out.

The hours went by and Martha did not wake.

He began to doze and the sounds blurred, not from the spreading of straw, but the falling of snow already making its own blanket across the dark city, white and silent in the streetlight.

Larry's father had wanted him to follow him into the diplomatic service. He had been attached to the American embassy in London for most of his career and, watching his son grow into handsome manhood, felt that he would have a great chance for success as a diplomat or perhaps a statesman. But Larry did not pay much attention to his school work and was more successful in his appearances at his father's side when he was representing his chief, Whitelaw Reid, at receptions for visiting dignitaries.

One of his father's duties was to arrange for the presentation of young American girls at Court. The lists for this social honor were submitted to the Lord Chamberlain months in advance and reviewed scrupulously by the staff at the embassy. In the spring when Laurence was seventeen, an important senator, the chairman of the Foreign Relations Committee, arrived in London with three of his four daughters. Two were not yet in their teens but the eldest, Sarah, a small and gentle girl, was the senator's favorite child and on the liner coming over he decided that the high point of their trip to Europe that summer would be to present this red- headed blue-eyed charmer to the king and queen. Sarah did not care about it one way or another; what excited her was the possibility of roaming around a city that had been real to her from her reading and re-reading of Charles Dickens and Arthur Conan Doyle.

Senator Lettington put through his request the moment the family was settled in their suite at the Savoy. Whitelaw Reid explained that the list was full, but anxious to please the senator, said that he would have his aide look into the matter. Laurence made all the correct calls and a few on his own to no avail. One evening after work at the embassy he walked over to the hotel, asked for the senator's room number, called him on the house telephone, and introduced himself. The senator, feeling sure that young Mr. Parrish was the bearer of good news, asked him to join the family for tea in the lounge. Ten minutes later they stepped out of the lift, the youngest girls standing back to allow their handsome mother to pass, then the senator, and then Sarah who looked directly at him and smiled.

"Poppa, it's not going to work. It isn't, is it?" she asked the embarrassed Laurence who was attempting to introduce himself to this attractive, noisy family. The senator did not hear her question. He welcomed Laurence to their group, and they sat down to a delicious tea, talking of the various plans for the women while the senator did his work, and making arrangements for theatres and operas for them all to attend in the evenings. The subject of the presentation was saved until last. Laurence felt Sarah maneuvering the conversation toward other things, saving his life or at least his job. When the senator beckoned to the waiter to remove the tea things, Laurence began his feeble explanation. The senator looked disappointed but not angry. Sarah's mother repeated, "It don't matter, it don't matter," in her twangy, attractive Midwestern American accent.

"I tried my best, Mrs. Lettington, Senator, Miss Lettington —"

"Sarah."

"Do you think you'll be coming back to London next year?"

"I'd like to come every year. Or live here," said Sarah.

"That don't sound like an American girl to me," her mother said and laughed.

"I haven't felt American since we got off the boat, Momma. In fact, on the boat the stewards made me want to change the way I talk. I love the sound of English voices. You sound quite English, Laurence Parrish. Even your name sounds English to me."

"I've lived here most of my life. I'll be going back to America for the first time in seven years next fall."

"Well, maybe I'll go home with Momma and Poppa after all."

The bill was signed, good-byes said, and the incident of the failure to be presented at Buckingham Palace seemed forgotten. Larry went home feeling he had handled it all rather well, and the next morning was astonished to be sent for by Mr. Reid and scolded unmercifully. This was not the way things were done at the embassy. The call was in the worst possible taste. It would have to be reported to the foreign secretary. Laurence was preparing to lose his job when Mr. Reid paused to answer a telephone call. It was Mrs. Lettington asking for the nice young man's address and telephone number. She wanted him to join them for a day at the races on Sunday. Mr. Reid started to laugh before he replaced the receiver and Larry joined in with relief when he understood that his gaffe was not only forgiven but seemed, for the present, to be approved by his mentor.

The Reids invited the Parrishes and the Lettingtons to Crichel, their estate in Dorsetshire, for a weekend.

For Sarah it was not like falling in love. There was no falling sensation at all. It was evenly spaced, her emotions rising and subsiding with his in a most natural, pleasant way. Often they tried to think of the moment when they knew they would marry, but neither could say for certain. Their first encounters were constantly supervised by parents or servants, but at Crichel, walking through the empty ballroom, without embarrassment Larry took the opportunity to embrace her, and her warm lips returned his kiss as if it were one of many dear kisses, not necessarily the first. How lovely, how comfortable, how friendly it was. Sarah had a few twinges of fear. Her mother had told her, "To find someone so dear means you will lose him. I always keep a tight rein on your father."

Laurence and Sarah were married on March 7, 1916, four years after their first meeting. They remained married throughout their lives, had children they loved, and were envied by their friends.

They made it look easy. They combined his career at the Morgan Bank with a social life that included travel and pleasant entertainments. They both loved racing and boating and they were evenly matched as partners in doubles on the tennis courts or as part of a foursome at golf. They read each other's signals swiftly in every game they played. Sarah made him laugh when he was sad. He contented her.

Neither his wife nor his lover would have changed the balance of their triangle if it were in her power to do so. If there were times when either of them thought of conceding to the other she did not, because it would have destroyed the man they both loved.

When Martha recovered she told him, "You heal me. You make me well." When she was with him — or when her ability to imagine herself with him was strong enough to make time's shape change and *be* with him — she was not afraid of life and did not judge her own too harshly. But in the times between, the stretches of days, weeks, sometimes months when there was no sight of him to reassure her, she fell into the habit of hating her life. The same life she loved and chose and worked to make perfect became a source of poison and pain to her. Her accomplishments were as nothing, her hopes empty. What did it mean, after all, to arrange rooms and houses and furniture for people? How necessary was it that anyone be surrounded by lovely things? Why not always the simplest and — yes, she had to ask — why not what cost less rather than more? And what of the men and women she spent her hours with? Not simply her clients — the rich, the attractive, the clean-smelling, easygoing, fast-disappearing upper class — but the other decorators, the men who did not seem to be men, the women who were more like men, the workmen in the shops who cared less and less about the quality of the work done and the date delivered?

Now, like Miss Deane, she had lived long enough to see rooms she had decorated destroyed by time or fire or more often by change of taste. The children of her clients rarely called on her; more often they simply threw out what she had done and started over. Precisely what *she* had done in many cases at the beginning. Was it time for her to stop now? Let others take over? No, she had too many ideas. No matter how the nightmares of uselessness tortured her, when the day came she would want to try again. To find the perfect color, the most beautiful lamp with a shade that enhanced it, a rug that could draw the room together in a subtle, comfortable way, a pair of white Staffordshire saltglaze hawks to grace a mantelpiece.

"The silliest thing I ever did as a professional decorator," Martha told Larry, "was to let Mrs. Conway's sister-in-law, Elida Nugent, buy some of the chintz I had chosen for her living room at Bar Harbor. It was an outrageously bright blue and red affair

— hibiscus red against the blue of the sky. The stunning thing was these big shocking pink flowers. Well, Elida begged me for the number of the sample about three months after I finished her house. It was out of stock and there were endless phone calls and finally, finally three yards of the damn stuff was found and sent right off to her. She took it to a fancy dressmaker. The dress was ready in time for Elida's housewarming party and the first glimpse we all had of it was when she came down the stairs to greet her guests. Two huge hibiscus made her bosom look as if it had caught fire, but the worst thing." Martha laughed. "The worst thing was her — ass! If the two blazing flowers looked absurd on her buz, what do you think they looked like spread across the generous dimensions of her bottom? And when she made it to the couch and sat down on the original brilliant blooms! If she had planned it, it couldn't have been funnier. It was the sort of thing that was even funnier if one didn't notice straight off. As the evening wore on, everyone was sharing in the joke and loving it. I never should have given her the number of that sample." She wiped away a tear of laughter. Larry filled her glass with champagne and laughed with her.

"I want whatever skill and taste I have to connect me with people; all decorators do, of course," said Martha smiling. "But it's one of the easiest professions in the world in which you can make an enemy in a moment. Unless you're able to lie, or dissemble, you're always hurting others' feelings. Someone asks, 'Do you like this?' and forgetting to edit yourself, you say, 'No' and that's the end of a friendship."

"You exaggerate," said Larry.

"No, honestly. I've seen it happen. I mean, to myself. I came into a room once and the walls were so green I thought I'd burst into screams. I heard my own voice say, 'This green is *too* green!' and the man standing next to me turned on me and said, 'Too green for whom? For what? For you, you silly bitch?' He was the decorator!"

"Did it matter?"

"Yes. I was so sorry I'd hurt him, but worse was to come. He sort of dined out on the story and made me sillier and more fatuous each time he told it. By the time it got back to me, I had thrown a fit in the room and had announced to everyone in it that he had no talent. I think he succeeded in losing me some clients just through ridicule. It should have taught me a lesson but I know it wasn't the last time I've talked when I should have kept my mouth shut."

"It's a nice mouth. Let me kiss it. I hate green walls."

When they exchanged memories, he often felt like an Englishman. His life in London as a boy was so unlike hers at the Camp and in the city.

"At Chesham Street we had a butler *and* two footmen. My mother entertained beautifully. I was not aware of the cost of food or clothes or servants then. Nowadays it would seem we lived like some of the royalty she entertained. Even as a boy I knew that precious things must be guarded. I used to sneak down to the kitchen at night to see Joshua, the servant, who slept in the washtub. His job was to guard the silver. I watched him sleep by the light from the cloudy skylight over which — eventually — my father had a bathroom constructed. That made the house a place of luxury on a par with any one on the street. But the addition of that special room meant that the kitchen, scullery, and pantry were darker than ever. The coal fire was kept burning day and night in the long winters of rain, mist, and thick yellow fogs. Being below the level of the street there was little chance for the air to circulate and the odor of the previous meal hung in the room for hours. Only on baking day did the lower floor smell the way I thought a kitchen ought to."

"Most of my clients think kitchens can still be that way. But it's one of the first rooms I deal with. I love to make them bright and clean and, most of all, cheerful. The best one I ever did, for a Chicago town house, had a day bed in it — in a sort of alcove. Why shouldn't the cook or the butler or your poor silver-watcher have a place to rest once in a while?"

"Odd. I never thought of you doing kitchens."

"*And* bathrooms! Of course we take them for granted now, but I can imagine the excitement when your father added yours to the house. I pick out everything, my dear, the towels and bath rugs, everything!" She beamed with pride in her work.

Martha knew how funny she must have looked to her clients, but she could not resist pushing their couches, tables, and chairs around the rooms she was decorating until the relationships were congenial. She had done it as a child in playrooms and schoolrooms and now she could hardly enter a room without yearning to shove a piece of furniture a few inches this way or that, or to move a piano from one part of a room to another. She knew she should wait for help and for the opinion of her client, but she could not. She knew where things belonged. That's what they were paying her for, weren't they? But she caught herself at it sometimes — her rearranging — and could see how awkward and ridiculous she was.

It was, she thought, the only time she could be caught in an undignified position. She had trained herself to be always in control of her feelings and her body. To avoid making faces of pain or pleasure, to hold back the sounds these emotions evoked, to go through life as silently as possible. To live without conflict or noise or show. For this reason she was often spoken of as serene when her heart was pounding within her chest and beads of sweat were forming under her perfectly pressed clothes and spotless underthings. Her toes might be curled into claws inside her polished shoes but her brow would be smooth, her hands folded in her lap. Her stillness was her strength.

Once Larry told her how unsettling her composure was.

"It's a family trait I think," she said. "You should look at my mother's and sister's faces. And especially at Nell's. Even my father — I remember how comforting it was to look up and see him looking at me with calm eyes."

Her calm meant quiet for those around her. People sought her out so that they could take something of her inner peace with them. And they sought her out because it was maddening to find this control in someone who certainly had to deal with the same problems of daily living everyone else did. Why in God's name didn't it leave a mark on her? When they were schoolgirls, Natalie threatened to slap her unless she showed some feeling. "I *am* feeling," said Martha, defensively, knowing what the trouble was. You have to feel what the other person wants you to feel.

Martha resembled the portrait of her grandmother, Eleanor Pringle, that hung in Nana's living room. Some of her strength must have found its way to mix with the sperm of her gentle grandfather and eventually spill into the lives of those living now. Not enough. They were weak compared to her. Eleanor impelled the family across the country, forced it to grow and thrive on an island of its own in the midst of a glorious lake in the Adirondack Mountains, and led the little band to the city of New York whenever she felt it necessary to spend her money and her strength to influence her relatives to do what she wanted them to do. Once, only once, her husband was heard to murmur "slave driver," but the embarrassed guests had pretended not to hear. What they heard was the sound of money in her curiously gentle voice. "Please try it my way" was her way of giving an order. Martha had inherited her strength, but her best features reappeared in Leonora — as if the cells had been split — to rejoin with greater power and appear a generation later in the countenance of her sister's only child. She heard Larry's voice again.

"I was going to say your look is perfect. But that isn't a word you can use for anyone is it?"

"It shouldn't be. And I'm not. I'm just trying to get through one day to the next."

"But were you always like this? I mean, as a child?"

"I can't remember. I can't see myself as a child. The only time I ever made a decision not to show what I was feeling is too ludicrous to talk about."

"Talk! I've told you so much about my life. Tell me yours. Anything."

"Everything?" Martha smiled and decided to tell her slave story.

"When I was six, I think, or seven, I lost my soul to my brother Harrison in a game of marbles." She paused and sipped her drink.

"Wasn't he the one who —"

"— drowned? Yes. It broke Nana's heart."

"And you?"

"Oh, darling, it's so strange, but what I'm going to tell you is almost my only important memory of him."

"Tell me."

"He had the most beautiful collection of glass marbles and although I didn't collect anything and I don't think I *really* wanted them, when he offered to lend me a few to play with I accepted and I did win a few of his in the first few tries. We played marbles constantly. I liked it. I hated races and ball games and even swimming didn't interest me, but sitting cross-legged on the lawn shooting immies was fun."

"Did you talk a lot, too?"

"No, that was part of what I liked. He didn't say much. We just concentrated on the game."

"And then what happened?"

"Hmmm?"

"The slave thing?"

"Oh. He wanted to play for pennies, but I hated to gamble. We played for matchsticks for a day. Then we went back to trying to win each other's marbles. I'd been pretty good in the beginning, but the more we played, the more I lost. I guess I was getting tired of it, but I didn't want to admit it. How he made me agree I don't know, but he said after he'd won my last marble — a lovely amber glass one — 'Now I'll play you for your right foot!' "

"Your *foot*!"

"Yes. He said if I lost the next set, he would win my foot. I didn't think of what it meant and we played and I lost and from that moment on, whenever he wanted something, he'd say, 'I want my right foot to go and get me such and such.' "

"And what did you do?"

"I laughed at him. I said my foot couldn't do anything without the rest of my body agreeing and we got into a terrible argument, which he won, and for the rest of that day, perhaps longer, I did what he told me to do. I didn't mind at first. It was like a new game. But it went on and on and the next morning I didn't want to play it anymore. He insisted and I refused. We stopped talking to each other. I felt guilty and silly. He sulked. Finally he suggested we play marbles again."

"You didn't."

"Yes, I did. When you're six, you don't think about what has happened or what might happen. You think, 'This will give me a chance to get my own back.' "

"Your *foot* back."

"We had a nice time playing again. I won a few of his immies, and thought I was getting better at it when he started playing in earnest and won everything again and — you won't believe this — when we got to the last marble this time he said, 'Now I have won your soul. You have lost it to me. You are my slave.' He picked up the marbles and poured them like liquid into his chamois pouch and walked away. Instead of leaving him alone, I followed him and questioned him and he just kept saying, 'I own your soul.' He wouldn't talk about anything else and he wouldn't play with me anymore and the next thing I remember was that we were both on the piazza, not talking, and he gently took my hand and led me to the edge where he had set down a coil of rope. 'Stand here,' he ordered, 'between the posts.' I did what he told me and slowly, methodically, he tied me up. He put the rope carefully around each arm and leg and pulled it tight and I was sort of splayed out between two posts of the porch."

"And?"

"Well, I thought it was part of another game. It was awfully uncomfortable and after a time I began to beg him to let me loose, but he walked away. I don't remember how far he went or how long he was gone, but as I tell it to you, I see the sun going down and the air getting cold and the next part I remember is my father walking toward me, seeing me there on the porch, and going white with rage, demanding an explanation and, of course, there wasn't one. I had none and neither did Harrison. I couldn't explain it then and I can't now, but I know that after that I never took a chance or risked anything or placed a bet or accepted a dare." She bit her lip and then her face was still again. Not a sign of discomfort. Her hands were folded quietly in her lap.

"And when you were freed from your bondage, what then?"

"My father took me into his library. I thought we were going to have a long important talk and I was afraid he'd ask me questions about Harrison I didn't want to answer. We children never wanted to be guilty of telling on each other. But he never mentioned it. We had a cup of tea and the afternoon faded away. I haven't thought about it in years."

"But it was important. There's something about it that's very important that you don't recognize."

"What is that, the fact that I enjoyed it?"

"My God! Yes. I didn't think you realized how obvious that was."

"I realized it as I told it to you, and of course I see that it *was* exciting. And I know there is a part of me — is it the same with all women? — that likes to be told what to do and to do it well even if it's painful. I think it's why we're better at our school work in the early grades. We love to follow the assignment and be praised."

"And boys choose to avoid the work and deal with the chastisement? We think we can get away with more?"

"I'm not sure. Certain girls — beauties and charmers — get away with a lot from the beginning, too."

"Who are you thinking of?"

"No one."

"Your sister?"

"No. Really, no."

"Yourself?"

"No. From the day Aunt Clara gave us the doll house I seemed to know what to do with my life. I wanted to arrange it. Leonora wanted to live in it. We turned it into a world that seemed more real than home or school or anything else. We were so close then."

"And when did it change?"

"I'm not sure. She was terribly upset by my father's death and Nana's marrying Andrew so soon afterward. Then she met Stephen and I think she was completely in love with him but — it all went wrong."

"In the bedroom?"

"I'm just a decorator, darling. I can't tell what goes on in private rooms. Actually I think that was the best part of it for them. It was out in the world where they felt uncomfortable . . . and then, Nell."

"The niece you love?"

"Yes. She was both a disappointment and a saving grace to them. She was perfect and marred. Oh, God, I can't talk about her without wanting to weep. She is everything and nothing."

"Because of her illness."

"Oh, Larry, she's not *ill*." But she knew it was Nell's existence that set Leonora apart from her husband, her mother, and herself. They were all playing a game — with Nell as the prize — but no one understood the rules or how to keep score.

"Do you wish you'd had a child, dearest?"

She answered gravely, "It mattered to me what other people thought. That I might be barren or frigid or whatever. I've never felt that I was. I think if my life had been different" — she smiled at him — "I mean if I'd been married, I would have had several children. Perhaps there was a time, long ago, when I thought about it, but I never ached for motherhood, never longed for it. And as I realized that I did not have the ache or longing, I began to feel guilty. If it was the natural thing for a woman to dream of, was I unnatural not to? Now that you ask me, I have an answer. I don't know if it's the truth. I never know if I'm saying the absolute truth, but I know I'm saying what I feel at this moment."

"Say it."

"I don't think I would have been a good mother."

"That's nonsense. You're the most maternal being on the face of this earth." He was thinking of times in bed when he was her child, when they seemed to give birth to each other at the same moment, when he sucked at her breasts until her nipples became stiff and later she would tell him, "They hurt, they hurt and I love the feeling."

"Oh, I would have been able to take care of a child, or children. But what I mean is this. I have nothing in my spirit to give them. I have only my own life, no knowledge of other lives. I'm practically illiterate."

He laughed out loud, but did not protest because he was anxious to know what she was searching to express and did not want an interruption to throw her off her twisting thread of thought.

"I got through school and I must have read and written what was required, but I don't remember any of it. I can't tell you the names of any but the title characters in a Shakespeare play, I can't identify any great music except by a cliché theme." She sang a bar of "The Moonlight Sonata" and switched in tone and volume to the important four notes of Beethoven's Fifth. He wanted to laugh again, but this time stopped himself. She was getting so close to a truth about herself it made him want her and he made a cradle of his hands so he would not reach out and touch her. "I know the famous works of art from reproductions, but I rarely visit a museum and I certainly can't discuss a painting or a piece of sculpture. The only real history I know I've learned from my interest in furniture and clothes. I can't tell you what the last book I read was about." Tears were streaming from her eyes, but she did not make crying sounds, and did not look ugly as she wept. The tears were simply a release of her feelings, of the pouring out of her small truths and it was healing her as she did so. "If I had children, I would have no inner life, nothing but my own small selfish life to share with them. And that wouldn't be enough."

"You share it with me."

"That's different. You have your own intelligence to feed on, you don't need mine." She was silent for a while, thinking of her sister. She shuddered.

"What?"

"I suddenly felt a little jealous of Leonora. But for the wrong reasons. Because how can I tell if she does share something special with Nell? Maybe she doesn't. Maybe my whole theory is nonsense. Still, if I had a child, I'd want him to have a talent for accomplishment — to be able to *do* something. I wouldn't care what field it was in. I suppose the greatest thing of all would be to have a talent for living, but I've spent my life *just* living, not contributing anything. When I think about my life that's what I'm left with. It makes me sad. You think that as a parent you'll set an example. My father worked very hard. Nana was just my mother. She did her best with all of us. But what is sad now is that the only thing that interests her is money. She doesn't know the world and neither do I."

Until he met her, Larry had little interest in families other than his own. There was no doubt in her mind that he was a good father and she knew in her head and heart how good a husband he was. She was a student of his life. How he spent his time and the way his thoughts returned to his wife and children, far from being painful to her, made him dearer.

"I know my place," she told him.

"With me."

"Yes, with you, my darling. But I meant I know where I fit in with Sarah and your sons. I think there was a time when I was — what? envious, jealous — not of them but of the time they took. I'm not sure when I began to know that without them you would not be fulfilled. Even if I'd known you — before —"

"Don't."

"Oh." She laughed. "You think I'm going to turn sad on you and spoil our hour? I'm not. I'm only saying these things now because I feel so strong, so confident of all my feelings about us."

"Well, then —"

"You've achieved a kind of rhythm of life that makes your relationships with your family consistent, growing. But with Leonora, her husband and child didn't know where they were with her half the time."

"Moody?"

"Yes, but it's more than that. She's the quietest person I've ever known, but inside the small scope of her outward emotions there's an intensity that frightens people. Nell knows how to deal with it, but it drove Stephen away, and her silences ended her relationship with Nana."

Trying to explain Nana to Larry, she told about the Christmas night when Nana's heart seemed to break like a child's, and her children watched her run from the dining room blinded with tears.

His reaction surprised her. "Martha, my love, I think your mother had a hard time of it. She set standards that were impossible to keep. I'm amazed she didn't explode more often. But it's the team really, isn't it? My parents were *together* about everything. If you asked one a question, the other would stand by the answer."

"That's rare. But weren't they terribly dignified, too? All that peerage and embassage!"

"Oh, but there were funny times. The evening we got back from a trip to Ranelagh. They were resting in the parlor, when Joshua, who had not had a chance to change his clothes and put on his white gloves, rushed in and announced, "The Austrian ambassadress is on the telephone and wishes to know if she can still expect you and Mrs. Parrish to dinner?" There was a panic. The invitation had been received but forgotten. There didn't seem to be time to bathe and change, but somehow they did. Luckily, the residence of the ambassador was only a block and a half away. It was hilarious to see these calm, even-tempered people who were my parents literally change color and sound and even shape before my eyes! My father pulling on his clothes the way an awkward child dresses when he's late for school. The wrong arm in the right sleeve, his waistcoat buttoned incorrectly giving him an odd paunch in an odd place, his fly button left undone until the last embarrassed moment as he called 'good night' and rushed out the door!"

He spoke of his early life with contentment. He described London for her and made it a living city. They were to spend many of their happiest times there.

"I don't know my own country or my own town or my own street. I can't feel myself growing anything except older and I don't know how to change the course of my life or whom to go to for help," she mused.

"It's something you have to figure out for yourself."

"Yes."

"You will."

"I wonder. I wish I hadn't told you."

"Why, dearest?"

"Because now you'll feel sorry for me and you can't respect someone you pity."

"Are you telling me what I can and can't feel — about you?"

"I didn't mean to, but I guess I was trying to influence you *against* me. Silly."

"I don't think it is." He reassured her. "From what you've told me about your parents I don't think they put you on the track of an intellectual search. They left you alone to find your own way and you found it, and your sister hers. That's the way life is supposed to be. If you'd had children you would have found ways to educate them and in so doing educate yourself further. But it isn't important. What is important is that you do not regret the lack in your life."

"You fill my life. I don't need anything more."

"But there is so much time when we're separated."

"I keep you with me."

Everything about Martha's rooms was feminine. Light colors and fabrics, flowers in the patterns of materials, and cornucopias of flowers in vases. There were delicate plants, ferns and lemon leaves on the wide sills inside the windows in the living room, and a hanging plant in the center of the bedroom window. Caring for them gave her pleasure. When she was alone the most used piece of furniture was certainly her chaise longue. A lovely, Louis XIV piece discovered in an apartment that was for rent on the same floor of her building. She offered the owner a generous cash payment for it. The doormen, highly tipped, brought it to her the next day and she set about having it recovered with pale blue velvet, which was now gently aged. Here she would attend to her telephone calls and using a desk-tray, answer much of her mail. Always a poor speller, she kept the dictionary on the side table. It puzzled her that she had to look up the same word more than once or twice without learning it. She seemed to learn the *wrong* spelling and keep it in her head. She played spelling games with Nell, who always won them.

Her closets were immaculate. Each garment in its place, always clean, ready to put on. Shoes, handbags, hats all in order. Sachet tied around the necks of hangers filled the crowded space with sweet smells. Rose leaves in bowls scented the rest of the apartment. Sun streamed in all the windows in the mornings. The plants thrived and she woke early with the day, never needing or setting an alarm.

Elma Stout came to the apartment twice a week. She kept the place clean, washed the clothing Martha left in neat piles on the kitchen table, and returned it to the same place in perfect condition, mended if need be, and smooth from ironing.

They communicated by note. Martha wrote her in large block letters. Elma answered mostly by circling Martha's words and adding yes or no. Martha left her pay in cash in an envelope at the foot of the bed.

The bed was too large for the bedroom, but it was a fine one. Large, canopied, covered with linen sheets and a soft Swiss comforter, it invited rest and sleep. The carpet beneath it was soft, too, an Aubusson patterned with pale blue and yellow tulips.

All of this was, she knew, out of key for Larry. She planned rooms for him in her head. Leather chairs, wide couches, dark rugs, bookcases filled with books that would interest him, space for him to walk around as he talked, paintings of ships where her flower prints now hung.

He protested that he loved the place and it was true. It was an approach to her, her femininity, and sometimes while he waited for her to bathe or dress he lay on her chaise longue and grinned at her, not feeling out of place, but in her place. Her offers to change things were refused.

"This is your home," he said. She wanted it to be his.

Nothing she had accomplished gave her more pleasure than decorating Hopecroft — his home. The fact that Sarah approved of her choices was the crowning delight. She was even able to solve the masculine-feminine dilemma, as Sarah and Larry had separate rooms.

She wanted to tell Larry about Elma, but hesitated because it might trouble him. She knew that some men could not bear the thought of women touching or being close. She noticed their reactions to effusiveness among her friends, and remembered Nana describing Natalie as "manny." Her voice sounded the same as when she talked of thieves or criminals. Anything hidden had the taint of error, of an unspoken sin; closeness between women friends had the semblance of something unnatural to her mother.

With Elma, it had started on a rainy night when Martha came home after a weekend of getting the furniture settled in the Slade mansion. She had driven herself from Cold Spring and, although she had eaten lunch and had champagne to celebrate the completion of the job, she arrived at her apartment hungry and too tired to do anything about it.

Elma opened the door before she had a chance to find her key. She had been waiting in the hallway, coat and hat on, reading her prayer pamphlet. Martha wondered if she had forgotten to pay her.

"I thought I'd wait until the Lord stopped the deluge!" she murmured. It sounded sweet and funny.

"When do you think that'll be, Elma?"

"Soon, darlin'. Why'n't you take off yer things and rest a bit. You look all in. I'll fix you somethin'."

"Oh, it's too late. Let me give you some money for a cab."

"No. I don't want to go yet."

"I mustn't take advantage of you," Martha protested without meaning it, as she let Elma help her off with her coat and guide her into the living room. Elma lit the fire, started supper, and was lighting the candles in the sconces before either of them realized she still had her coat and hat on. They discovered it at the same moment, and Martha helped her off with them.

A sense of being cared for lulled Martha's senses. She found herself with a glass of claret in her hand and sipped it slowly. Presently a dinner tray was placed before her and she ate the cold lamb, mint jelly, and endive salad with delight. When she finished she was about to say the polite words of dismissal again but Elma was in the bedroom turning down the sheets, so she took her own tray into the kitchen and started to take off her blouse and unzip her skirt as she scuffed her tired feet toward the closet door.

"Let me, honey." She stopped her by kneeling down and removing her shoes. I should be embarrassed, thought Martha, but I'm not. In the bedroom the curtains were drawn. Martha was in her slip and Elma handed her a pink cashmere wrapper and helped her tie it around her waist. Their hands touched.

"Lie down, honey."

She did. Elma stayed near the bed and rubbed her neck and shoulders. Martha kept her eyes closed. She felt Elma undo her garters and roll her stockings. Instinctively she lifted herself up and felt her garter belt being removed, but not her underwear. She lay on her bed half-clothed and Elma continued to massage her back and occasionally run her hands down her thighs and legs until she fell asleep. When she woke at dawn the lights were off, her coverlet from the chaise longue had been put over her, the room was still, and no one else was there.

It was not until several weeks later that she saw Elma again.

In the meantime the notes with instructions were followed out and a small round handwritten "Thanks" was left on the note pad on the days she got her salary.

The weather might have had something to do with it. Because the next time she found Elma waiting was a stormy afternoon when Martha could not get a taxi from the restaurant where she was wooing a client to allow her to try something new for a summer cottage in East Hampton. Her idea was to upholster all the furniture in either the thinnest-wale blue corduroy or denim. The rugs: straw. The walls painted white and the ceilings blue. The furniture low, wooden, modern. It was a complete departure from her traditional style and she wanted to try it with this wealthy couple who had been sent to her by the Slades.

It was exhausting. To sell them without seeming to sell. She wanted a yes that afternoon so she could begin at once. The project excited her. She tried not to drink too much, and ate sparingly, but it was important to make them feel comfortable. They arrived at the restaurant at one sharp and did not leave until three-forty-five and somewhere between those hours the storm broke. No one was prepared for it. She did not want them to leave the meeting in a downpour, so when the doorman got one cab after long whistling and waving, she insisted they take it. The young man embraced her roughly, and said, "We'll call you. We'll talk it over a little bit more, and then we'll call." His pretty wife smiled, took her hand, and said, "Thank you for the most perfect lunch. Good-bye." They ran into the taxi and Martha felt the deal was probably all right. She did not want to wait for another cab, and risked getting drenched, walking under the awnings and overhangs until she reached home.

The water squished inside her shoes and the fur on her collar reeked. Her face was as wet as if she had been swimming.

Elma opened the door and laughed out loud before she realized how embarrassing the moment was.

"I *know* I look a sight! Help me out of all this wet mess."

Together they removed each article of clothing and Elma took it with her to the kitchen to hang on the drying rack. Martha put on her wrapper and Elma quickly offered the slippers. "Oh, no thank you, I'm going to lie down right now."

As if a signal had been given, the ritual from the last meeting was repeated. This time Martha was aware of what was happening and surprised herself by not protesting. She returned several of the loving strokes with caresses of her own and once more fell asleep.

She wanted to ask Elma what her life was like, what she went home to, what she wanted. Surely taking care of other people's homes must have been drudgery. One morning quite by chance she overheard her talking in the hall to another maid. Elma was collecting the mail, the other woman was probably doing the same thing. She could not see either of them, but Elma's voice was clear. "Mine's a good job, 'cause she's no trouble. Neat, ya know. And quiet." Then the other voice, muffled. Elma again: "When I walk out of here I feel — satisfaction." The other voice asked a question. Elma went on. "I love prettiness and when I leave here at night, it's pretty. Everything shining and smelling good and in its place. I feel like it's my place when I clean it and take care of it."

Martha went back to her room so that she would not be standing in the hall when Elma re-entered. She thought how alike their professions were. I choose things to make people's homes pretty and she keeps them that way. But neither of us is really *connected* to the people we work for. The connection, tenuous, unspoken, kind, would not last. But she would not forget it. And when she remembered it, with Larry, she wanted to share it but did not dare. She had to remember it alone.

Martha was happier than she had ever thought of being. She was living in a perfect time. But in the instant of recognition, the fear that it would end as accidentally and suddenly as it had started poisoned her thoughts. She imagined Larry with someone else, not his wife. She accepted and made peace with his relationship with her, but another partner in his bed, talking and laughing with him and — most easy for her to see — loving him as much as or more than she did.

It was to take more than weeks or months — in fact all their years together — for her to live comfortably with the idea that he might not be hers alone. Might Larry suffer from the same illness? The jealousy that comes before any reason for it has appeared, the uneasiness that overwhelms the blessed realized moment of joy shared when they joined together and fell apart with delighted exhaustion? She knew that no matter what happened she would not seek another. Better to have nothing, to remember what life was like with him than to try to replace him. It was the knowledge that the search for that partner, that person, that constant life-giving companion was over that made her feel young, strong. And that, more than the creams and exercises and cool cloths, smoothed the furrows from her brow.

And yet try as she would to accept the nature of aging, it hurt her to discover fresh proof of it every day. It was no longer possible to ignore the changed color beneath her eyes and the puffiness that seemed to hold it there like new features of her face. The skin was delicate, opalescent. It hurt to draw a line with a dark pencil over it. There was sensitivity on her upper lids as she stroked the lashes with mascara. She wanted to give it up. The endless recoloring of her hair bored her, she wondered if it was worth it. To him. What would he say if the next time they met she had gray hair and no false colors on her face? She had seen old women of extraordinary beauty on the street, in restaurants, in photographs. Would it be possible for her to achieve the kind of serenity that always belonged with the nakedness of these pure faces she admired so much?

She continued to struggle against the marks of age with wasteful products from beauty shops that crowded her medicine cabinet and the top of her dressing table.

In bed, in love, after a bath, there was no artifice for either of them. His dear face changing, growing more sensitive with his years — nothing on it but the occasional slap of bay rum or witch hazel or, if he saw it near, a drop of her cologne. What soap do you like? she asked him once. He answered that it did not matter. Flavor of toothpaste? Color of walls? He left it to her. She wanted to search the world for things to please him until she realized that to have exactly the same scents and touches and sights he saw at home would make her rooms less an Eden for him.

Hating herself for it, she sometimes compared herself to Sarah, imagining man and wife sitting together talking, laughing, reciting the day's events. Sarah's warm, twangy voice animated and vivacious, her face deliciously mobile, impossible to imitate.

Sarah's face and body, too, must be aging and changing. How? She smiled at her thought: sensibly.

She looked up as he walked quietly back into the room, and lay down beside her. She opened her arms in greeting, her mouth welcomed his tongue. His kisses punctuated their meeting and undressing.

"Tell me what you're thinking." Her lips touched his ear.

They loved to talk while he was inside her. He wondered if he should tell her exactly what he was thinking or modify a bit.

"Tell me. The truth. We can say anything when we're like this, can't we?"

"Yes," he answered. "No need to shade or shape the truth, love. I'm thinking that you are my animal."

"What?" she said between laughs of contentment. "What?"

"We're told how natural animals are, how they react to stimuli without thought — if only human beings could be like that."

"Oh?"

"I'm not hurting you, am I?"

"Never. What? Animal?"

"You. I know everything about you now. Without talking. I know what you like and what to do and I know your bark and your purr and your growl."

Now she was laughing out loud and trying to make the sounds he suggested.

"No, my angel. Not like that." He wanted her familiar sounds and he moved and changed in her and she made them effortlessly. And later when she was able to think, it was with pleasure. She told him, "I wanted to be your goddess, your princess, your dream. But I am much happier being your —" He interrupted her with his fingers in her mouth, touching and holding her tongue and then wetting her nipples with his hand. He put his tongue in her mouth again before he licked her body. The room was their cave. They heard the wind outside, the fire dying in the hearth. He thought he would like to take her somewhere outside, in the country, and asked her if she would like that. She answered with her animal noises that were now part of their language.

"What happened to my quiet girl?" he asked.

Martha felt she was dying of love. A kind of suicide. Now she knew why men and women drove themselves to death or madness because of the great joy withheld, or the agony given, by feelings that could not be returned or situations that could never be resolved. But I could never do it, she thought, because I believe somehow it will be possible to have a real life, a daily life with him. He could never do it because he has made a bargain with himself and Sarah and me, and he will always keep his part of that bargain. He will not hurt her by leaving her, he will not destroy me by forgetting me.

"Happy — everything, every place happy now?" he asked.

"Yes."

She fell asleep in his arms.

She had taught herself to let things go. In time the attachment to her favorite objects in the shop lessened and she was able to sell them without regret. There was, however, one thing she wished she owned, but it belonged to Sarah Parrish.

Larry had come with her to Christie's to an auction of eighteenth-century glass. The tables were arranged with glasses of all kinds on view before the sale. The light from the windows and the ceiling glistened and glittered on the perfectly proportioned goblets. Martha wanted to pick up each one separately, lovingly, and toast the unseen artisan who had made it.

"Look at these, darling. Look at this table."

He led her gently toward a set of glasses nearly nine inches tall with drawn-trumped bowls and long thin stems. "Do you know what they were used for?"

"*You* do, tell me."

"They were called toasting glasses. My father had several. But there are very few sets, because the point was to toast your lady love with champagne and then snap the glass between your finger and thumb and throw it into the fireplace!"

"You made that up."

"It's absolutely true. It was because there was to be no lesser toast given with the glass. Just one. I would drink that toast to you."

"And break the glass?"

"You wouldn't let me."

Only one of the toasting glasses from Larry's father's family survived. It was kept in a cabinet in the sitting room at Hopecroft. No servant ever dusted or washed it. Larry could not remember the last time it had been touched.

"When I die, you must go to Hopecroft and take it."

"Never."

"Sarah doesn't care for it."

"No. It belongs in your house."

He bought Martha two glasses at the auction.

In New York Leonora looked at the glass Martha was telling her about. She felt a pang of jealousy and a wish to know more.

"But you only have *one* glass. Is it Sarah's?"

"Of course not, you goose. It's mine," said Martha.

"Did you snap and break the other?"

"In a way we did. We left the glasses on the table near the couch and —"

"Say no more."

"Yes, that's exactly what happened. And we didn't do a thing about it. We stayed together and let the beautiful broken thing lie there. I was astonished. At myself, I mean. Even now I can hardly believe I didn't jump up to try and rescue it!"

"And did you save the pieces and put them in a box with a label with the date on it? That's what I would have done," said Leonora. "I would have hoarded the pieces for the rest of my life."

Martha and Larry drank too much and knew it. Neither could help the other slow down or stop. They planned to, just as they planned diets and exercise programs, knowing they would not follow them. "Hedonist!" he called to her when she was dressing for a party and sharing champagne from their precious, remaining glass.

She went to him and surprised him by holding on to the lapels of his dinner jacket and looking at the ruby shirt studs Sarah had given him for their last wedding anniversary. "I'm bad for you, aren't I? All I want to do is be good for you, but I'm not. I'm leading you astray."

"I'm too old a dog to lead astray," he replied knowing she would hear an echo and laugh.

"I'm laughing, Larry, but I'm serious. We're both too old to be so silly." She didn't tell him how much she drank when they were apart, or that she had started to smoke occasionally and enjoyed it. At Hopecroft she imagined him eating regular meals, sleeping sensible hours.

"We are good for each other. Let's not question everything. We may not have all that much time."

"You're not going to leave me?" she asked jokingly.

"I'll die someday."

"So will I."

"No. Not for a long time."

"What will I do without you?"

"There must be something you'd like to do or *learn*. I'll bet there is. We'll give it some thought, serious thought. It's much more interesting than playing bridge or whist. We'll give it thought and time."

"Thank you."

"Put on your things, darling. We'll be late for cocktails."

Part Nine

BECAUSE FAMILY holidays were impossible to share, Martha and Larry invented an anniversary of their own, the September day of their meeting at Natalie's. Through the years they did not miss talking on that day even during the war when Larry was in London and Martha was working with the Red Cross.

Later Larry scheduled bank meetings in New York on the day or Martha flew to London on business for the shop. In New York they always included Dwight and Leonora and Stephen in the party, although Stephen rarely accepted. After her divorce, Leonora surprised her sister by suggesting that Natalie join them. She arrived each year with a different escort, sometimes with her hair a different color, and always left early, a little drunk, saying, "Let's go somewhere for a nightcap."

When Nell was twelve, Larry sent her a telegram inviting her. Arnold was not included and Leonora was relieved. Close as she felt to him, there was something so intimate about Martha and Larry on these occasions that she feared it might embarrass him.

Nell wore her black velvet dress with the lace collar and patent leather shoes. Her bangs were combed away from her brow and fastened with small tortoiseshell barrettes, and Leonora buffed her nails with talcum powder. It was going to be a grown-up evening.

Supper was in the private room at Giovanni's, the menu and

wines chosen by Martha in advance. Separate arrivals meant that drinks were served for an hour before the first course. Dwight drank, Larry tippled, Martha and Leonora sipped Dubonnet, and Nell was given her first glass of sherry. "I like the glass more than the drink," she confided to Larry.

He could not stop looking at her, this child sitting next to him about whom Martha talked and wrote and dreamed. He saw the others in her face and hands and body. Martha more than Leonora, which surprised him. She might have been his love's child. He was not aware of anything odd about her, whatever troubled the family about Nell was not apparent to him. Throughout the evening he kept her at his side, and she in turn watched his every move with her wide cat's eyes.

Nell remembered Giovanni's for the rest of her life as the place she stopped being a child. The little rules were being broken through the years — she did put her elbows on the table, she was allowed to do two things at once, and small lies were permissible — but at the restaurant she learned to play with fire.

When the grownups were having café-filtre, a waiter brought Nell a glass of milk. She implored Leonora with a look and it was waved away. Giovanni appeared with a bowl of pastel-colored round toys that turned out to be Italian macaroons, each wrapped in blue or red or orange tissue and inscribed with the name Amaretti di Saronno. Inside the wrapping were two biscuit halves made into a circle. Larry unwrapped several and straightened out the delicate papers so Nell could read the writing and see the drawings of medals and two-masted ships that graced each one twice. "Watch me now," he whispered as the others went on laughing and talking.

He twirled the paper into a column and stood it on the edge of the table where it moved slightly but did not fall. He reached into his pocket for his gold cigarette lighter and flipped it open, started the flame, and touched it to the top of the paper column. The flame burst out, diminished quickly, and crept down the length of the paper. Signor Giovanni made no move to stop him, and just as the flame reached the base of the paper and nearly touched the white table linen, the blazing paper rose in the air slowly like a golden butterfly and the sparkling wings turned to ash and the last gray remnant of it soared to the ceiling where it paused for a moment before returning to Larry's hand as a pinch of dust.

"Do it again," begged Nell. Larry repeated the feat three times. As the last ashy ghost reached the ceiling he looked from Leonora to Martha to Nell, picked up his snifter of brandy and toasted them: "Loveliest of women — sweet, embraceable —" the silent "you" was a long look to Martha.

Sentiment got the better of the adults, and while the waiters were clearing, they began to sing. Larry started it, unwittingly, by humming a few bars of "Embraceable You." Natalie took it up and before long they were all spoiling the enchanting song with the wrong words and notes and enjoying it immensely. Even Nell knew it because it was Martha's favorite song and she had taught it to her at one of their early tea parties.

"Sing with us, Nell, darling," she urged and Nell tried to get it wrong in order to get it right, to find the foolish rhythm they chose to repeat in chorus. She wondered what the waiters were thinking.

Larry smiled at her. "They don't give a fig, my dear," he said, but she thought they must.

It troubled her to see her aunt not quite in control, and yet she saw something else, something new. Happiness spreading over her face and staying there like a perfect mask. Her mother was quiet and sad. She did not sing. Her eyes were filled with sorrow and envy. Nell looked away. It was safer to watch Larry Parrish and enjoy the warmth of his hand when he touched her and the comfort of his blue eyes.

At the antique show at the Armory, Martha was cornered by the ubiquitous Peter Holczer.

"Larry Parrish," he said.

"What's *wrong* with him?"

"Nothing. I was just going to say that I heard he's moving from the Morgan Bank to Goldman Sachs, a wonderful opportunity . . ." and he went on to estimate the amount of increase in salary and other "benefits." In time she heard what he was saying, but it took several moments before she recovered from the terrible feeling that he was going to tell her Larry was dead. He had a way of beginning a sentence with someone's name and pausing, usually to make the good news or bit of gossip seem more dramatic, that made Martha anticipate an obituary. Peter had an actor's voice and used it. The simplest statement was given a variety of tones and stresses, more than were necessary. When he was being witty, it was a delight; when he was reporting something, it was irritating. She encouraged him to keep talking about Larry anyway. In Larry's absence, just to hear his name gave her pleasure. She asked all the right questions about Sarah and the children and managed to keep him on the subject for a while, grateful to him and sorry for the times she had mentioned him unkindly in letters to Larry.

If she should hear of something terrible happening to him, what would she — could she — do? Wait. Be still, like Leonora. She had seen her sister live through the pain of her marriage and divorce and wondered how she had done it. They should talk about what to do if —. If. I wish I could be a child again, she thought, before I knew there was an end to anything. Without his life, there would be an end to hers.

"I mean it's fine for old Larry to get on with it. Take a chance. See what happens. I think he'll be over here several times a year from now on, don't you? They do *so* much business in New York . . ."

She wanted to hug him, to reward the bringer of such news. But what if it were *not* so, just an idea of his? He might be making conversation. If only he would leave so that she could dial the overseas operator. No, she would not do that, but if she were alone she could wait for a call. A night, a day, another and another. Eventually the insistent bell would mean not a client, not a tiresome friend, but that impersonal cherished voice of the operator asking if she would accept a call from . . . "Yes, yes, I will. Put him on."

When it rang, when the voice she waited for talked to her saying the most ordinary things, her whole being melted. The object she circled, avoided, loathed, now was a living thing, cradled and kissed. The letters, the snapshots, and the flowers — oh, God, the flowers — were all wonderful, comforting, but that damned telephone was a person in her story with Larry. It was part of him.

"I've lost my audience, haven't I?" asked Peter. He wanted to be friends. "Shall I drop you? I think we've both had enough of these horrors." His arms reached out to embrace the Armory full of furniture.

"Come and have a drink with me, Martha. We decorators ought to stick together more. We've got lots of problems but no union."

"You don't want to try to *start* something like that, do you?"

He took her question as a show of interest. "Let's go to my place."

"I really don't have time, Peter."

"Don't you want to see how the other half lives?"

For as long as she had known him, Peter set little traps in the form of jokes, and Martha was never sure how he expected her to approach them. She knew that Peter lived with a younger man, but it was not clear whether he wanted Martha to behave as if she knew and approved or to accept his self-mocking jests without comment.

"I don't care how you live, Peter, as long as you're happy."

"I've always envied you, Martha. I've watched you ever since you took over Flossie Deane's little establishment and for a long time I hoped that circumstances would allow us to work together. I've even thought of asking you if you wanted or needed a partner. You seem so *alone* in the world."

"I am not alone."

"I know, I know. Old Larry. But that's just a safe bet, isn't it? What are you risking? You're sure of him because he has Sarah and everyone knows that a marriage like theirs just goes on and on no matter what. For the sake of the children and all that nonsense."

"They adore the boys."

"Ha, ha! Well, what I mean is, you have it *arranged* haven't you? Or are you just waiting until —?"

"Peter, stop it."

"Well, the point is, what makes you think a man like Larry Parrish can live that stodgy life in London and Paris and see you once in a while and not — you know — *experiment*?"

It was at this moment that Peter's friend appeared.

"Ellis Graves, this is Martha Ives." A man in his thirties with grace and dignity lifted her hand to his lips, and looking at Peter, said, "Have you asked her, Peter? He told me to keep away for a while because he wanted to proposition you." They all laughed lightly. "I mean he wants you to go into business with him."

"I think you're a very talented man, Peter. I'm flattered that you would want me as a partner, but I'm going to say no. I have my life in balance now — both my lives." She looked at her watch as she pulled on her gloves. Ellis adjusted the fox fur around her shoulders.

"Oh, Martha, give your nice sister my best," said Peter. "Does she still live in that monstrosity — Oak Hill?"

"No, she rents it now. She and Nell live in New York. She said you had some lovely ideas for Elm Hill."

"That husband didn't approve. Did *you* finally do the job?"

"No, not really. I gave her a little advice. She did it on her own. My sister's rooms really don't need much decoration."

"What do you mean?"

"She isn't aware of the look of things. She lives in a world —" She did not know how to describe her sister's isolation. "— of sensations and thoughts. I really must go. I'm expecting a call."

Peter shook her hand and held it. "You're awfully nice, Martha. Please give my idea some thoughtful consideration."

"I will. Good-bye."

"Friends, then?" He often asked this question instead of saying good-bye.

Martha's telephone was ringing as she turned the key in the door. She ran to the bedroom and picked it up saying, "Darling, darling, darling" before she realized the operator was still on. She heard Larry's laugh. As they talked she pulled off her coat and let her shoes fall to the floor. She was with him at last.

For two weeks there were no trans-Atlantic calls and no letters. Then a radiogram was delivered on a day Martha spent at an auction of English furniture at Parke-Bernet. Everything she saw reminded her of Larry — and of Sarah — at Hopecroft. She was startled to find herself on East 67th Street, while her heart was in London.

As she leaned down to pick up the message her purse fell open, she pushed the contents back with her trembling fingers and tried to steady herself as she struggled with the familiar lock. Everything seemed changed. She leaned her weight against the door to swing it open and stepped into the room, putting off the moment of reading the news.

LARRY GRAVELY ILL STOP YOU SHOULD BE HERE STOP PLEASE COME WIRE COLLECT S.L.P.

On other flights to London she had filled the monogrammed silver flask Larry had given her with brandy and nipped on it with secret pleasure. And when he met her and kissed her he used to say "Courvoisier, my love? Warming, warming" and they were already so close she could not breathe. This time there would be no one there. This time there would be no lips and tongue to taste her lips. I will not cry. He hates tears. She left the flask in her satchel.

Sarah was at the gate at Heathrow. She came forward and took Martha's overnight bag, and pulled the checks for the other bags from her tight fist. Larry's driver was waiting; in the car was a basket of fruit and cheese and wine. Sarah was polite, tenderly formal with her. Martha supposed royalty behaved in much the same way at state occasions. Certainly she had never experienced such grace before. It was not necessary to talk in the car. Sarah simply remarked, "You must be too tired to chat, my dear. Close your eyes, we'll be at the Connaught soon." The Connaught, yes, not Claridge's, by now she probably knows that when I have been there, he . . . Oh, God, I *am* tired. Too tired to think.

She slept in the car and Sarah managed to get the chauffeur to help them into the hotel lobby swiftly. No need to check in, all had been arranged. Sarah had the key. A small suite with a fire in the grate, more fruit and chilled wine on a table, the bed turned down.

"I'll call you first thing. I'll come and get you."

"Oh, no —"

"Around nine, then. Good night, my dear. Bless you for coming. He's lived for it." Without a touch of hands she was gone and the door clicked. Martha bathed and slept and woke before the floor waiter knocked with the breakfast Sarah had ordered for her.

Little at Hopecroft was changed. The patterns had faded from years of sun, a few of the ornaments and several lighting fixtures had been replaced, but each piece of furniture was there to welcome her. If everything around him was well, then he must be well, too. Let him be, dear God, please.

He was in the guest suite. A nurse had her quarters in the sitting room and he was lying in a hospital bed in the flowery, pretty bedroom. The sun was shining.

His skin was clear and clean and as pale as seashells. His eyes were closed. Sarah stood at the door for a moment before she said, "I'll be in the morning room. Just sing out if you need me." His old phrase.

"I know I'm dying, darling. I wanted to say it and now we don't have to avoid saying it. I can't get the doctor to tell me how long I've got. I guess he doesn't know. I think I do."

"How long?"

"A few more mornings and evenings and a few more cups of tea."

He took her hand. The reach was gentle, his grasp was sure but without any demand. She leaned near him. He could smell her perfume and feel the warmth of her breast against his cheek.

"I want you to find someone else afterward. Promise me, will you? I want to know that you'll be with someone."

She could not consider a life with anyone but him. "Will you?" he insisted.

"Yes, my dear love. Yes."

"I know you think it's *un*thinkable at this moment. I want that. I want you to be mine in your thoughts and deeds until the last moment. I'm talking about — after."

"I know."

"And I have your promise?"

She took his other hand. "You've never asked me to promise anything. Why now? Trust me," she said, knowing that in this one thing she would betray him. The promising and lying made her feel lightheaded, unable to look at him.

"Turn to me, darling," he said.

If I turn my head now, he will be dead. If I keep looking at his hand in mine, he will live. But she looked up and their eyes met and locked and he smiled. "Can you come back after the doctor leaves?"

"I'll be here."

She waited.

He had spoken of death often in the relaxed way he discussed items of interest from newspapers or magazines. The deaths of his friends — more each year, sometimes two or three in less than a month's time — did not depress him. He used to read her the obituary and spoke of the person thoughtfully and easily, remembering what was vital and important about him. No sentiment, no emotion. He made up his mind he would die before her and before Sarah, too. He had knowingly misused his body when he was young. He had eaten the wrong food, drunk too much, smoked from the time he was thirteen, continuing long after the doctor told him it was hastening the end of his life. He always had coffee near at hand, black fragrant cups of it, sometimes ten or fifteen a day.

"I don't mind being old and I don't mind dying. I liked being young well enough but I was always anxious to be an adult. I hurried through my youth — to meet you, my dear, perhaps — and I have no regrets. I've never wanted more than my share of anything, so I can't want more of life." He said this when he was feeling well, but he meant it and she remembered it when he fell ill. She wished she could share the saneness of his ideas. Death, the thought of it, terrified her and made her sick at heart. And his death, for which she had been preparing from the moment she fell in love with him, represented for her the threat of the end of all life. His absence would leave so great a gap in life, she would fall through it like a parachutist and float down to a place where everything would end. She had no sense of joining him, seeing him again in some mystical afterlife, just nonbeing. In a way he had prepared her, she could not have had these thoughts before she knew him and loved him.

The *Herald Tribune,* open to the obituary page, on the hall table announced the death of Laurence Parrish to Nell before Leonora had a chance to tell her. Nell read the headline LAURENCE PARRISH, HERO IN TWO WARS as she put her schoolbag down. The photograph did not resemble the Larry she remembered, nor was it as handsome as the one in Aunt Martha's bedroom. He was wearing an Army cap and there were decorations on his chest. The paragraphs related his career as a banker, as a soldier, as the husband of Sarah, father of two sons. Nell looked for Martha's name. She took the paper into the sitting room and the look on her face made Leonora gasp. "Oh, Nell — I wanted to tell you. I left the paper there when I was trying to call London. I'm going to try again in a little while. Will you speak to her?"

"Is she there?"

"Yes, darling. She's with him. With them."

Never having read an obituary, Nell thought of it as an article describing someone living. She tried to imagine the man she knew so well through Martha's words doing the things the writer chronicled: An American born in 1895 in England, going to school there and to boarding school in Massachusetts. Graduating from Princeton. Leaving the university to enlist in the Army in the First World War. Wounded in the Argonne. Awarded the Croix de Guerre. A lot about banking, then another war and more medals — the photograph was from the second war — names of generals, campaigns: North Africa, Sicily, Normandy. Campaign ribbons, battle stars, bronze stars. "He is survived by . . ."

And by her aunt Martha, too.

Nothing Leonora thought of to do calmed Nell. The realization that Larry was dead had the effect of speeding up all her daughter's languid movements and an entirely new person emerged prowling from room to room without a purpose.

"Sit and have coffee with me, darling. I'll make the instant." That invitation usually took precedence over any other plan.

"Not in here."

"Why?"

"I don't want to look at the picture of grandfather."

Leonora crowded the tray with cookies and fruit as well as the still steaming coffee and called Nell. "Let's go up to your room." It was the first time they had sipped coffee there. They sat on the bed, the tray between them.

"What's wrong with my father's picture? I thought you liked it."

"I love it, but —" Nell turned away, holding the corner of the tray so as not to shake it, and looking out the window at the snow, still saw the oval frame with its five portraits set in the rose moiré material. Her mother with long hair and a big white bow set on one side of her head like a hat, Uncle Dwight looking wicked and happy, Aunt Martha whose eyes looked as if an artist had drawn a soft black line around them, Nana with a long string of beads cascading down her proud pigeon breast, and in the center, her grandfather, looking exactly like Laurence Parrish with an added lush mustache and beard. "I don't like to look at it now that I know he's dead."

"Dearest, he died before you were born."

"When I look at your family portrait, everybody looks like someone else."

"You mean we look like each other?"

"But who is who? I am you and part of Aunt Martha, you are you and part of Nana, Uncle Dwight isn't related to anybody, Nana is Nana, and your father is —"

"Larry Parrish!"

It was a remarkable likeness, Larry and Lemuel Ives. More in the picture in the paper than in the frame, but of course Nell saw something beyond just the looks. She was what Martha saw, what Martha waited for all those years and finally found at a house party on Sand's Point. What Nana would call an accident.

"What am I going to do with you, bright eyes? How am I going to get through my life when you're not around to make me see the things that are in front of my face?"

Nell pulled herself off the bed and resumed her roaming. Martha's grief was in the room with them. "I wonder what time it is in London now? Let me call the overseas operator and see if we can reach Martha."

"Oh, thank you, yes, *please,* do, do it, please."

It took over an hour to get the call through. Nell tried to read,

Leonora pretended to do the double crostic in the *Saturday Review.*

"It's the overseas operator, ma'am," said Sarah's maid to Martha after a gentle knock on her door. It must have been obvious to the maid that this house guest had had too much to drink and she hesitated to disturb her.

"Thank you, Lilly. I'll take it right here."

Leonora's voice sounded like Nana at first. A moment later when she realized it was her sister she cried out, "What is it? Is Nana all right? Is Nell?"

"It's nothing, Martha, but *you.* We're thinking of you."

Leonora talked quietly. Martha could barely hear her. "It is Nell in a way, Mart, she's terribly upset and doesn't understand —"

"Let me talk to her. Thank you for calling, Leo."

"Aunt Martha?"

"Nell? Dear Nell. Are you all right?"

"Are you?"

"Yes. He talked of you. He sent his love. It wasn't sad, it was — beautiful. You are not to worry, darling. I'll be home soon. We'll meet, first thing."

"Shall I hang up now?"

"Yes. Thank your mother. I'll be there tomorrow night."

On the plane to New York Martha thought of her life as someone else's story, and wondered how it would end. She wanted to plan an ending that Larry would like to hear. Where should she go? To the Camp.

Once she was settled it would be a simple thing to take herself back to the time when they were children and all the influences of her life were at work on her, and sort them out, make sense of them at last.

That is what she would do, thinking it was the beginning of the story she would find there, not knowing it was beyond the grasp of her knowledge or imagination. It had begun generations before and she was never to know, never to find out why this thing happened or did not happen and who the men and women were who made up the real beginning of her story or Nana's or Leonora's or Nell's or anyone's. "I'm drunk," she thought, and took another deep swallow of brandy from Larry's silver flask.

Nell lay awake for a long time, remembering the sound of Martha's voice on the telephone. Did she imagine that she heard the waves washing through the words? A watery sound that was not tears.

Leonora called Arnold and he came over to see Nell. They talked about Larry, and what his life had meant to each of them and why a newspaper sets down the facts and not the heart of a man's life when it is over.

Nell scanned the columns again for Martha's name and then cut out the article and put it in her box where she kept her school reports, a photograph of her father on a pony taken in a studio in Brooklyn when he was five, the results of her yearly tests from the neurologist's office, and three folded Amaretti tissues.

Part Ten

JUST AS ERMINA was getting used to what she termed Martha's widowhood, the appearance of gray thoughout her luxuriant hair, her more frequent telephone calls, a death that was to age and widow her occurred. Andrew Dennison died in his sleep.

His death did not cause anyone great sorrow. He was a kind man who had lived a long life. His going was as quiet as his living had been and the family gathered to mark the event at a funeral in the chapel of the Church of the Good Shepherd. What no one was prepared for was the expert job the undertaker's cosmetics would do to the face that in the last years had sagged with folds into jowls and now was pulled smooth and tight over the bones giving it a youthful, slightly effeminate appearance — the lips rosy, the cheeks pink, and was there a touch of mascara on the lashes? They looked without comment at the apparition lying in the tufted-satin coffin until Dwight guided Nell toward the bier. Staring down at the embalmed figure, she gasped, "He looks so *funny*!"

After the ceremony at which the rector referred to the deceased as "Renfrew" Dennison, after the shrill singing of a small choir of boys, the family grouped itself outside the church and plans were made to meet for lunch at the Golden Anchor. Some walked, some rode. They arrived and greeted each other as if they had not met earlier. A party commenced. There was the usual confusion about ordering too much food, and too many drinks were consumed while it was being prepared. It was past three o'clock when the first ones got up to leave. At four o'clock, a telephone message from Nana told them that he had been interred. Then all were solemn for a time, the bill for lunch was divided up and paid, and the family parted not to meet again until the next birth or death or holiday.

Martha called Nana to tell her about the lunch. "We drank your health, Mother. We drank to Andrew, too."

"That's very sweet of you," said Nana without feeling. "I simply couldn't face looking at another mourner. I went home because I thought I'd laugh out loud or yodel or bark like a dog. I think I'm going mad."

"Did you eat anything?"

"No."

"Well, that's it then. Please get Evans to fix you something."

"I've sent him home. There's nothing here but Andy's invalid food. It's like eating Gerber's. I've been eating it for days."

Martha thought she was talking to an old woman. A tone of self-pity mixed with mockery colored Nana's rambling about the food and the family. She told Martha she could not reconcile the events of her life with her own behavior and the outcome of all her close relationships. "I've not failed, have I, Mart? With you, with Leo — my second chance. I know I failed Lem, I didn't know enough. I was good to Andy — but what happened to Leo's marriage? What's going to become of Nell? You *won't* tell me about yourself, so I'm not going to ask. And Dwight." Martha heard the sucking sound that meant Nana was circling her tongue around her teeth.

"Mother, did you have anything to drink today?"

"Dwight's the drinker."

"Mother — I'm going to get in a taxi and —"

"No, don't do that, Mart. I'm perfectly fine. I'm going to bed and tomorrow I'm going to look over my will and then —"

"Yes?"

"I'm going to send for that Arnold Leveen."

"Why? It isn't about Leonora is it?"

"No, ninny. It's about Nell."

Nana was seated on the couch with both cat and dog vying for room on her lap. It alarmed Arnold to see how drawn her face was and that she was inhaling a cigarette from a long holder. He had not brought cigarettes with him out of deference to Nell, but now he wished he had one.

"Sit down, Mr. LeVine. Arnold. 'LeVine,' odd name, always meant to ask you —"

"It was Levine, Mrs. Ives, but my father felt he would get along a bit faster in business if it weren't quite so obviously —"

"Semitic?" She said the word for the first time in her life. Arnold grinned.

"Exactly."

He wondered if she was as ill as she looked, and was about to inquire about her health when she said, "Dwight is no good to me anymore, I'm sure you know that, and where Stephen Tannenbaum is these days is anyone's guess, so I have decided that you will be the one to take care of my money after I'm gone."

"Be an executor?"

"Yes. For Nell."

It surprised him that he did not mind being asked. He welcomed the chance to do something for Mrs. Ives, though he did not like her. She was grateful for his ready acceptance and knew it was for Nell's sake, not her own, and not even Leonora's.

"I'll put you in touch with my lawyers. There won't be that much for you to do, but I simply felt that a member of the family —" She came to a dead stop. This time Arnold did not grin — the look of astonishment on his face told her everything. "You're quick. You're smart. I like that."

"And I'm Jewish," he added to her sentence. She pushed her tongue around her mouth.

"Do you and Leonora discuss Nell's condition frankly?"

"We always have."

"She won't talk to me about it. She thinks I want a miracle drug to cure her."

"Nell's not ill, Mrs. Ives. She has what is called minimal brain dysfunction. Her neurologist tests her regularly."

"Neurologist? Why not a psychologist?"

"*He* sent us to the neurologist."

"Us?"

"Them." She was making her impatient face again. "Listen — Ermina — the last time Nell saw the doctor he said something very important to Leonora. He knew she was thinking about Nell's future. Becoming part of the adult world, he called it. And he said, 'There is absolutely nothing wrong with the architecture of her brain.' "

Ermina Ives's face relaxed into powerful beauty. Arnold reached for a cigarette from the monogrammed silver box on the table in front of her as Evans appeared with a lighter. He put the cigarette down and asked for a glass of water. His throat ached.

"Would you rather have a drink?" asked Nana.

"No thanks. Just a sip of water, please."

When the glass was empty it was time to leave. Arnold thought he might never see her again and wished for a way to reach her. She looked so dignified and sympathetic sitting under the portrait of her mother.

"I like that," she said in a soft voice he had not heard her use before. "The architecture of her brain."

Arnold went over his meeting with Nana as he walked near the Hudson River. He wanted to report it honestly to Leonora and he wanted to get it straight in his own mind. What seemed to obsess the family was not the money, for no one was in need. It was Nell. How clear it was now after spending time alone with Nana. None of the women felt she was enjoying a worthwhile life and each wanted to have Nell as a part of her life to give some meaning to her days.

He had never made a date with Leonora. He knew now he must set a time and place and that Nell must not be with them. He tried to sound casual when he invited her to lunch at the Algonquin, but his rattled arrangements made her suspicious.

"Is something wrong, dear?"

"No. Nothing wrong at all. I just need to see you alone and talk."

They met. Both were prompt, both nervous. Leonora laughed, "Our first date — after how many years?"

"That's part of the problem, Leo . . . years . . . and love . . ." he stammered. "And, of course, the coin of the realm. All the things poets write about and real people *don't* say." He wiped his face with the still folded table napkin.

"You're not going to propose to me are you, darling?" Leonora laughed again and touched his arm.

"No. It's much more complicated than that. I am going to ask you what I didn't have the courage to ask your mother. I want your permission —"

"— to marry Nell."

Arnold looked as if he might cry. "Oh, God, Leonora. Make this easy for me, but not *too* easy."

"I'll just listen. You know the questions I want to ask. Answer them and then we'll go to Nana."

"No, to Nell. I don't think this can be something I can achieve in your mother's lifetime. I think she would hate it so much it might kill her. It's all mixed up with my being Jewish, being around you so much of the time, not having money. She'd think I was an adventurer."

"In a way you are. You'll be choosing something out of the ordinary to do with your life and most people will think you are mad."

"Do you?"

"No. But what about my questions?"

"The difference in our ages? That hasn't been what's kept me from wanting to marry *you,* Leonora. It's because of Stephen I've never considered myself as a possible husband for you, not because I'm eight years younger. The fact that I am more than twenty years older than Nell does not trouble me. If she tires of me, if it doesn't work out the way she wants it, I'll let her go. But until that time I want to be the one to care for her."

"And love?"

"Can I say this to you? She wants me to be her lover. She has shown me that many times. Looks, touches, sounds. Little things. All clues, and she knows I've seen them and felt them and returned them. I am more attracted to her than to any woman I've ever known. It's true. I don't tell you who I see when I'm not with you because you never ask and because it has never been important enough to share with you. When I talked with your mother and saw that she trusted me, I knew I was going to take the chance to ask you for Nell. I have had enough experience to know myself. I will be good to her, true to her. Not out of pity. Listen, we better order something or they'll throw us out of here."

"No, let's go somewhere. Take a walk. Keep talking to me, please."

They went out and turned toward Fifth Avenue and walked the familiar blocks back to the apartment.

"Being married, having a ceremony, will change so little. And it may not be for some time. Your mother's a formidable woman."

"I think she's weakening, somehow. I think that's why she sent for you. The odd thing is, except for your being what she calls 'Jewy,' I think she would consider your wild plan eminently sensible."

"You sounded *just* like her then!"

"I don't want to sound like anyone else or be like anyone else today, Arnold. I lived with my mother for so long of course I echo her and I echo Stephen, too."

"So do I."

It was certainly because of Stephen's interest in the field of mass communications that Arnold became interested in radio and television as outlets for his writing. Often when Leonora read his newspaper articles she found some of Stephen's toughness in Arnold's approach to advertising, politics, and news coverage. When he said that Stephen had prevented him from marrying her, she felt angry. She might not have accepted him, but it would have made her happy to know he thought of her as more than Stephen's wife or Nell's mother. She tried to stop thinking about herself. "I wish you'd spoken to me about Nell long ago, Arnold. There are certain considerations, you know."

"Like what?"

"You know better than anyone else. She's got to be looked after, taken care of."

"Leonora, listen to me: She has been taken care of too long. You say one thing, that she's healthy and strong, and you do another, you wrap her in cotton so the world can't hurt her. The world must hurt her if she's going to turn out to be —"

"—somebody?"

"Yes."

"That's Stephen talking. Everyone had to be somebody, do things, make things, accomplish things. No one was worthy enough just as they were. I know I wasn't and I'm not now. But Nell *is*. You know that!"

"Don't yell at me, Leo. I'm not trying to threaten you or Nell. I agree we should have had this talk a long time ago but I just wasn't ready. I mean somebody *on her own,* when I use the term. I mean she has to take chances. Chances you never took."

Leonora had come from her mother's house to Stephen's apartment with almost no experience in between. She had avoided — whenever possible—every conflict with the people in her life. She was tense from holding in her cries of discontent and now when she wanted to be sensible and quiet she heard herself raging at Arnold.

"Why does everyone want to change everybody else? Why can't Nell be Nell, just the way she is?"

"That's what I'm asking *you,* Leo. Let her free, let her go. And I promise to do the same thing. We have to stop planning for her, thinking for her, answering for her. Both of us. I'm just as guilty as you — and your sweet sister. I'll tell you something, I defended you to your mother, but your mother's strength is a wonderful thing —"

Leonora interrupted him with a look that made him stop walking as well as talking. She transformed her face into Nana's and glared at him. The tears of anger had not dried on her cheeks. Her eyes were shining and looked young and vulnerable, but her mother's power had taken hold of her and controlled her outburst.

"My god, Leo — I thought you were going to say something in your mother's voice!"

"Only to make you laugh at me? No, it's too easy and it's mean to make fun of her. Nell's so good at it it's spooky."

"Yes, when I told her about the financial stuff she imitated her perfectly. She said, 'But Arnold, I don't want a *pinny* of Nana's *minny!*' "

"She doesn't. And neither do I and neither do you. But there it is and it looks as if we're going to take it into consideration from now on. It's her power, whether she lives or dies."

"Leonora!"

"Oh, don't you see why I hate it so? She has never had any need of me because of it. She thinks she can run Nell's life because of it. It is an awful barrier and I know how ungrateful I sound."

"I said time and love *before* I said money. I want to spend my time and love on Nell. It's *for* Nell. And because you are so much a part of her, my beautiful Leonora, I *am* proposing to you, too, aren't I? Will you take your best man for a son-in-law?"

"Yes. When the time comes. Yes. And until then —?"

"We go on as before."

She thanked him for their date and he touched her cheek as was his habit. They entered the apartment together. In the living room Nell was reading and listening to a Schumann quintet. She smiled at her mother and moved slowly into Arnold's embrace. "I've got lots to tell you," he said, but he did not speak again until the record stopped playing. Leonora took off her things and went into the front room and closed the door. She could hear the music and then Nell's voice and Arnold's.

"Nell, if you could choose any person to live with, who would it be?"

"You, Arnold."

"I'm talking about a whole lifetime."

"I know you are."

"Marriage."

"Yes."

"Have you thought about it?"

"Sometimes when I'm reading I imagine myself as the character. And so often the woman is in love or —"

"Can we talk about loving?"

"I love you, Arnold."

"And you would be my wife?"

"It would be the best dream of all. Shall we tell my mother?"

To celebrate, Nell planned a complete dinner of delicacies, Leonora's favorite music on the phonograph, the apartment shining with lemon-waxed tabletops and polished mirrors. Candles and flowers.

"What have you done to the room, darling? It looks as if your aunt had been here! How lovely."

"It's a party. For you, for us, all three."

"Is Arnold here?"

"He went to get some wine. He'll be back in a trice."

The wine was poured, before dinner, and Arnold said, "Let me make the toast. To both of you. My loves, my darlings. To you, Leonora, for the best part of my life so far, and to you, Nell: my future."

Leonora drank a sip of wine before she looked at them smiling at her. "Have you decided, children?" She had never called them that before.

"We want your permission —" said Arnold.

"You have it," said Leonora. Fighting not to cry, her sobs were strangled. Arnold and Nell put down their glasses and went to her and held her until the shaking stopped.

"I'm crying because I'm happy, you know that don't you?"

They believed her and she believed it, too.

"I am going to do something new," said Nell. "New *and* different."

Arnold looked at her and grinned. "Tell me."

"I am going to dial Nana's number and ask to speak to her and I am going to tell her my — our — news."

"So what's new is the news?"

"No, what's new is that I have never called her before and I have never been the first to tell her something, and what is strangest is I've never had this impulse."

"You'll probably get Evans and panic and tell him."

She touched his dark hair and went slowly to the telephone, planning what to say. She dialed and waited and spoke for a moment to Evans and then her voice changed. "Nana? This is Nell. Fine. Wait . . . no . . . wait, I want to tell you something. I have a nice surprise for you." There was a brief silence and then Nell hung up.

"She said she didn't want any surprises," she said. And so, as with every other event in her life, Leonora would tell Nana and Nana would behave as if she had known it all along.

Leonora was longing for September. It was the month she had always loved most. The heat would subside, the smell in the air at the Camp was sharp with pine, and future plans seemed to sail in on the breeze as Nana told them to start cleaning up their rooms and packing what they did not use every day. It was time to go back to the city, to start school, to begin that life they shared with other people. Real people, Leonora thought, as if her family were somehow invented by her. But now, there was nothing to look forward to. She knew she must wait for Nell and Arnold to settle into a pattern of living before she could expect to be a part of their world. There was no friend she particularly wanted to see. Jerry Walters called occasionally and suggested a meal, a concert, a film, whatever would please her, but she found excuses and avoided him. There was no Stephen to be afraid of.

One night she dreamed he came to the door. She mentioned it to Nell, who said, "It is *your* door." Leonora's weekly visits to Riverside Drive were disappointing. Even when she told her about Nell's wedding plans, Nana kept the radio playing, and Evans hovered like a male nurse until he ushered her to the door. Nana's voice stopped her in the perfume scented hall. "Don't worry about Nell now, Leo. She will survive."

Because Martha was grieving for Larry, Leonora felt for a time that staying away was the best thing to do. Now she knew it was not.

"Let's go to Albany on the train the Monday before Labor Day. We'll hire a car and spend the holiday at the Camp. What do you think?"

"We'll do it," said Martha. "Let me make the arrangements." That meant a picnic basket of delicious food and an exact timetable of departure and arrival for a smooth, easy trip.

In the darkness neither sister recognized the young man who met them at the shore of the lake. "I'm Phil. Abe Langhorn's grandnephew," he said, making it sound like an apology. He loaded their suitcases and packages and guided the launch across the quiet, starlit lake. While Martha kept looking back at the land, Leonora turned to face the island.

"What is that strange smell?"

"Can you still smell the fire?" asked Phil.

"What fire? When?"

"Last weekend. Some campers left their charcoal pit burning and the whole north shore went up in smoke. No one hurt, though."

"And the island?" asked Leonora.

"Not a spark. Everything's O.K."

Suddenly Martha wanted to suggest turning back, but at the same instant Leonora touched her hand.

"You go first," said Leonora, and Martha reached for the frayed rope ladder on the pier.

At sunrise they took their coffee out to the porch and with Lem's binoculars surveyed the acres of blackness across the water. The tall pines were like huge charred matchsticks against the sky; the white birches, dark stalks. When the wind came up the smoky scent overcame Martha and made her eyes water. "I'm not crying, I don't feel sad. I think we were terribly lucky. I have an idea. It kept me awake all night."

"About the fire?"

"Yes. We've got to find out just how serious the damage is, how many acres have been spoiled, and then we must figure out how to go about planting new trees. And at the same time I'd like to know how much granite we have on our shore land. If we have enough we should get someone to help us mine it."

"Martha, have you gone crazy? Do you want to live here?"

"We don't have to live here. But it isn't right to let the land die. Father wouldn't want it that way."

"I was thinking about him last night." Leonora had spent an hour in Lem's study while Martha was roaming through the other rooms. When the logs in the living room fireplace cracked and fell into the grate, the sisters, startled by the sound, met and went up the stairs to the bedroom they had shared as children.

"Nell told me you started to write something about what she calls 'the olden times.' Did you ever finish it?"

"No, not really. *You* thought if I had a room to work in I'd create something of value. But I'm not a writer. I wrote a few things to please Nell and impress Arnold and for a week or so I thought I'd found something I could do. But I made the mistake of looking at what I had written after reading a chapter of Arnold's new book and I realized how pitiful my attempts were."

"You should have kept on. Not to be published, but for us, for Nell."

"I thought of that too, Mart. I made myself go into the room and sit at the desk, but what I wrote was even worse. It was like the text for a translation."

"They can be pretty funny! Remember Benchley's? And Beerbohm's?"

"Martha, you've been reading behind my back!"

"No. I picked up things from Larry, special things. Because he liked them, I read and remembered them."

"Stephen was like that, too. He taught me about baseball, to care who won!"

"I never caught on to cricket — no matter how much Larry explained it — but I cared who won at Ascot. I wonder if we have that effect on people, our tastes, I mean."

"You do. You know you do. And I suppose I have with Nell. But I don't think women change people. I think men do."

"Men change?"

"No, *they* change *us*. They alter our perceptions, as Arnold says."

"And why don't they change?"

"I'm not sure, but I think people change because they *want* to. Women are more likely to want to, and so they adapt. They — or do I mean we, or just *I* — try to please. The only person I've known who doesn't have that weakness is Nell. She goes her own way."

"With guidance." Martha said. Leonora flinched. Years of defending her constant care of Nell to Stephen, Nana, teachers, doctors, and well-wishers had made her wary. Martha added, "And with love."

They walked through the woods, past the cove and around the rim of the island. Leonora, wrapped in a winter coat of Lem's and a scarf they identified as Dwight's, reminded Martha of photographs of Nana in the album. Her figure obscured by the heavy garment and her gray hair framed in reddish-brown wool resembled their mother in every respect but the height, in her fur-trimmed boots Leonora's long legs looked stocky.

"Why are you staring at me?"

"You remind me of someone."

"Is this a game?"

"No. I thought you hated games."

"Grown-up games."

"Do you ever play the list game?"

"Yes, sometimes. With Nell. When I gave up on the writing and she kept asking me about the past, I'd let her choose a subject and I'd write a list."

"Remember Dwight's lists?"

"Cars!"

"And ours?"

"Everything."

Leonora knew that even her lists for Nell were lists of lies. There was no way to write the words to describe the early years with Stephen. The good times were harder to define than the terrible ones. And she knew that in her remembering of her father she chose only words that would endear him to Nell, so that she would have a perfect person to put in the part of her grandfather. Leonora excused herself from using the Tannenbaums in the game by telling Nell she hardly knew them. Nell's Uncle Dwight list was a combination of humor and despair. She guessed how he spent most of his time and Leonora was sure it was the main reason why her daughter never drank more than one glass of wine at family celebrations.

"I wish I'd saved Nell's lists. I think I'd know more about all of us — the truth — if I had the words she chose. Even if I don't write things down, Mart, I am going to try to tell the truth about things from now on. I've been afraid of it for too long."

"I wouldn't want to see the list after my name," said Martha.

"Yes, you would. Our whole past would swim back into your head. And think of what you could add to it."

"And a Nana list? I suppose if I made one it would be quite different from yours."

"What amazed Nell was not how different things were for us, but how much they were the same. She knew we had cotton or silk stockings, but when I told her our summer dresses were made of lawn or dimity she didn't know the words. I told her Nat used to chew Chiclets and we had Droste chocolate —"

"— I've told her that."

"I know. It's still 'your' brand. We use plain old Baker's downtown. But there were so many things she sees in magazines now: Mennen's talcum, Packer's tar soap, that 4711 white rose glycerine Nana used. What else? Oh, White Rock soda, A-1 sauce. Arnold joined in and named cars. And cigarettes."

"Remember the time Nat stole her father's Murads?"

"How is she, Mart?"

"Don't know. Lost touch again. I think it's a safe bet she's not alone."

"But how is that possible? Here we are, utterly alone — that way."

"Because for her it's never a real commitment, is it? I don't think she could remember them all if we asked *her* to make a list." They laughed. "I miss her, in a way. She always seemed to be having such a good time, even when she was doing things I disapproved of."

"Nana liked her."

"Nana was amused by her, which is more than she could say for her own daughters. Strange, but it's hard to think of Nana laughing now. I suppose she laughed with father and with Harry. I can see her smile perfectly but I've forgotten her laughter."

"She convinced me that I had no sense of humor and that I was tone deaf. So I gave up jokes and singing at an early age."

"Leo, you can say that to a friend but not to me. Nana isn't responsible for our seriousness about things any more than she is for our passions."

The word seemed to float in the air. "She doesn't think we're capable of deep feelings," said Leonora. "She thinks she was the only one ever hurt by death or disappointment or loneliness or failure."

"Darling, deep feelings breed cruelty in everyone. I'm sure

that Larry and I wounded Sarah, though we swore we wouldn't. I would have been much kinder to many more people if I hadn't been so wrapped up in my love for him. The time you were married to Stephen — happily or not — you were a stranger to the rest of us."

"I was hiding my panic while you were hiding your happiness."

"But we all knew."

"And I knew, too. About you, I mean. And about Nana and Andrew, and I'm so ashamed of my jealousy that it hurts to think of it. I used to spy on your happiness and hers. I tried to find out everything Nana did so that I could blame her for betraying Father. I used to ask Nell to tell me all about Larry so that I could imagine you with him. I wanted to learn how to be good with men from you and Nana. My life with Stephen was supposed to be normal. I don't think it was, and yet I look back on even the strangest times with pleasure."

"Are you a masochist, Leo?"

"I think we all love our unhappiness or we couldn't bear it. Don't tell me you were happy all the time."

"Don't ask me to tell you that. It's a foolish question."

"But we never stop wanting, do we? Wanting to make someone happy?"

"Oh, Leo, if Stephen really did come back and knocked on your door, what would you do?"

Leonora started to raise her shoulders in a gesture of helplessness and heard her mother's voice: "Never shrug, girls, it is so common. Give me an answer, but do not shrug." She sat still and looked at her sister for a long time.

"I don't know, Mart, I don't know," and she shrugged her shoulders like a lonely child. "What will we do now? It's getting late."

"We have time. When we're here at the Camp we don't have to hurry through the days. It's the first time in years I haven't been waiting for the telephone to ring or the mail to come. I wonder what I am waiting for." She frowned. "Larry made me promise to find someone else. He wasn't very realistic about a single woman in America. I told him I'd try to. I don't think I'm going to be able to keep my promise, but I can't live with the idea that he could look down and see me rocking on the piazza."

"Who are the women who sit and rock on the porches when we drive up here? They've all had lives with men and children and work in them. We'll be like them, won't we?"

"Why? I can go on working. And if it would amuse you, you could help me. We'd be partners. I'd rather have you than prying Peter Holzcer."

"You're the one with taste, Martha."

"And I was wondering if Nell might like to help, too."

"Have you asked her?"

"No, I thought you'd be furious!"

"I'm not as bad as I used to be, am I?"

"No, or I wouldn't have dared joke with you about her. You know she's safe now and you're not so jumpy about her, are you?"

"I think things have worked out in the most magical way."

"And Arnold?"

"I love him, you know that."

"Explain."

"I've never been in love with him, but I love him in every other way and he returns that love. He's the best friend I ever had."

She could not tell Martha of the times she had wanted to get up from her chair and shake his shoulders and beg him to respond to her. Those times she kept hidden in her heart, in such a private place that even now it shocked her to remember how frightened she was by her feelings for Arnold. Until she realized that he was waiting for Nell, she could not understand how he could know her so well and ignore her desire for him. Had she kept it hidden from him, too? Perhaps he had never known. Too late now, too late. But for her daughter, the possibility of everything: friend, husband, lover, father. The sentences she could not write about Lem formed in her mind, seemed almost ready to be spoken and then drifted out of her thought's reach.

They sat in silence, thinking about the men they had loved. Leonora, still in the habit of imagining Stephen's reactions to things, wondered if he would approve of her working with her sister. She felt sure he would find the replanting of the forest and the search for granite interesting because eventually the trees and the stone would represent money. The way she would find out how Stephen felt was to discuss the plans with Nell. In time Nell would be questioned by her father. Time and money would transform his daughter into an object of interest at last.

Through the door they heard the hall telephone ringing with their signal on the party line: two long, one short.

"Long distance from New York City, for Miss Ives," said the operator, and before she could say the name, Martha heard Dwight. Not a word exactly and not a cry, a moan that sounded like her name.

"Yes, yes, operator, I have it. Thank you. Dwight? I'm here, talk to me."

"Sis, is Leo there?"

"Yes, do you want her?"

"I have to talk to you both," he said and Martha could not tell if he was sober or not. The words were muffled and the connection crackling with static. She beckoned to Leonora who was standing at the top of the stairs, thinking the call might be from Nell.

"She's here," said Martha. "Leo's right here."

"Mother?" It was Nell's voice.

"Oh, Nell, it's Martha."

"Aunt Martha, Nana's dead —" Then Arnold's voice came on, explaining that they were at Riverside Drive. Evans had called them an hour before. He had left her sitting under the portrait listening to her favorite radio serial. He found her there, her hands folded in her lap, her head bowed, when he brought in her afternoon tea.

"I can't go back with you," said Martha. "You'll have to manage with Dwight and Evans and Arnold and Nell."

"You'll be all right, I'll take care of you."

"I'm not sick, Leo. I just can't face another funeral."

"You can't stay here alone and drink."

"*Leo.*"

"Darling, if I pretend not to notice is it better? Ever since Larry's death you've had a glass in your hand. I noticed it at the shop, and Peter Holczer told me —"

"He's just a gossip."

"He's your friend, Martha. He told me because he's worried about you. But he didn't have to tell me, I see it myself. Do you want me to say I don't?" Leonora watched her rise to refill her half-empty glass of sherry. "All right, we don't have to talk about it, but we do have to get ready. There's a night train we can make if we start now. I told Phil we need the launch. He'll be ready in fifteen minutes."

Martha looked around the big room and suddenly loved it. The ugly furniture, the stuffed deers' heads, the junk of all their lives on the shelves, made her want to stay at the Camp alone without any responsibilities. Leonora pulled her gently from the chair and started toward the stairs with her. "Let me help you. It's my turn now."

During the night Martha opened the silver flask from time to time and offered Leonora a sip of brandy; it sweetened the hours and took the place of rest. When they got to New York, Arnold and Nell were there with Nana's car. Dwight was at the Church of the Heavenly Rest waiting for them on the wide stone steps.

The meeting with Dr. Deerfield was brief, the arrangements simple. The following morning the service would be held in the chapel of the Beloved Disciple. The body would, he said, be cremated "according to dear Ermina's will and her ashes preserved perpetually in the columbarium."

Arnold held Nell's hand. He was not sure what the slight smile on her face meant. Pain, amusement, embarrassment?

It was confusion. The fact that she had felt so much when Larry died and shared the grief with her aunt and mother made the hours after the news came seem real. This death, this loss, had no sense of reality for her, and as she watched her family, she sensed that they were experiencing a lack of emotion. There was nothing to fill the emptiness. Not a tear was shed, and hardly an expression altered. It was a new kind of death.

Evans had prepared lunch at Riverside Drive. Sandwiches and coffee and fruit and champagne. Dwight refused the tray with his glass on it. Evans offered it again. "No thanks, Ev. I think I'll pass this time." His sisters exchanged a look. "I'm swearing off for good."

Martha laughed, "Then I am to inherit the mantle of the drinker of the clan!"

"Don't, Mart," said Leonora.

Martha reached for Dwight's glass and set it down beside her own. "One for Larry and one for me." She drank them both slowly. When it was time to leave, she said, "Why don't we all have dinner together tonight? Come and have it with me."

Arnold looked at Nell who nodded and at Leonora who saw the nod and said, "How dear of you. What can we do to help?"

"Just come. Elma will get things ready. Now go home and get some sleep. Nell, make your mother rest. She's had a long night and day. Dwight, can I drop you?"

Nell asked Arnold what had happened to Martha. She knew it was much more than fatigue. "I think it's as much Larry as her mother, dearest. She hasn't recovered from his death and she wasn't prepared for your grandmother's. She needs to rest, and I think she needs you."

"Shall I go there before dinner?"

"Why don't you call her in an hour or so? If she says yes, I'll take you up there and meet you later with your mother and Dwight."

The space of time between her mother's funeral and dinner at Martha's loomed in front of Leonora and frightened her.

Nineteen years before, when she knew she was pregnant and

the test said she was not, she had sought refuge in a movie. It was the middle of the afternoon and many seats were vacant. In front of her she thought she recognized a woman but it was not until she rose to leave that she was sure who it was. She had been sitting at the film only two rows behind her mother. She needed to talk to someone, to confide her joy and fear about having a child, but she let the imperious figure walk up the aisle without making any attempt to catch her attention. She justified her lack of action by imagining that Nana would have been embarrassed to see her. But she knew that any real daughter, true daughter, would have gone to her at once.

Now there was no one to go to. Nell and Arnold were still at Riverside Drive. Dwight was at the Century Club, Martha certainly needed to rest. She was alone and wanted to weep but could not. She started to walk down Park Avenue and did not stop until she was in the Village. She had just enough time to go upstairs, bathe, change, and take a taxi.

In Martha's apartment little had been altered in the year since Larry's death. The lovely goblet was now in front of his photograph on the side table, the vases were full of green leaves instead of flowers, and not as many lamps brightened the room.

Elma was taking Nell's sweater when Martha called from the bedroom. "Come in here, darling." It was like walking into the past. Her aunt in a pale pink dressing gown stretched out on the chaise longue. The lights dim, and in this room the scent of flowers. Elma had brought them. Funeral flowers. Nell wondered what to do with the carnations in her hand. "Put them with the leaves on the mantel, darling. They'll look perfect there." She did so and when she came back to Martha a transformation had taken place. The tired mask was lifted and the face she loved and remembered looked at her as before. "Let's talk, shall we?" Sit beside me."

Comfortable and easy now, they had time to talk of Nana's life and death.

Nell spoke of her life with Arnold and of her hopes for him. Convinced of his talents as a journalist, she felt that his work would take them to places she longed to see.

"I'll be able to help him. I touch-type now, and I always make him two carbons. I am his partner."

When Martha asked Nell about Leonora, her replies diminished to monosyllables.

"Do you want *not* to talk about your mother, darling?"

"I feel I am going to betray her." Leonora's word.

"That's not possible with me, Nell. I'm your mother's friend as much as her sister. You mustn't feel we're going to say things that will hurt her. I want you to be able to say anything you wish to her about me."

"I have never told her what we talk about here, Aunt Martha. I don't know why. My time with you here has always been secret."

"That's probably why your mother resented your coming here so often. She's possessive and I don't blame her."

"She wants to possess people's thoughts, and that isn't possible."

"But she can *read* mine," said Martha.

Nell smiled. "Mine, too. For as long as I can remember. It used to make my father furious. 'Let Nell speak for herself,' he'd say, and then I'd say exactly what my mother had said for me!"

Nell asked about her parents' divorce and Martha told her of the journey downtown to Jerry's office.

"Jerry pursued my mother, you know. He called all the time and wanted to come over. Once he brought phonograph records and tried to make her dance with him."

"How do you know that?"

"Because I was there. He acted as if I weren't in the room when I was. I think he thought I was stupid, backward — you know. He'd pat my head. I tried to be polite to him."

"And your mother?"

"I think she was very lonely then, don't you? I wanted her to have a friend and it was a long time before Arnold started coming to see her again. When my father left, everything seemed to stop. I don't count Jerry." Nell turned back to Martha and made a face that caricatured him devastatingly. Martha bit her lip to suppress a smile, which Nell caught.

"Then, thank God, Arnold."

"Your Arnold."

"My mother's. Hers. He was wonderful to her and that made me happy. It was always lovely when he was there. But the times when Jerry wouldn't go away were difficult. We'd all go out and have dinner together. Four of us. I couldn't swallow. I felt *I* was in the way, but Jerry was *more,* much more. I knew it, I'm sure my mother knew it. What was so hard for me to understand as a child was how a grownup could *not* know it."

"He may have known it, but if he cared for her he couldn't help himself."

"Ah."

"It's devastating to be the one who cares too much. If you have nothing else, you hang on to the person even though somewhere in your heart you know you should let go."

"Has that ever happened to you, Aunt Martha?"

"No, dear, I don't think so. The beautiful thing for me with Larry was the equalness of our feeling. We shared even the unhappy things in the same way."

"Unhappy times together?"

"Well, yes, darling. It was perfect, the best thing in my life, but it was difficult, too. You can understand that now, can't you?"

"No, not yet. The bad times must be ahead of me."

"I'm not a Cassandra, Nell. What I mean is that no matter how much you love a man and he loves you, it can't all go just the way you plan it."

"Nana used to say, 'Life has no plan, it's a series of accidents.' Remember?"

"Yes, I do. She said it too often."

"But when she got married, do you think she felt the same?"

"I don't know, Nell. She didn't confide in us. And my father was very careful to protect her, to be on her side in everything. They never argued in front of us. I didn't know that married people quarreled until I heard Dale and Vernon Hammel scream at each other. I thought they'd gone crazy."

"Weren't they happy?"

"They were loveless."

"I thought that was what was wrong with Nana and Grandfather."

"That's because your mother cannot believe that they were ever 'equal,' but I'm sure they were. And they loved us all, too, when we were young. But your mother doesn't trust those feelings anymore." Martha sighed. "I'm working on that with her!"

"But with her father — your father — she was comfortable, wasn't she?"

"Yes. He was a dear man. And just as Leo can read your thoughts, that's the way it was for me and my father, and Leo."

"And Nana?"

"No, darling. I think Nana cut herself off from our thoughts — I mean, especially Leonora's. It had a lot to do with your uncle Harry and a lot to do with your grandfather. Those deaths. Now we have Nana's and I have no idea how that will be resolved for Leo and Dwight and me."

"Resolved?"

"It takes a long time to get used to death, to loss of any kind. It took Nana nearly a lifetime to get over Harrison, and it will take me the rest of my life —" There was no need for her to finish. Her thought-reader took her hand and presently they got ready for the dinner party at which Leonora was hostess for Martha in her softly lighted living room.

Arnold picked up his mail and noticed a St.-Tropez postmark. He did not know anyone there, and there was no return address. It was a letter from Stephen. He had heard that Ermina Ives had died. He needed money and guessed that his daughter was about to hit the jackpot. Arnold wondered if Leonora would laugh.

"I told him once he might need Nell," she said seriously. "But I didn't mean money. I thought one day he'd simply want to have his daughter in his life again. But this makes me sick. Because if it's a way to get back to her it's the wrong way, and if it's just for the money . . . Well, I have nothing to do with it."

"You have everything to do with it. You have to advise me. You have to talk to Nell. Just because your mother put my name on a piece of paper doesn't mean I am the only one to make decisions."

"I don't want him back in my life or hers. I'm still afraid of him. But I feel sorry for him. What do you suppose he's doing in St.-Tropez?"

"He says." Arnold turned the letter over. " 'I have a sweet chick with me . . .' "

"Oh, God. It never ends, does it?"

Nana's money was beginning to make trouble for them all. It was better when she hoarded it. Now that it existed as a tangible asset, Leonora despised it.

Leonora, Arnold, and Nell discussed plans for the wedding. It was understood that because of Nana's death whatever celebration occurred it must be a solemn one.

"Mother, I've never been to a wedding and the ones I've read about are never lovely enough. I want to invent one of my own."

"What kind?"

"I mean, I don't want the wedding to change anything, I just want the three of us to go on living and loving each other —"

Arnold saw Leonora's concern and interrupted Nell, "I think what Nell would like is for us to go away somewhere, get married in a quiet, simple way, and come back here in a month or so."

"Aren't you going to live at Riverside Drive? That's Nell's now, too."

"We thought — wouldn't it be better for you to have that place? It's an Ives place, Leonora, it's so — Ives!"

With her mother's blessing, Nell got into the hired car that took her to meet Arnold in the judge's chambers. David Markewich had known Arnold's family and came in on his day off to marry the grown man and childlike woman. The only witness was the guard who prowled the halls of the building all day long. "Happy to help out," he said, and signed his name to the certificate. Arnold hummed the wedding march as they got back into the car and told the driver to take them to La Guardia Airport. They had their tickets and boarded the plane quickly. Arnold explained the seat belts, the air vents, and the constant attention of the stewardess to Nell, who had never been on an airplane.

They flew to Bermuda where another car was waiting to take them to the pink cottage on the grounds of the large hotel Arnold had found for them.

It became a secret, warm, safe paradise for them. He taught her what she had waited so long to learn and she practiced each move and returned each caress with a tenderness he did not imagine even she possessed. They were one now and it was as simple and sweet as he had hoped and prayed it would be. Man and wife, man and woman, lovers at last.

While Martha finished up one of her "easy" jobs, decorating the lobby of a small bank, Leonora worked on her plan. She called Peter Holczer. She discussed the possibility of Deane-Ives merging with his firm and offered her services as Martha's liaison.

"I ran an art gallery in California when I was young, Peter. I carried out the instructions of a very demanding woman and I think I did well. Looking back, I think I liked it, too. But I wasn't sure what I wanted to do then — a career seemed so unlikely — and I haven't worked since. You and Martha would have to train me. You would make all the artistic decisions, but I could deal with the painters and carpenters."

Peter thought she was funny. He did not think his work had anything to do with art.

"Where did you get that idea?" he asked her.

"From Martha, I guess. Not that she's ever said it in those words but there's something about the way she works and thinks and creates atmospheres" — she remembered Peter's phrase from long ago — "that makes me believe her work has something to do with making other people's lives better. And that's what art does, or should do."

"I asked her months ago to join me. She was rather skittish then."

"Let me suggest it again. You can write down anything you think I should say."

"Well, we don't need two places and Deane-Ives is still the nicest shop on Madison. And Ellis will want to know that Martha wanted to work with him, too. He's my other self, Leo."

"She knows that. She likes him."

"Well, do your work, and we shall see."

Phil Langhorn's shyness disappeared gradually as he became used to the Ives sisters consulting him about what they called "the trees." He tried to teach them what he knew and called the State Forest Agency when they asked him questions he could not answer.

They talked to him of the future and it baffled him, since he was used to living from day to day. Now he was faced with a time he could not conceive of that had something to do with Leonora's daughter's children. "We are thinking in terms of generations, aren't we Martha?" she said, and the older sister nodded, smiling. Phil tried to share their plan.

"I think you'll be able to reap substantial benefit from a sustained yield, miss. We'll harvest the mature trees that escaped the fire. There's still plenty of them, thank the Lord. And we'll replant the land that wasn't too deeply burned."

"And the rest?"

"Nature will take care of it, I guess, and time. It takes as long as three years for the seeds to mature after fertilization."

"Seeds?"

"We'll plant young trees, miss. But the wind — the same wind that spread the fire — will carry the seeds of new trees, the spruces as well as the pines, don't you know, and those children you're talking about will see some green again. From the second growth. But they'll have to learn how to leave them alone."

Leonora thought of Nell and interrupted him. "I think they'll have to learn how to harvest them. The cutting will be hard for my daughter to imagine."

"Well, the young trees you buy will be the capital in a manner of speaking. She'll want to protect that, naturally. The older trees are useful. Not just as timber."

Phil recalled what his father had told him about getting turpentine and resin from the wood, of the possibility of selling some of it for pulp.

Martha interrupted. "Could we buy a young elm, Phil? One beautiful white elm?"

Leonora smiled. "An elm for me, and for you —?"

"Paper birches. We could plant them on the shore and hide the scars of the fire."

"You could order several kinds, Miss Martha. The gray and the yellow and the sweet."

"Silviculture!" said Leonora.

At precisely the same moment Leonora and Martha began to sing the forestry song they had learned as children. The words that at one time had no meaning now delighted them.

" 'The names of trees, oh, the names of trees!' " Martha laughed.

"Think how surprised father would be if he knew what we were planning for his beloved lake and lands!" said Leonora.

Together they rushed through the final verse:

"I'll learn the names of fish and bugs, fish and bugs,
Of birds and butterflies and slugs, flies and slugs —"

Now their laughter was contagious and Phil joined in with the last line,

"And the names of trees will never bother me,
When I have studied forestry!"

February 6, 1964

My darling Mother,

This is the first birthday in my life I have not spent with you. But you are with me — with us — and at the end of a fine day I am writing to you because I could not say enough on the telephone. You asked me if I felt old and I said no. I meant to say yes and no. I feel grown up at last. Arnold helps me to be that now, just as you did. What I remember most — the most vivid moment of feeling the future — was with you, but I am not sure exactly when. I do know where. We were walking to Nana's, crossing the street, and I gave you my hand as I always did and you didn't take it. All through the afternoon I thought I had done something wrong and that it was your way of telling me. I thought and thought and could not figure it out. When I looked at you, you smiled at me. That smile I love. But I couldn't smile back because I was so puzzled. When we left Nana's, we took a taxi so it was not until the next day when we were walking again (we must have gone to Nana's on Saturday and this was a Sunday) and the first time we came to a corner I tried again.

I reached for your hand and you did something with yours, pulled your coat closer or something. I wanted to grab your arm or hit it with my fists. I did not want to stop being your child. I have stopped being your dependent, haven't I? But never your daughter.

Happy Birthday and love,
Your Nell

Arnold circled Nell's "love" and printed his initials beside her name.